To my niece Esther Tuttle

PREFACE

One of the world's last great wild rivers remains unconquered. Only one man has ever attempted to kayak it: Rex's legendary, domineering grandfather. At seventeen, Rex is determined to conquer it in hopes of carrying on the family legacy. He flies to South America and hires an attractive female guide with her own agenda – and secrets – who shrugs off his advances. Then the guide abandons Rex. Chasing his grandfather's footsteps brought him this far, but now he must re-examine his motivations and find a way down the Furioso River.

CHAPTER ONE

When the shot rang out, I leapt from my bed, lifted a corner of the bedroom curtain, and looked down on the river bend. A fresh crack in the humpbacked ice jam glistened in the morning sunlight, like a wet wound. I squinted at it carefully, feeling my pulse rise. My mind flashed back to other rivers and other springtimes, reminding me that spring breakup can sound like gunfire.

I shaded my eyes and looked upstream towards the wall of sandbags. My back still ached from hefting them into place. All last week, I'd worked alongside most of the town's able-bodied population for long hours, proving how very strong I am for seventeen. Not that my grandfather took much notice.

With one hand still on the curtain, I swept my eyes along the half-mile ribbon of steaming black water formed by the release pipe from the pulp mill in Milltown, Alberta. Fringed on both sides by fragile ice shelves, the dark open patch was followed by solid ice downstream. As I shed my pajamas and reached for my wetsuit, I spotted a boy on the far side of the river's edge. I frowned. He was playing on an ice shelf along the water warmed by the pulp mill.

Not smart, kid, I thought, zipping up my wetsuit and reaching for my paddling jacket. *Where're your parents, anyway?*

I checked my paddling jacket's pocket for the good-luck charm I keep there – a necklace my famous grandfather once got off a starving native woman in the Andes. Far better than having a famous grandfather is having this necklace, which no one but him, my mom, and me know about. Plus I have the actual journal that he kept on that journey. I keep it under my pillow and read bits of it before I fall asleep.

I patted the necklace again and made my way towards the back door.

"Morning, Rex." Mom smiled at me as I grabbed a banana off the kitchen counter. "You're up early for a Saturday. I'll cook up brunch after your training session. Be careful, now."

"Thanks, Mom." I headed down the hallway, nearly slamming into Gramps' tall but emaciated frame as he stepped out of his bedroom.

"Can't you ever watch where you're going? Where the hell *are* you going, anyway?"

"Sorry, Gramps. I'm off to paddle." As if my wetsuit didn't make that obvious. As if he didn't see me paddle every morning. Gramps is Gramps and I try to shrug off his temperamental outbursts, but it's harder to do that lately.

"What's the point of training? You didn't make the cut."

For a split second, the steel-edged remark hit exactly like he meant it to. But I took a deep breath and silently counted to three. He crossed the hall and slammed the bathroom door shut behind him.

Mom appeared with a sympathetic smile. "Don't mind him. He's . . ."

". . . not himself since Grandma died," I finished for her. I refrained from saying that he'd always been testy and it had been a month since the funeral. But, like Mom, I try to give him lots of slack.

When I was a child, he was my hero – from the time he first showed me photos of him in *National Geographic*. Those faded photos still hang framed on his bedroom wall, above his dust-covered expedition medals and trophies. But I don't go into his room anymore. I've got my own growing collection of trophies to look at and, someday soon, maybe, my own mug in *National Geographic*. And yet, well, a part of me still wants to worship him, this crotchety old man.

Mom smiled. "At least he's coming out of his bedroom more. Have a good session, Rex. *I* admire your discipline on these cold days."

I grinned at her as I peeled my banana. "It'll be warmer in South America. *If* I come up with sponsors for my expedition."

She winked and returned to the kitchen. I ate my banana and took the stairs to the basement's rear door. Stepping into the backyard, I hurried towards the boat-house as frosted grass crunched under my neoprene boots. I puffed a cloud of steam into the frigid air. *It'll be a* lot *warmer in South America*, I reminded myself. *And I will land the final sponsor who'll pay my way there. More important, I will, I hope, one-up Gramps' career while launching my own. As in finish the one and only expedition he failed. Write my own entry into the yellowed pages of the journal that rests under my pillow.*

When I reached the boathouse, I shrugged into my life jacket and spraydeck, buckled up my helmet, and lifted my lightweight slalom race kayak and paddle down from their racks. I felt my biceps, pleased that the sandbagging had added to their firmness.

The fact that I could paddle on a short runway of liquid this time of year, instead of just lifting weights, was courtesy of the local pulp mill. As tough as it had been to move here from Montana in the middle of my senior year of high school — so Mom could help look after my ailing grandma — I was glad, at least, for this preseason strip of water to paddle.

I lowered my whitewater kayak off the ice into the water and squinted at the kid on the ice shelf on the other side. *Eight, maybe?* Dressed in a thin parka, jeans, and runners, he was trailing his mittenless fingers in the frigid water, unaware how dangerous his position was. Or maybe he didn't care. He was probably native, from the reservation across the river.

"They let their kids run wild," Gramps likes to say. "And they live in filthy, overcrowded houses."

I don't like how he talks about people from the reservation — or reserve, as they call it here in Canada. *Just 'cause Gramps is from here doesn't mean he's right, does it?*

I stretched in the cold air and seated myself in my boat. Silently, I powered across the dark river. "Hey, kid!" I addressed him in my friendliest voice as my kayak drew near the reserve's side of the river. "I think you should get off the ice. You could fall in and drown, you know."

He sat up and narrowed his blue eyes at me. A frown made his forehead bunch up. He crossed his little arms over his chest, curled his lower lip, and mouthed, "F— off."

That's when the second shot sounded from upstream, like a rifle. As the startled boy scrambled to look around, a louder crack reverberated from under him. His ice shelf broke off the bank and lurched into the river, nearly pitching him off. His eyeballs bulged as he clung to his breakaway floe.

Someone must've seen it happen from the fire-station tower upriver because, as I sprinted over to calm the poor kid down, the town siren let loose full blast to call volunteer firefighters. The boy started bawling.

"It's okay, I've got you," I said. "Just sit still."

I nudged the bow of my kayak against the edge of the floe and tried to push his square of ice back towards the far shore. But the kid twisted around, and the movement made his floe bob out of my reach. Even as I chased him, his floe hit the main current, which made it wobble so much, I was sure it was going to pitch him into the drink.

"Don't move! I'm coming!" I said, half-deafened by the siren.

He sat stock-still for a moment, but as my kayak drew up to him, the boy panicked and tried to leap right onto my boat. It tilted and capsized, just like that.

Man, it was cold. Brain-freeze cold. I did a quick roll, spinning the kayak all the way back upright in less than a second. I take pride in never missing a roll.

As ice water dripped down my face, I watched the boy's flailing hand reach towards the side of my boat. I planted a sweep stroke just in time to whip the kayak away from his grasp. One dunking was more than enough.

"Listen, kid," I said, as I watched him dog-paddle to keep himself afloat. "I'm going to turn my boat so that its tail end is near your hands. Hold on to that end, only the tip. Okay? Don't try to crawl up until I tell you."

Flashback of Gramps saying that to me when I was little, so very many times. When he was less grumpy. Or maybe I just hadn't seen it for adoring him so much all those summers Mom and I spent with him. He was the dad I'd never had.

"O-k-k-k-kay," he said between chattering teeth, clinging to my stern like his life depended on it, which it did. By then, we'd managed to drift towards my house, on the other side of the river. Firemen were running down the bank as I half-listened for further cracks from upriver. I had to get this kid and me to safety.

"So," I said to my young client, "you're going to stretch your arms towards my waist and pull yourself up onto the boat. Keep your weight even, or I'll flip. Got it?" I've had dozens of coaches, some good, some bad. I know how to sound like one of the good ones when I need to. Not like Gramps.

"G-g-g-got it."

"Good. Now lift yourself very slowly out of the water until you're lying on the back of my kayak, hands around my waist, feet trailing in the water. That's it — *no! Balanced!*"

He shifted himself just in time and clung so tightly, he squashed my ribcage.

"That's better. Good stuff, little buddy. Now don't move one inch till I get us to shore. Deal?"

"D-d-deal."

I struck out for shore, my double-bladed paddle slicing rhythmically through the icy water. The entire kayak trembled with the shivers of his little body. I watched puffs of condensed air from my own breath float calmly away. Everything was under control.

As we drew near the ice shelf onshore, I heard his small voice whisper, "Thank you."

"No problem."

A fireman lay down on the ice shelf and reached to pull the kid off my kayak. "Attaboy," the fireman said, "I gotcha." He wrapped the boy in a blanket and handed him off to another fireman.

"You need to get him back to the reserve fast," I suggested. "He's shivering badly."

"The reserve?" The fireman's eyebrows arched. "This is Joe MacDonald's son. He lives two houses from me. Must've had a sleepover there last night."

"Oh," I said, avoiding his eyes and feeling color creep into my face.

The first fireman reached out to pump my hand. "You're Malcolm Scruggs' grandson, right? Lucky you were there."

"No worries." Luck had nothing to do with it. The river – *my* river – had prearranged it entirely, had even woken me up to make sure I was there. I gave the kid a thumb's-up. He was soaked, but basking in the attention of people running towards him. He waved good-bye to me.

"So your name's Rex," the fireman continued. "I've known your grandparents a long time. Sorry about the loss of your grandma."

"Thanks." I was still in my kayak, shivering.

"I heard you won the national championships."

"Yeah." I smiled broadly. One part of me felt great about the rescue I'd just done, but I also had a gnawing feeling that I needed to get away. I had to get home in case the ice jam really was about to break.

"Must've made your grandpa proud. He used to be famous himself, eh?"

"Still is," I added dryly. *At least in his own mind.*

"What for?" challenged a little girl, listening in.

I smiled at her. "For being the first one down a bunch of wild rivers. It's called a first descent. Mountain climbers dream of doing first ascents; kayakers like my grandpa and me do first descents."

"Have you done one?" the fireman asked.

"Not yet, but someday. Sorry, but I really have to get home," I said as I used my paddle to back away from shore. With the noisy siren still blaring and half the town's population streaming down to the riverside, my nerves were on edge. Whatever the crowds might think, and whatever I might want them to think, it had been an easy rescue. I probably could've done better, as Gramps was sure to point out if he'd seen it.

As I headed downstream, I glanced up at our house. The living-room light silhouetted Gramps watching me, Mom behind him. Under his gaze, I felt a need to sprint harder, faster. When I was halfway to our beach, someone turned the screeching siren off. I breathed deeply of the quiet – only to be jarred by what sounded like the mother of all gun battles from the ice bulge upstream – *Crack! Zing! Bang!*

Adrenalin surged through me like electricity. I went into a high-speed sprint, knowing that the ice jam behind me was splitting apart as surely as if someone had blown it up. I didn't need to look to know that the pent-up river beneath it was about to explode, like lava from a volcano. If the first push of broken ice reached me before I neared shore, I'd be churned like meat in a grinder. I'd seen TV news footage of breakups before: ten-foot-long ice chunks tossed so violently that they acted like saw blades, ripping up vegetation, tearing entire trees up by the roots.

But I was an athlete – fast and experienced for my age, even if Gramps would rarely admit it. I had a shot at outrunning the surge. And, somehow, I knew it wasn't my time to die yet. I had the good-luck necklace in my paddling jacket pocket, after all.

The juice and pistons in my arms worked overtime, trying to close the gap between midriver and shore. If people were screaming, I was only vaguely aware of it. If Mom was tearing at her hair while Gramps was gritting his teeth, I had no way of knowing. My world for those suspended moments was just me, the river, and the thin crust of ice lining the bottom of Gramps' riverfront property. When the bow of my kayak was about to hit the shoreline's ice edge, I leaned back, put in a super-powerful stroke, and let the kayak slide up and over it.

The second my boat touched frozen mud, I leapt out and lifted the kayak by its cockpit as I ran up, up, up our yard. Behind me, the thud and crash of giant ice blocks tumbling over one another thundered like boulders being spilled from the shovel of a monster bulldozer. Still more ice chunks were clawing at the riverbank, with a shriek like fingernails-on-a-blackboard amplified by rock-concert speakers. The water surge spewed these chunks onto the frozen river below the mill's strip of meltwater. That's exactly where I'd have been pummeled and crushed if I hadn't outsprinted the water.

Only when I reached the house did I drop my kayak and turn. Ignoring the warfare of ice, water, and shoreline below me, I searched the crowd I'd left behind for any sign of panic. People were huddled watching, shaking their heads in wonder, even though they'd seen spring breakup dozens of times before. No one was screaming or pointing, which meant no towns-people had been caught. That's all I needed to know.

I spun around and walked into the house, one hand pressed against the pocket that held my necklace. On my way up the back stairs, Mom nearly knocked me over in her rush to reach out and hug me. She clung to me with a tear-stained face.

"Rex, Rex, Rex, I can't believe you . . . what a fright . . . you saved that boy . . . oh, my crazy, crazy son. . . ."

I worked to free myself from her embrace. "Mom, chill, okay?" *The kid is okay, the kid is okay* was the only thought going through my adrenalin-saturated mind.

"Sorry, dear," she said, releasing me slowly. Mom's okay, really. She understands me, is proud of me, and mostly supports my goals, even the ones that would freak most moms. I gave her a quick kiss on the cheek.

After I showered, changed, and arrived at the kitchen table, I was startled to see Gramps joining us for the first time in days. He was staring at me with something that felt almost like respect. My heart picked up. Then he looked away, busying himself with a cup of black coffee.

"You got lucky, Rex. Shouldn't have risked your life for a kid you don't even know," Gramps said.

I looked away, disgusted.

"You did the right thing," Mom said, reaching for my hand.

I swept my eyes over Gramps.

Gramps stirred his coffee vigorously, added sugar, glanced at me, then at Mom. "On the other hand, Rex, that was quite the sprint. Makes me think I've made a good decision. A decision your mom and I have been preparing to tell you about."

"A decision I've agreed to only on two conditions," Mom cut in, her eyes on Gramps.

"Yeah, Gramps?" *What have I done wrong now?*

"I know it was hard on you, not making the cut for the Olympic team."

Hard? To miss it by one slot? All he'd said at the time was, "I knew you weren't there yet, Rex."

"Uh-huh," I said, frowning.

"And maybe because you don't have those credentials, you haven't been able to get enough sponsors to pay your way to Colombia."

"Not yet, but I will. I've got fifty percent of the sponsors I need." I looked him in the eyes. "I'm seventeen. Same age you were when you got your first sponsor."

"Exactly. And I rewarded that sponsor with a first descent that launched my career." His voice was sharp, as if he were rebuking me. *Or do I detect a fragment of fear? Is he afraid I might finish what he hasn't? That the history books will herald my name in future mentions of the Furioso River of Colombia?*

Mom stood there, shifting from one foot to another, her eyes on me. "Mother's passing seems to have put a streak of craziness in your grandfather," she said, with fondness in her tone.

I stared from Mom to Gramps. Gramps ignored her. "I've decided to sponsor you, Rex. Foot half the expedition. Especially since you're obviously no good at getting enough sponsors."

My breath left me in one long gasp. I wondered who'd taken possession of my grandfather's body. Then I caught a look that passed between Gramps and Mom. She'd made him. She'd talked him into it. *How did she do that?*

I rose to wrap my arms around his bony chest anyway. "I'll do it, Gramps. I'll finish that river for you." From over Gramps' shoulder, I looked at Mom, at the pride that was tearing up her eyes, and I beamed her a heartfelt smile of thanks. No other mom in the world would have done that. Not one.

"Not just for Gramps. For the Scruggs family legacy," Mom said, gathering Gramps' withered palm in one hand and mine in the other.

Gramps' chin sank, like he was suddenly very tired. I tried to pretend that it had been Gramps who'd just uttered those words. In all my childhood daydreams of someday living up to his reputation, I'd never once heard him encourage me. Gramps dispensed only hard-boiled criticism.

"On two conditions," my mother added, still holding our hands like we were an inseparable threesome. "That you, son, arrange for at least two other qualified expedition members to join you, and that Gramps and I determine the region is safe to travel in."

"Agreed!" I promised quickly, my mind leaping to a mental Rolodex of South America's best whitewater kayakers.

"Gramps wouldn't agree at first," Mom said.

"I told her you were still a boy," Gramps' gruff voice spoke up.

"And I informed him you're nearly a man." Again, her eyes were teary.

"Well, you're the same age your mother was when she had to drop out of high school to have you," Gramps spoke up, pulling his hand out of Mom's.

I watched Mom's crimson face. *Why does Gramps have to be so cruel?* Mom had told me ages ago she didn't even know who my dad was. So she'd made a mistake when she was young. *Is Gramps going to hold that against her forever?*

"Anyway, try, and if you fail, maybe it'll be out of your system," Gramps said.

I refused to let his words sting me. This was my chance, my big chance, to prove myself to Gramps, my mom, and the world. I turned and hugged Gramps and Mom in turn. "I'll be fine."

Gramps eyed me soberly. "There's one other condition."

I waited.

"That necklace of mine."

"Still have it." I pulled it from my paddling jacket pocket. His hollowed-out eyes locked on it.

"Did you know I got this off a starving Indian? Traded her an avocado sandwich for it."

"You've told us lots of times, Gramps."

"I want you to try and locate the family that gave it to me, the Calambáses. They live along the river you're aiming to paddle."

I hesitated. I hoped he wasn't going to ask me to return the necklace to them. He didn't know how attached I'd gotten to it, how I believed it kept me safe. And I couldn't tell him because he'd think that was a sign of weakness.

"Tell them you're my grandson."

I shrugged. "Of course, Gramps."

"They might be able to help you hire a guide, someone who knows the area. Even better if they speak English."

I breathed easier. No more mention of the necklace. "Okay. You're the best, Gramps. I'm totally going to *own* that river."

"Or you'll come back with your tail between your legs. But you'll come back either way, I reckon. That's what I promised your mother."

CHAPTER TWO

The same day in southwest Colombia, Myriam Calambás set her bucket of dirty clothing beside the rushing river, lifted her calf-length wool skirt, and stretched a toe towards the water's coolness. Tumbling waves splashed their way around the river's boulders. The seventeen-year-old knew every inch of the land on both sides of the river for miles, but this was her favorite place.

She sang softly, in English. It was her way of practicing her best subject at school without getting disapproving looks from her family. A rooster's first crows sounded down the hill. She paused to listen as she breathed in the familiar, earthy smell of dust and humidity, tinged with the fragrance of pine and eucalyptus trees.

This was her special time of day. Every morning before dawn, she'd rise from her bed, dress quickly, and tiptoe out of the adobe hut. Without a backward glance at her four younger sleeping brothers and sisters, she'd hurry past the *hacienda*, which served as the reservation village's community center, towards the river. Her bare roughened feet traveled firmly over the courtyard's flagstones as hens cackled and geese waddled out of her way.

Her father disliked her coming to the river alone. He'd warned her again and again. But Myriam prized her moments of quietude here.

She flicked her long black braid over her shoulder and cocked the felt hat on her head just so. Shifting her wool poncho, she stepped forward and curled her toes into the mud of the little eddy. Then she gazed downhill at the mists that clung to the sides of her mountain, like tufts of sheep's wool caught on branches.

The tap of small claws on the rocky path behind told her that Capitán, her family's small mutt, had roused himself to follow her. She smiled and stooped to scratch his ears.

Filling the bucket with river water, she crouched to scrub her family's clothes. As the oldest child, Myriam had the most chores. But all the people on her reservation worked from sunup to sundown. Hard work was all that stood between them and starvation.

I would like to cross the river and run around free and happy for just a few minutes, Myriam thought, *without fear of stepping on a land mine or being grabbed by a soldier.*

Something about the tumbling mountain river pushed that reality away for a few moments each day. Myriam liked to imagine that her river whispered secrets. She liked to imagine her grandmother, her great-grandmother, and hundreds of great-greats before that pausing by this river each morning with clothes, food, and children to wash. She liked to imagine how peaceful life must have been before the Spanish conquistadors had come. Before the Spanish colonialists had herded up her ancestors and turned them into serfs to work the land around the ranch houses, called *haciendas*, they built. And before fifty years of civil war had killed or displaced what was left of her people, the Andean *indígenas* of Colombia. "Dirty Indians," some Colombians called them.

Myriam had just finished her washing when Capitán emitted a low growl, the hair on his back standing on end. She tensed. As she glanced across the river, Capitán's low growls turned into barking and his snout pointed accusingly at the far shore.

"*Shhh!*" Still crouched, Myriam placed her hand against the dog's coarse fur, her eyes searching the far shore. She could see nothing, but there were many large boulders behind which a soldier could hide. She knew soldiers sometimes lurked there, scouting land for the coca fields that supported their cause, or maybe just spying on her people.

She decided to heed Capitán's warning. In one swift move, she turned and fled, running in a zigzag motion, fast as a puma, adrenalin coursing through her veins. Zigzag is how she'd been taught to run from soldiers' bullets from the time she was a small child.

In the minute or two it took to sprint to her community, she recited silently: *Leave us alone. We are no threat. Let us live in peace.*

As she rounded a head-high slab of stone above her community's courtyard, she slammed into Alberto, her boyfriend, which sent her washing pail crashing to the ground.

17

"Hey! Watch where you're going," he teased her, reaching long arms down to pick up the bucket of clean clothes, letting his hands linger on hers as he returned it to her. He looked hurt when she pulled away. Then she noticed what he held in one hand.

"Alberto! You caught a rabbit!" Her mouth watered at the thought of rabbit stew.

He started to smile, then frowned at her pail. "You've been to the river alone. I've told you not to. Why do you do it?"

She drew herself up and reached for the stiffening rabbit, avoiding his eyes. "I don't take orders from you, Alberto. But everyone will be happy your trap got a rabbit."

He released it into her hands, although his face still wore a pained expression. "I could kill a rabbit every day if I had a gun."

Myriam held the rabbit at arm's length to keep blood from dripping on her clean washing. "If you had a gun," she reminded him, "we'd all be dead when the soldiers found out."

Silence hovered between them for a moment. "You've been avoiding me, Myriam," Alberto said, watching her as Capitán scurried away to chase a goose in the courtyard.

She stepped back. "Just busy," she said quietly.

"Myriam!" her grandmother called from inside the *hacienda* community center, downhill from the adobe huts the villagers lived in.

"Sorry, Alberto. I have to go." She turned and walked through the courtyard, hens clucking at her heels. *Why can't I just say the words I practice every night, the words that will end things between us?*

————

Hurrying towards the community center, Myriam realized the place had come alive since she'd snuck away at sunrise. The smell of *arepas* – cornbread patties – frying in a pan mixed with the yapping of dogs and the laughter of her aunts and uncles. Everyone was organizing goods and children for the walk to market. The women had strings of herbs, piles of hats, and bundles of woven goods they'd made. The men – most wearing the calf-length skirts that served as the community's traditional male clothing – had burlap sacks of potatoes, maize, coffee, beans, carrots, and fruits they'd harvested.

Before ducking into the run-down former *hacienda*, Myriam waved at her tall powerful father as he lashed sacks onto their mule. Papá's weather-beaten face, paler than most of the other men's, was so serious when her mother was away in the next village of their reservation, visiting Myriam's other grandmother. His green eyes – so unusual in the community that they probably enhanced his power as leader – were downcast.

"Abuelita, you're coming to market?" Myriam was astonished to see her grandmother in the *hacienda* doorway, organizing small fiber bags of herbs – chamomile, mint, and medicinal – that she had dried. Some days, the old woman hardly stirred from her bed in a dark corner of the part-dirt, part-concrete floor hut up the hill that Myriam and the six members of her family shared. Other days, she used her knowledge of herbs to tend to villagers that were ill. Sometimes she even pushed her stiff fingers through Mamá's loom to help with weaving crafts, or carded sheep-wool strands on a wooden spindle whorl for the younger women to knit with. It had been months since she'd insisted on accompanying the family to the market to help them sell their goods.

"Of course," Abuela replied, her ancient face wrinkling into a toothless smile as she stepped back into the *hacienda*. At that, the tiny, shawl-wrapped figure lifted herself onto tiptoes to remove her felt hat from a wooden peg. She dusted it off, perched it on her head, and grinned wider, stray whiskers poking out from above her puckered lips.

Then her face turned serious, and she plunked herself down in a plastic chair with a colorful, hand-woven cushion. She motioned for Myriam to sit in one beside her.

"Myriam," she said, reaching for her granddaughter's hand. "It is time for you to leave school and marry, and for me to spend more time teaching you about herbal medicines."

"No, Abuelita," Myriam protested, her heart sinking. She'd known this was coming for a while. "I want to go to university." She dared not tell her abuela that she'd already filled out applications, with her teacher's help.

Abuela fixed her eyes on her bundles of herbs and on some shirts piled in a chipped enamel washbasin in the corner of the room. She shook her head. "Schooling does not help you cook, work in the fields, and look after little ones. And there's no one else to take over my healing work."

"But, Abuelita, Rosita wants to be a healer. She wants you to teach her."

"Rosita is only twelve," Abuela snapped.

"Abuelita, I want to go to university to help keep the soldiers away. With my English, I can tell foreigners about

what they do to us – tell them on the radio, on the Internet."
Myriam sank to her knees on the concrete floor and
directed imploring eyes at her grandmother. *Does Abuela
even understand what the Internet is?* She certainly knew that
the radio station was a long, dangerous bike ride away.

"When I was your age, Myriam, I was already expecting
your father. Your mother left school in fifth grade. *Indígenas*
do not go to university, especially *indígena* girls."

Myriam rose on unsteady legs, head bowed, fists clenched
tight. Every nerve in her body wanted to defy her beloved
grandmother, but *indígena* girls were raised to be respectful
of their elders. So she mumbled only five words – a sen-
tence that didn't count, she told herself, because she said it
in English.

"I will find a way."

The effect on her grandmother startled her. Her frail
body went rigid. Her glassy eyes grew crystal clear. She
stared at Myriam as if confronting a ghost.

"No, you won't!" she responded, wagging a bony finger
at her granddaughter.

Myriam stumbled backwards out of the community
center, shock hindering her movements. She had imagined
that exchange. Guilt had surely made her imagine her
abuela understanding English.

"Myriam, Papá's ready!" shouted Rosita, dashing into
the courtyard with the two-year-old twins, Flora and
Freddy, in tow.

"I'm coming," Myriam responded grimly as the two girls
each hoisted a twin onto their backs, tucked them under
their ponchos, and secured them with long, brightly colored

woven sashes. Mamá, of course, had taken the youngest, a baby boy named Alejandro, with her.

Abuela emerged from the community center's doorway, barefoot, wearing her hat and wielding her cane, eyes on the party ahead starting down the mountain. Alberto was with them, looking back at Myriam. The girls picked up bags of embroidered tablecloths, put on their rubber boots, and sidestepped some kittens to escort their grandmother to the rear of the group.

A desperate thought entered Myriam's mind, a thought she'd first battled away when Alberto had proposed to her. *If only I can keep the money from the goods we're selling and use it to escape. Or find a way to earn money of my own. I need to get out of here.*

At the front of the group of more than two dozen people, cheerful Andean music floated from Alberto's battery-powered radio, his proudest possession. He and some of the teens sang and swayed to the beat, as if on their way to a party, while the adults shook their heads, bemused. Myriam liked the songs, but wasn't in the mood as she negotiated the steep switchbacks and long spiky grass.

After an hour of walking, the trees began to thin. She felt a tug on her skirt and turned to see Rosita looking at her. "Myriam, soldiers."

Myriam looked up, heard the radio switch off, and noticed a commotion at the front of the line. Her father, by far the tallest and strongest man in the village, halted the mule. Everyone was staring at a group of men and youths whose faces were half covered in black bandanas. Wearing green camouflage uniforms and military boots, they stalked towards Myriam's group with sophisticated U.S.-made M60 machine guns and AR-15 rifles swinging loosely from their shoulders. The bandanas and boots meant they were paramilitary soldiers, hired by the rich to fight the guerillas, who supposedly fought for the poor. Guerillas – whom Myriam distrusted just as much – wore berets and cheap rubber boots. Myriam guided Rosita's hand into her grandmother's, then edged downhill, Freddy's sleeping head bobbing against her shoulder.

"We're looking for the people in your village who give food to the guerillas," the tallest soldier, the commander, said to Myriam's father. He leaned his sweaty face close to Papá's as his soldiers, including a few teenage girls, halted a couple of paces back and lifted their guns from their shoulders. Alberto was standing stock-still to one side, his face a frozen mask averted from the soldiers. Myriam feared more for Alberto, who was nineteen, than for anyone. *Please don't press him into your army*, she prayed.

"We have never helped the guerillas," Papá said in a firm, calm voice. "You know we don't get involved with either side. You know we are unarmed. We are neutral." He was standing with his feet planted widely apart, his face and voice revealing no aggression or fear.

"Neutral." The commander spit into the dirt in front of Papá's faded rubber boots. He shifted his eyes to Alberto. "You!" he shouted, lifting the butt of his M60 and pushing it without warning against Alberto's shoulder.

Myriam tensed. She saw Alberto do the same, but he did not speak.

"Look at your shoes," the commander jeered, pointing to where Alberto's dirty bare toes stuck through holes in his worn sports shoes. Alberto's gaze dropped to his shoes.

"You want boots? Brand-new boots like ours?" The commander swept his gun casually towards some of his soldiers, who'd lit cigarettes and were lounging with smirks on their faces. All wore smart-looking black leather lace-up boots. One was eyeing Alberto's radio. Another group of soldiers, standing farther back without smiles, included two *indígena* boy recruits. Myriam wondered what lies had helped recruit them. She knew they were powerless to stop this harassment.

"You want money? A gun?" the commander persisted, his mustache twitching as his eyes bore into Alberto's passive face.

Still, Alberto refused to answer or look the commander in the eyes. *He wants a gun, all right*, Myriam breathed to herself. *But only to fight what your troops do to our people.*

She saw her father open his mouth to speak and step protectively in front of Alberto. Suddenly a tiny pair of bare feet beneath a woolen skirt and poncho swept past Myriam and planted themselves between Papá and the commander.

Myriam's entire body went taut. Papá's chin dropped.

Her grandmother was a full head shorter than the commander, but that didn't stop Abuela from raising a bony finger up to the commander's face.

"We were here before you. We will be here after you. We help neither you nor those you seek. You heard my son. We are unarmed and neutral. Leave us in peace."

And then, as casually as an actress who'd completed her

lines and was scripted to head offstage, Abuela turned and walked back up the hill to Rosita, the bag of herbs strapped to her stooped back quivering.

The soldiers' cigarettes drooped from lowered hands, spilling ashes onto their boots. The commander, eyebrows raised, followed the swish of Abuela's dark wool skirt over her tough, blackened soles.

It might have been a second. It might have been minutes. But as Myriam's party stood waiting, the commander finally returned his attention to Alberto, snatched his radio away, and spit once more at Papá's feet.

Then his face lit up with an evil smile, and a deep belly laugh rose in the dry air, frightening Myriam more than his words or gun. His open mouth revealed crooked teeth, several missing. As his troops echoed the laughter, the commander whirled around, raised his gun, and shot wildly into the air. Lowering the gun, he walked back to his troops, the radio tucked under one arm. The soldiers retreated up the trail they'd come down, back into the woods, eagerly passing Alberto's radio around. Alberto, now with Papá's hand on his shoulder, remained rooted, but his dark eyes followed the men until they disappeared over a rise.

Myriam let out a long breath. Alberto had been right to stand still and not speak. And she couldn't help but be impressed that her abuela had delivered that speech in flawless Spanish. Women older than Myriam's generation had never attended school, and Abuela was one of the few who had taken the trouble to learn anything but their native language from the younger women. Myriam, like all girls her age, was fluent in both her native language and Spanish. But she was the only one in her community learning English from the non-*indígena* teachers at school.

"Abuelita . . ." Myriam scolded halfheartedly.

"Walk tall so Freddy doesn't flop about," her grandmother scolded back.

The party was tense and sober for the next hour's walk down the mountain to the nearest road, the sound of their footsteps broken only by the men talking in low voices. Myriam watched her father speak softly to Alberto, watched Alberto's chin jut out as he responded. Robbed of music, they eventually sat cross-legged in the dust along the roadside, waiting for the bus. Alberto dropped beside Myriam and offered her water from an old cola bottle, which she accepted. A few of the men – but not Papá or Alberto – sipped homemade sugarcane liquor from old glass bottles. It slowly eased the tension, and occasional laughter rippled through their ranks.

Two, then three brightly colored buses passed them, each packed full of standing passengers and cages of cackling chickens. More passengers sprawled on the buses' roofs, while a few stood on the rear bumpers and held on to the back door handles.

"Abuelita," Rosita said, breaking the silence among those sitting in the roadside dust, "tell us the story about the avocado sandwich."

Abuela smiled and placed her hand on Rosita's felt hat. "But you've heard it so many times."

"Please, Abuelita," Myriam's many cousins chanted.

"I was a young woman, Myriam's age," she began. "I was looking for berries in the field across the river."

"But couldn't you have been blown up?" a cousin asked.

"This was before land mines and soldiers," Abuela responded, her eyes far away. "A white man came hiking up the mountainside."

"Did he have a gun? Were you scared?"

"*Shhh.*"

"He pointed to my necklace, which my great-grandmother had given me. He held out some coins like he wanted to buy it."

"You had coins then? Not gold?"

"*Shhh.*"

"They were not coins I'd ever seen, so I pointed to his pack. I wanted food. He pulled out an avocado sandwich."

"But, Abuelita!" Myriam interrupted, feeling more rage than the last time she'd heard the story, years ago. "It was an unfair trade! How could you?"

Her grandmother moved fond eyes to her oldest granddaughter. "If I had not done this foolish thing, the necklace would be yours, it is true. But I was hungry."

Hunger. It's the same excuse she always gives. As always, Myriam failed to hear regret in the words.

Just then a bus pulled over, and Myriam's community stood and walked towards it, all except the men who would take the unloaded mule back up the mountain. The men of Myriam's community pushed the heaviest bags to the bus' roof, then scrambled up after them and lowered their arms to pull the women up. Papá escorted Myriam's grandmother to a seat inside the bus, ignoring the comments of non-*indígena* passengers.

"She smells. Let her sit outside. Those *indígenas*. Do them a favor and they take over. They used to know their place."

Minutes later, Myriam and Rosita, perched on the bus' roof, arranged their ponchos to keep the dust from making the twins cough. Myriam pretended to be unaware of Alberto studying her. No one spoke as the vehicle swayed and bumped over the potholes for thirty minutes, its radio blaring static-mangled ranchero music.

The moment the bus halted in the town's market, Myriam's group scrambled down and looked about eagerly. Myriam's heart always picked up in town. *So many people, so many market stands, so much noise!* As Myriam helped haul goods to their stall, Papá steered Abuela to a shaded place where she could sit down and display her herbs. Myriam wondered what he would say to her about her performance on the mountain.

Alberto, Rosita, and others opted to work the milling crowds — Colombians of many skin colors and white tourists — leaving Myriam on her own for a while. "Tablecloths," she called out, draping the wool fabric she'd embroidered in bright colors around her stall. "Only 10,000 pesos or $5.00 each."

"Those are nice," came a deep voice from the stall beside her. She turned and surveyed a new occupant: a tall, muscled boy of mixed European/*indígena* blood. A few years older than Alberto, he was leaning over the partition that separated them. A moment before, he hadn't been there. Or maybe she hadn't seen him because he'd been bent over, pumping up the item she could now see filled his entire stall: a giant rubber raft. It looked so entirely out of place there, sitting in the dirt of a mountain village, that she wanted to giggle. But, mostly, she felt dumbstruck by the unexpected friendliness of a non-*indígena* boy.

"Thank you." She raised her eyes. A sign on his booth read EXPEDICIONES DEL RÍO. River Expeditions. He'd hung up color posters of people in rubber rafts and kayaks, paddling down a wild river. She stared wide-eyed at the posters.

"I'm Javier Gómez, though my clients call me Jock," he said in Spanish as he extended his hand, prompting her to lift hers shyly.

"I'm Myriam." Gathering her courage, she added, "Is Jock an English word?"

"It is. It means, *um*, 'sporty.' I specialize in clients who speak English, so it helps to have an English nickname. I take them down the Magdalena River in rafts or kayaks. They have lots of money, you know."

She looked around to make sure no foreigners were nearby, then lowered her voice. "Sometimes they buy tablecloths from me. Sometimes I ask twice the price, and they pay it without bargaining. Especially if I speak English to them."

Jock laughed an easy confident laugh, nodding appreciatively. He indicated no surprise at meeting an *indígena* girl who spoke English. She warmed up to him. He raised his thumb. "Smart girl."

Smart girl. If only Mamá, Papá, and Abuelita would say that, instead of pressuring me to leave school. If only Alberto hadn't mocked me the one time I'd dared to mention university.

"Is that your baby?" Jock asked as Freddy stirred and started bawling.

"No, he's my little brother," she said, reddening as she loosened the sash and rocked Freddy in her arms. Jock obviously knew that *indígena* girls marry earlier than non-*indígena*.

"Where are you from?" Jock asked.

She told him, and he asked lots of questions about the river near her home, *El Furioso*, as if he loved rivers as much as she did. She described its rapids and waterfall as they chatted in between serving customers. Now and again she glanced across the road at Abuela, expecting a disapproving look to discourage her from speaking with a strange boy, but Abuela seemed preoccupied with selling her herbs.

"You spend a lot of time embroidering," Jock observed at one point.

"Yes, but I hope to go to university," she replied bravely. "I want to be a reporter."

Jock nodded. "University is free for *indígenas*, right? Even housing?"

"Yes," she said.

"That's good. You should go."

While her heart warmed to his encouragement, she knew he had no way of knowing that her family couldn't afford to get her to Popayán, the university town a six-hour bus ride away . . . even if everything else was free . . . even if they approved of her going, rather than fiercely opposing the idea.

When Papá and Rosita returned, Jock seemed to understand that he and Myriam could not keep speaking. Anyway, he was drawing crowds, and she could tell he had a knack for selling his raft rides. When she wasn't too busy herself, she listened to his English, which sounded fluent.

"You're from Colorado? Fantastic! I'd love to visit there! I hear you have some of the best whitewater in America! But wait till you raft the Magdalena River."

Her head jerked up when he added, "Now don't forget to stop at this stall beside me. Best embroidered table-cloths in Colombia, and she speaks English."

Myriam shot him an astonished look, and he smiled as the foreigners ambled her way, their white faces examining her tablecloths with interest. When Rosita busied herself rearranging the cloths, she looked a little uncomfortable as Myriam tested her English on the customers. Myriam reddened when she stumbled over the occasional word, but grew more confident with each transaction.

Standing in front of her stall, she'd just finished a conversation in English when someone touched her shoulder from behind.

"English is an ugly language," Alberto said in a low voice. "I hate it when my beautiful girl speaks that ugly language."

Myriam bristled, but held her tongue. Alberto moved in front of her, where he held up his empty fiber bag, blocking her view of Jock. "We sold all our potatoes, but your father says I shouldn't buy another radio."

"I'm sorry, Alberto," she said, "but maybe when he sees how much I made . . ."

Alberto moved quickly to snatch her bag and count her earnings. He smiled proudly at her. "You will make a good wife."

"I agree," Papá said with a smile.

Myriam clenched her teeth and stood staring past Papá and Alberto. Jock was gone, raft and all. He'd disappeared almost like he was never there. *If the university accepts me, I will disappear*, she decided. *I will have to run away.*

CHAPTER THREE

It was Monday, two days since I'd rescued the kid on the river. Two days spent e-mailing and phoning around the South American paddling circuit until I'd extracted promises from my top two choices: Henrique Coutinho and Tiago Fialho of Brazil. I was pretty psyched about that, and, better yet, Mom and Gramps seemed satisfied. Now I was rooting through my school locker for my books and sweating bricks over the fact that I might flunk this morning's Spanish test, when I felt a strong hand come down on my shoulder. I swung around so fast, I nearly knocked Mr. Peterson off balance.

"*Uh*, sorry, Mr. Peterson." *What is the principal doing beside my locker? As if my pretest nerves aren't bad enough.*

"Rex, I didn't mean to make you jump. Just wanted to congratulate you on your heroism over the weekend."

"My what? Oh, that." I shrugged, color creeping into my face as I noticed a few students slowing down, trying to eavesdrop.

"The kayak freak is sucking up to the principal," one of the football jocks observed to another in a raised voice, prompting chuckles. *Just what I need: the principal talking to me in the hallway. Like I'm not having enough problems settling into Milltown High. When I get back from Colombia, maybe I'll be a hero, at least in Gramps' eyes.*

"I just happened to be there. It worked out. No biggie," I said. I was about to turn back to my locker when I noticed a young man, neither teacher nor student, standing at Mr. Peterson's elbow. He had slicked-back hair and a leather jacket.

"Well." Mr. Peterson dared to clap his hand on my broad shoulder again. "We're proud of you, son. This is Thomas Graham, a friend of mine from the local paper. He said you didn't return any of his calls."

What? I remembered Gramps moving the phone into his room. I remembered hearing his low voice answering it a few times. He'd never once mentioned calls for me.

"I was wondering if you'd give him a few words now. You know, the press coverage looks good for Milltown High, given that you're a student here."

I felt the heat in my neck rise flaming to my face. I glanced left and right, searching for an escape route. There were only swelling bunches of students leaning our way while pretending to talk.

"Not now, please," I said. *Did it come out sounding like I was pleading?*

"Judging from the fact you're out on our river regularly, you must plan to race again this coming season?" the reporter asked, stepping squarely in front of me. His face was over-friendly and deadly determined, his pencil poised above a slim notebook.

"Hey, I've got to get to class."

"Not for ten minutes," Mr. Peterson asserted.

I sighed and looked at the reporter. "Yes, I'm training for slalom kayak races."

"Races," the loitering jock mocked in a stage whisper.

"He's my hero," the jock's friend responded in a high-pitched voice, drawing laughter from the gathered crowd.

If the reporter heard, he ignored them. "Your grand-father is Malcolm Scruggs, the kayaker who was the first to conquer a bunch of rivers in South America, right?"

I relaxed a bit, deciding to ignore my detractors. "Yes."

"And is it true you're headed to South America soon to tackle a first descent of your own?"

I drew in my breath. *Gramps has let that out of the bag already?* I pictured Gramps sitting at the local bar, saying, "Thinks he's ready for an expedition, foolish boy. Well, I've called his bluff by paying his way. Let's see what he comes back with." I blinked and tried hard to imagine him saying instead, "My grandson, ready to carry on where I left off." But the first image weighed heavier.

I stared at the reporter, tongue-tied. The jocks were moving down the hallway, their hands trying to mimic pad-dling a kayak as they wiggled their bottoms and laughed.

"Rex?" Mr. Peterson was grinning broadly. He wanted the headline MILLTOWN HIGH KAYAK-CHAMP BAGS A FIRST RIVER DESCENT.

Well, so did I, but without the "Milltown High" bit, and not before I'd earned it.

"When do you leave?" Thomas Graham was pushing, ignoring the fact that I hadn't answered his previous question.

I closed my locker slowly. First, I needed my new passport to arrive. Then Gramps would book the plane ticket. Cheapskate that he was, I expected a red-eye econo flight.

Before I could answer, the bell rang. "Call me at home at five, okay?" I said, then pushed past him and beelined for Spanish. I plunked down at my desk and studied the graffiti on it, waiting for my pulse to slow.

"Life sucks," someone had written. I crossed off "sucks" and replaced it with "rocks." Clearly, the graffiti writer didn't have goals, didn't know how to reach out and make life happen. A positive attitude is everything. *I* will *pass my Spanish test.* I will *kayak the river Gramps walked away from in Colombia.*

A long-legged girl from the reserve passed by my desk, a whiff of lavender perfume trailing her. I'd noticed her before. She was pretty hot and always smiling at me. I mean, a guy knows when a girl is giving him the *I-want-you* look. Especially when no one else had been very friendly to the new kid. *Or is it just that I don't have time to make friends, given the demands of my training schedule?* In any case, sadly, she needed to find someone else. It wasn't going to happen between us. My grandpa would freak. She was from the wrong side of the river. Unless I decided I wanted to freak him out . . .

Now I'd lost my concentration. Oh, yeah, I was telling myself I would pass the Spanish test.

Two hours later, she sidled up to me as I sat shivering on a bench outside the school's front door, waiting for Gramps to pick me up.

"Hey, how'd the Spanish test go?"

"Excellent," I lied, barely glancing at her in hopes she'd go away. But also half-hoping she wouldn't.

"Yeah, was pretty easy, huh?" She snapped her gum, grinned at me, and sat down.

I glanced around, noticing a bunch of guys huddled over smokes in the parking lot. I was torn between finding an excuse to bolt and asking her name. Sure, there's some mixing between the "rez" and town kids, but I'm not your progressive, cross-cultural, wade-in-and-to-hell-with-what-anyone-thinks type. Not yet, anyway.

Then again, who besides Gramps would care if I hung out a little with a looker who appreciated my . . . *my what? Physique? Mystery?* I had no idea why she was pursuing me. But the native/aboriginal/First Nations/whatever-you-want-to-call-them jocks glaring at me from the parking lot could stuff it. If she wanted any of them, she'd have let them know already.

"My name's —" she started.

Panicking as I sighted Gramps' black pickup truck coming towards us, I leapt up and moved a few feet away.

"Look, I gotta go. My grandpa's here." It was outrageously rude, and I instantly hated myself for it. "Talk to you later," I added lamely as she rose and stamped off.

"So," Gramps said with a leer as I climbed in and slammed the door shut. "You like the dark ones, eh?"

"Leave it, Gramps," I snarled, hating how old and out of it he was. "A charming old racist," my mom would purr. "He grew up in different times."

"Nah, good to see it in you, boy." He chuckled too loud, like we'd shared a manly joke. I counted to three as we pulled away. Then his face grew stern. "But leave it at the looking, if you know what I mean. There's plenty of white women in this town. We're not meant to mix with Indians."

I clenched my teeth so tightly, I wasn't sure I'd be able to pry them apart. But I dared not say anything to the person paying half my way to Colombia.

"Want to go hunting with me on Saturday?" he asked.

"Maybe, if training doesn't get in the way," I answered vaguely. I hated hunting. He knew it.

"Good. Black bear season's open. Let's get us one. I'll make a man of you yet."

Silence stretched as the truck bounced across muddy ruts.

"Gramps, why would I need a guide in Colombia?"

"'Cause it's impossible to get decent topographic maps – the local army doesn't want them circulating."

"The Colombian Army doesn't let maps out?"

"Well, Colombia's a bit of a mess. They've got guerilla soldiers trying to help the poor people and paramilitary soldiers trying to protect rich people from the guerillas. There aren't enough Colombian Army soldiers to keep the guerillas and paramilitaries under control, so it's been a free-for-all between the three armies for about fifty years. But the Colombian Army's just about on top of it now. That means there's a chance to get in and get that first descent."

"So it's safe where I'm going?"

"As far as I've been able to tell." He took a hand off the wheel and dug in a pack for some wrinkled Internet print-outs, which he shoved my way. I examined the map of

Colombia, with areas marked in white, gray, and black.

"White is *'currently deemed safe*,'" Gramps said. "Gray is *'pockets of military resistance.'* Black is . . ."

". . . *'closed: military zone.'*" I recited, studying the key. I let my index finger trace the portion of the Furioso River I was heading for and smiled. White, in between light strips of gray. Then I read the fine print at the bottom of the page. "'*Reliability of military updates varies. Check back frequently for reclassifications.'*"

"Some of the colored zones change every week," Gramps said with a frown. "But I've talked with the embassy, and where you're going has been white for months. They said this map is the best one there is. I wouldn't let you go if I thought there was danger."

"I know," I said. It was the one thing I was sure about.

"But any change once you arrive, I expect you to get yourself to the Canadian or U.S. embassy right away."

"Of course."

He swung the truck up to the house, braked, and idled the motor. "Your mom wants to talk to you. So I'm going to go get our hunting licenses. See you."

"Okay, Gramps. Thanks for the ride."

I jumped down, grabbed my backpack, and headed for the front door.

"Hey, Mom." She'd kicked off her running shoes and had her hand curled around a glass of fizzy water. I gave her a peck on the cheek. She was sitting on the new floral sofa she'd just talked Gramps into buying.

"Hi, Rex. Can we talk a minute?" Turning a concerned face to me, she patted the sofa beside her.

I shrugged and headed toward the fridge. "Sure."

"Why do you want to go to Colombia so much, Rex?"

I laughed, reached for a Coke, and plunked down on the sofa. "The river Gramps tried kayaking sixty years ago is one of the last ones left."

"What do you mean, exactly?"

"One of the last wild rivers in the world that hasn't been kayaked, but probably could be."

"That's because it's been a war zone all these years, Rex. You do know that, don't you?" She set her water glass down. Her hands twisted in her lap.

"Of course. And now it's not. Did Gramps show you the maps he downloaded?"

She nodded distractedly, running a finger along the rim of her glass. "And we spoke with embassy people together. They say it's safe at the moment, but to keep an eye on things."

"So there you go. That zone has been white for months now. The Colombian Army's chasing out the rebels." I popped the top of the can, then cupped a hand under it and gulped some down as Coke fizzed all over.

"I know I probably shouldn't worry, but . . ." She grabbed a tissue and dabbed the spray on my T-shirt.

I set the can down. "Mom, I know I can kayak that river. Gramps thinks I can too or he wouldn't send me. Right?"

"Right," Mom said like I wasn't there. She shook her head. "He's acting very strange, Rex. Muttering and ranting more than usual. I think it has to do with your grandma dying."

"Don't work yourself up, Mom," I said gently. "He's fine. It's all good."

"You're not like him, you know," she said, taking my hands in hers. I wanted to yank them away, but I didn't. She'd pulled up roots in Montana to help when Grandma fell ill, and now she'd lost her mom and was worrying too much about my trip and Gramps. And I was still in awe she'd persuaded Gramps to be my final sponsor.

"I mean, I know you want to be like him, or you used to anyway. And you *are* like him in some ways."

"Yeah?"

"You're strong, a natural athlete. Fearless, determined. But you're better than him in other ways."

"I am?"

"Sure. You care more about people. You have a stronger sense of right and wrong. You proved that when the ice broke up the other day."

I frowned. "That's not what Gramps said."

"Because he's jealous of you, Rex. I love him dearly, but he's a lone wolf – a stubborn, grumpy, old man. And you're young and full of promise, while he's getting old and frail."

I gulped down the last of my Coke. "What's your point, Mom?"

"I know how much you want that first descent, and your other sponsors think you can pull it off, and the embassy says it's okay, and you've got your two expedition mates on board, so I'm choosing to believe you are up to it." She turned to me with a fierce love in her eyes. My shoulders relaxed, and my heart felt warm. I gave her a big hug.

"Thanks, Mom!" I rose to head to my room.

"He was never really there for Mom and me, you know, Rex." I sat back down. "Always off kayaking, traveling the world. But your grandma's death has done something to him. You know what he said to me the other night?"

I said nothing.

"He said, 'Your mother was a good woman. And I was a lousy husband and father sometimes, Anne. I'm sorry. Guilt is a terrible thing to live with.'"

I raised an eyebrow. "Gramps said that?"

"He did. So you see? He's not himself at all." She sighed and reached for a pile of mail on the coffee table. Fishing out two envelopes, she handed them to me. One was registered mail.

My heart skipped a beat. "It came!" I tore the passport envelope open. Then I examined the other envelope. "From the Colombia Tourism Board. Hey, maybe they've decided to sponsor me."

I opened the envelope and read the letter aloud.

Dear Rex,

The Colombia Tourism Board is pleased to hear of your upcoming visit to Colombia. Regretfully, we are unable to sponsor your trip with funding as requested, but we are pleased to inform you that two of our business members have generously donated gift certificates. Enclosed please find

- a voucher for two nights' complimentary stay at the Magdalena Hotel
- a gift certificate for a week's kayak rental from *Expediciones del Río* (River Expeditions).

As explained in the accompanying document, Javier "Jock" Gómez, outfitter of *Expediciones del Río*, has also agreed to provide transportation between the airport, hotel, and river for you and your Brazilian companions if the three of you allow local media to feature you kayaking with him.

Congratulations. We hope you have a safe and pleasant journey.

Sincerely,

The Colombia Tourism Board

"This Jock guy wants a photo of Malcolm Scruggs' grandson," I said, grinning.

"Not of your Brazilian teammates?" Mom was quick to tease.

"I beat both of them last world championships," I reminded her. "Anyway, free kayak rental is worth something. So you're letting Gramps book my flight?"

"I am if you get permission to take your school exams early," she said, pursing her lips. "You need to qualify for graduation before you go."

"Consider it done." I smiled and rose to look out the living-room window at my river, now ripping down its course without a flake of ice to hinder it.

CHAPTER FOUR

The guerillas swarmed the community before breakfast. Myriam was up, lighting the fire in the woodstove outside the community center. The women around her were peeling potatoes and husking corn. The guerillas dragged a young boy into the courtyard and dropped him at Myriam's feet. His shirt was ripped, and his nose dripped blood on the dirt. Myriam guessed he'd been on guard duty and had fallen asleep.

Then a dozen soldiers – some of them not yet teenagers – ran about, shouting into the doorways of all the community-center buildings, ordering people outside at gunpoint. Abuela shuffled out in front of one gun, her head held high.

Their guns were Russian rifles, AK-47s. They wore berets and black rubber boots, not leather lace-up ones like the paramilitaries. When Capitán came flying out of the community center to bark at them, one of the guerillas' boots connected with his jaw, sending him yelping over to

Myriam. Her heart beating wildly, she placed a comforting hand on his head and held him near.

When she next looked up, she saw the soldiers applying their machetes to the community's garden, specifically to their coca plants. The government allowed *indígena* communities, but no one else, to grow coca in limited quantities for traditional medicinal and ceremonial use. This, of course, made non-*indígenas* – who grew it illegally to process into cocaine – jealous.

Alberto came running from the fields, well ahead of Papá and the men. He planted himself beside her. "Are you okay, Myriam?"

"Yes," she whispered.

He stood tall in the center of the courtyard and dared to nod at some of the guerillas as if in welcome. *Good thing Papá didn't see that*, Myriam thought.

"You've been talking with the paramilitaries," the commander shouted at Papá, who arrived breathless and without the hoe he'd been wielding in the cornfield. "You gave them a radio and told them where we're camped."

Papá looked at the roughed-up boy at Myriam's feet and ran his clear green eyes around his people in the courtyard. He shook his head. "We have no information. We gave them no information. They seized the radio."

"You lie!" shouted the young guerilla commander. He gave the boy at Myriam's feet a hard kick in the stomach that sent him sprawling dangerously close to the hot stove. Myriam watched the boy's hands rise to protect his head, but otherwise he didn't move from there or look up to meet anyone's eyes. He'd failed to sound the alarm. The community had worked out a system with whistles, and his signal should have prompted runners to the fields and huts. Myriam's community was good at responding quickly, at gathering almost instantaneously into a group too large for most soldiers to dare push around. But, this morning, the guerillas had found a weakness. Myriam knew that the boy, although only eight, was lucky to be alive.

"You gave them a radio," the commander accused again.

"They *took* my radio," Alberto declared.

"Quiet, Alberto," Papá ordered.

"They took it," Alberto repeated to the commander, hands on his hips.

The commander shouldered his gun and turned to smile at Alberto. "Did they threaten you?" he asked more gently, removing his beret to rub his head.

Alberto opened his mouth to respond, but caught Papá's eye.

"You need protection from them," the commander continued in a friendly tone. "They killed ten *indígenas* in the village just north of here last night."

Myriam's heart seized up. That's where Mamá was visiting Myriam's other grandmother. She looked at Papá and saw a flash of panic on his face, before he set his jaw. Alberto's eyes signaled that he also feared for Myriam's relatives.

"We don't need your protection," Papá addressed the guerilla commander in the same even tone he'd used with the paramilitaries. "We have our own system."

"What, unarmed boys who fall asleep?" the commander jeered in a raised voice, lowering his rifle and poking it at the boy still cowering beside the stove. "You need real protection, from those of us who are fighting for your cause."

"You know we don't get involved with either side," Papá recited. "We are neu – Alberto!"

The commander surveyed Alberto directly, sending a shudder up Myriam's spine. Papá should never have used Alberto's name in front of them. "Alberto, you know we protect *indígena* villages from the paramilitaries."

You used to a long time ago, before you turned corrupt, Myriam thought.

"And when boys or girls from those villages join us, we give them guns, uniforms, food, money. And send money back to their villages."

Myriam knew the last bit was a lie.

The commander shot a glance at some of the guerilla kids standing around, three of whom were *indígenas*. "Isn't that right?"

"Yes, comrade," they replied, smiling mechanically at Alberto.

Myriam watched Alberto's feet shift uneasily.

"Those who do not support us sometimes suffer," the commander added. "It is not necessary to suffer. If you don't give us soldiers, you need to pay us a *vacuna*."

Myriam drew in her breath. It was the first time the guerillas had demanded a "vaccine," or protection money from further attacks.

"I'm asking you to leave," Papá said, pulling himself up to his full height. The other men in the village stepped forward and formed a line across the courtyard, Papá in the middle. Myriam noticed Alberto moving into place slower than the rest. He alone would not raise his eyes to the guerillas now. The men and boys in the line carried no weapons, yet their faces revealed no fear. They were willing to die, if necessary, to retain their neutrality. Anything but neutrality was death in any case, Myriam reminded herself, and *indígenas* had been dying at the hands of outsiders for hundreds of years.

"For now, we'll leave," the commander said in his overly friendly voice. But he approached Alberto, placed a gentle hand on his shoulder, and smiled. Then he turned and pointed at a pig snuffling in a corner of the courtyard.

"Use your machetes," he ordered the boy soldiers who'd spoken earlier. "That will be our supper."

The boy soldiers chased the squealing pig until they had it secured between them. Myriam looked away as their machetes fell and blood sprayed.

Within minutes, the guerillas exited the mutilated garden with their commander, the pig's carcass hanging from a pole between them. They headed toward the bridge that crossed the river not far from Myriam's community. Myriam noticed that one of the boy soldiers had a hole in the bottom of his left boot. But he had boots. And soon, he'd have pork in his belly, while her family would go hungry.

Myriam waited until the guerillas were gone. "Breakfast will be ready in a few minutes," she announced in a quivering voice as the line of men broke up. "Abuelita, I'll help you back indoors."

"Not until I've tended to this boy's injuries," she replied.

"They say the Colombian Army is starting to win the

war," her father said to no one in particular. "That's why both the guerillas and paramilitaries are getting more aggressive where they still have strongholds, like here."

"The Colombian Army will never come up here," Alberto retorted. "They don't care about *indígenas*. Do we have enough money for a *vacuna*?"

"We'll never pay a *vacuna*!" Papá said. "If a village pays a *vacuna*, the soldiers only come back for more money, and more again, until there is nothing left.

"You," Papá ordered two men in the community, "hurry to the next village and find out what happened." They nodded and jumped on their rickety one-speeds, pedaling hard up the dusty trail.

Abuela, who'd finished treating the boy with the bloody nose, stood and leaned on her cane. Papá bent down to offer a hand to the boy. "Come with me," he said sternly, then threw a dark look at Alberto. "You, too, Alberto."

"Do you think Alberto will get in trouble?" Rosita asked Myriam in a strained whisper, her face serious. "Do you think Mamá is okay?"

"If Papá gives Alberto a talking to, it's because he has too high an opinion of the guerillas," she replied. "And Mamá? Of course she is okay. Maybe she'll be home by the time you return from school."

"Abuelita hasn't changed her mind about you going to university?" Rosita asked.

"No," Myriam said bitterly. "She found out I have enough credits to graduate without finishing the year, as long as I complete one more exam from home. But please ask my teacher if she has a message for me." *An acceptance to university — on condition I pass that exam — even if it rips me apart from my beloved family*, she prayed silently.

An hour later, Rosita started herding up children for the long walk to school. Then, chewing her braid and giving her older sister a mournful side glance, she took Myriam's former place at the head of the little procession.

Myriam's heart swelled with sorrow. *No more school. No more English. Trapped here forever, unless . . .*

The men came back in from the field at lunchtime. Their body odor filled the courtyard as Myriam and the women stirred a pot of watery rice broth and pulled cheese bread from firewood burning in an ovenlike cavity between three large stones.

Mamá arrived on her bicycle from the opposite direction, sandwiched between the two men her husband had sent, baby Alejandro on her back. Beneath the shadow of her hat, her long braid was askew. She looked like she'd been crying.

Papá hurried over to embrace her. Myriam followed suit, the twins at their heels.

"Mamá! Mamá!" Flora and Freddy sang in unison, dancing a toddler dance until she lifted and hugged each in turn.

Over lunch, as everyone leaned close to hear, Mamá related what had happened. The paramilitaries had shot and killed two groups of five guards each, who'd challenged them before more guards could arrive.

"Then the soldiers set fire to some of the huts. That's when a boy stepped forward and volunteered to join the troop."

"Did his parents not try to stop him?" Papá demanded, face taut as he eyed Alberto, who was listening intently.

Tears leaked from Mamá's eyes. "His parents were killed by guerilla land mines last month, and he'd threatened many times to join the paramilitaries. His grandmother let him go because she said there was not enough food to feed him."

"The land mines could have been paramilitary land mines!" Alberto spoke up with vehemence. "He should have joined the guerillas, who protect the poor, not the paramilitaries, who protect the rich."

"We cannot trust either," Papá shot back. "There will be no peace for us until both are gone from this area."

Alberto held his tongue. Papá looked from him to Myriam, with those penetrating green eyes. "Myriam, now that Mamá is back, you need to check the trout tanks. Alberto, go with her."

"But I don't need Alberto. . . ."

"I said, Alberto will go with you," Papá insisted.

"Me, me, me, too!" Freddy sang, reaching his chubby arms up to Myriam.

Papá smiled distractedly as Alberto reached over to tickle Myriam's little brother. "And Freddy," Papá added in a warmer tone.

Although Myriam would have preferred to walk alone to the river, a part of her was relieved to have Alberto along after the morning's tension. He circled around her to make faces at Freddy, who giggled and squirmed on Myriam's back.

"Freddy, I'm a condor," Alberto teased, flapping his arms like wings as Freddy squealed with delight.

"Freddy, I'm a puma," he said, dropping on all fours and growling softly.

Condors and pumas, Myriam thought. *Numerous in these mountains in Abuela's time. Now both nearly extinct, thanks to land developers and soldiers.*

When they reached the river, they located the eight trout holding tanks the community had built during a work party. Bit by bit, the *indígenas* were improving their lot in life through *mingas,* occasional work-party projects partially funded by the government.

"Hordes of fish," Myriam enthused, peering down to watch tiny trout darting about, glistening in the afternoon sun. The villagers had built the tanks – each a little larger than Myriam's family's entire hut – along the riverbank so that the community could use diverted current to sustain the fish.

"They'll fetch good money in the market," Alberto said. "And taste good, the few we'll keep to eat."

Myriam flashed back to the long day in which the men had mixed and poured cement to build the tanks. She, like all the women and girls, had stayed in the village and cooked massive amounts of food for the after-work-party feed.

It was at the feed that Alberto had drawn her aside and asked her to marry him. He was still waiting for her answer.

"Tonight we'll celebrate Mamá being home," Myriam told Freddy.

Alberto shrugged. "Except for those of us on guard duty. The paramilitaries have been harassing us more and more. We have to step up patrols. But that means fewer people to do the work that needs doing."

He dipped into his woven shoulder bag and produced handfuls of fish-food pellets to pour into Myriam's and Freddy's outstretched palms. He guided Freddy's hands to a position over the wire-fence-topped tank. Freddy opened his palms and watched the food drift down to the tiny fish, which went into a feeding frenzy. Freddy smiled and clapped his hands, and Alberto hugged him and gave him more. Birds sang to them from the nearby treetops. Myriam felt she should be happy, but all she could think about was whether the university would accept her – and what she should do if it did.

When he'd emptied his sack, Myriam walked a few steps upriver and strode into the water, letting the mud squelch between her toes. "I love this river," she murmured.

"Me, too," Alberto said, tentatively circling her waist with his arms.

She whirled around and stepped sideways. "Abuelita and Papá have made me quit school."

Alberto smiled. "I know. It's good. School's boring, and it means you and I can –"

"It's not boring to me. I like school, especially English."

"But why?" he asked, clearly perplexed.

"School is the only place I can use the Internet. Sometimes I write reports in English about what the soldiers do to us and send them to places."

"What places? Who cares?" Alberto said in a raised voice.

Freddy shifted on his sister's back.

"Foreigners, especially *indígenas* in other countries, care. Sometimes they answer me and say they are sending my information to reporters and politicians there. Those people will pressure the Colombian Army to protect us."

Alberto shook his head. "Myriam, I know you want to help, but letting the guerillas protect us is the only way."

"It's not! The guerillas tell lies to get children to join them. And they torture or kill anyone who tries to quit after they've joined!"

"Myriam, those are just rumors. You don't know what you're talking about. You got those crazy ideas from school. It's just as well you're done going there now."

She crossed her arms and glared at him, watching his face turn even more serious.

"Myriam, I think it's time I join the guerillas. The pay could support us, you know."

She felt her jaw stiffen. She wanted to pound his chest. "No, no, no! You know how I feel about that! You know how Papá feels. Why do you keep bringing it up?"

He lowered his head, but his shoulders remained erect. "Okay, let's not fight now. Myriam, my untamed sweetheart, follow me."

He lifted Freddy from Myriam's back and tucked him under one arm, then grabbed her hand and pulled her to shore. They headed upstream. Trying to swallow her anger, Myriam struggled to keep up with his long strides as they wound their way through brush and trees to a small cliff face overlooking the river. There, still holding tightly to Freddy, Alberto started to scramble up small indentations in the rock that someone had made with a pickax many decades before. Myriam, concerned for Freddy's safety, sprang up the footholds after Alberto. Hunger made her grab some figs off a wild fig tree on the way.

"Why are we going to the cave?"

"*Shhh*," Alberto said, turning with a grin. He ducked into an opening in the rock. Freddy was still under his arm. Myriam wriggled in after them, mindless of the dirt on the jeans she wore. When her eyes adjusted to the dark, she noticed a blanket and water bottle in one corner. She frowned at Alberto.

He grabbed the blanket and spread it out, then coaxed Freddy to lie on it. He offered him a sip of water from a plastic pop container, which Freddy guzzled greedily. Myriam produced the figs, and all three munched on them while lying stomach-down on the blanket and peering out the cave's opening.

From this commanding perch, Myriam could see a long way across the field on the other side of the river. She could see the daisies soaking up the sun and the high grasses waving in the wind. She could smell the pine and eucalyptus trees and hear the roar of rapids that stretched endlessly upstream and downstream. She hadn't been in the cave for years. Lying here reminded her that nowhere else offered such a sweeping view of her river.

"It's beautiful up here," she acknowledged.

"Like you," Alberto said, studying her face. "Will you say yes, then? We have your parents' blessing, you know."

Myriam's insides churned. "No! I'm sorry, Alberto, but no."

"You need more time," Alberto asserted with a confidence that made her want to push him off the cave ledge.

Just then Freddy pointed. "Puma," he whispered.

Relieved for the distraction, Myriam looked across the river. At first, she didn't see it. Then she heard Alberto's excited whisper, "It *is* a puma!"

The blond cat moved stealthily through the long grasses, stopping to sniff every few yards. Myriam had seen one only once before, as a child. Mostly she'd seen pictures in books and heard the elders' stories. Her senses were on fire; she felt extraordinarily privileged to witness its primal grace. When it reached the river, it sipped cautiously, ears twitching and head lifting. Clearly it had no scent of them in the cave far overhead.

Myriam hardly dared breathe. Alberto looked entranced.

Then Freddy shouted, "Puma!"

It turned and leapt away so fast that Myriam barely had time to register its flight. She saw only the tips of its ears and its tail as it ran through the grass. One leap, two, and then came the deafening explosion.

Myriam's entire body convulsed with horror. Alberto placed a hand over Freddy's eyes as the boy began to scream. His other hand sought Myriam's.

"Land mine," they uttered in fractured voices.

CHAPTER FIVE

I've finally arrived in southwest Colombia. It feels safe and peaceful here. Nearby is a snow-covered, inactive volcano with wild-looking streamlets running down its sides. It doesn't look too steep for hiking – a walk in the park for me! My host here is a light-skinned Mestizo – which means of mixed breeding, Spanish and Indian. A pleasant sort of fellow with good manners. Far preferable to the poor, dirty Indians in town who wander about barefoot, begging for work. Many of the males wear hideous skirts and are drunk from bottles of homemade sugarcane brandy they hide on them. Their womenfolk wear ridiculous black felt hats, heavy skirts, and ponchos. They are not what anyone would call beautiful. – Malcolm Scruggs

I smiled as I closed Gramps' journal and returned it to my backpack. *Gramps, you'd never dare write like that these days,* I thought. I stifled the notion that maybe no one should have in the mid-twentieth century, either.

As I looked at the mountains and rivers beneath the plane's wing, the seatbelt light came on and the flight attendants asked everyone to prepare for landing. At least, I thought that's what they requested as I shrugged off a humiliating sense of being back in Spanish class on exam day.

So I was just about there, finally, in southwest Colombia — land of Gramps' attempt on the Furioso River sixty years before. I sat up straight and proud. *Show me what you've got, Colombia!*

The plane taxied to a halt. I glimpsed tropical vegetation and smog. Somehow, I'd made it through customs on my marginal Spanish when I'd changed planes in Bogotá. No one had questioned the paddling and camping gear or the antique necklace in my backpack. As I walked into the greeting area here in Neiva, I spotted a fit-looking dude in his midtwenties, waving a sign saying WELCOME, REX SCRUGGS.

"Jock? I'm Rex." I pumped Jock's hand. "Thanks for meeting me. And for donating the kayak rental."

"No problem! Good to meet you, Rex. Welcome to Colombia. Henrique and Tiago fly in tomorrow morning and are getting to my place by bus. I'm excited to show you guys the Magdalena River."

"Perfect."

We chatted on the way to Jock's nearly new red Toyota Hilux pickup truck, me relieved at the guy's fluency in English. The air was hot and humid, the sky clear. The high elevation made me noticeably breathless. I needed to get used to that fast.

"I hear your rivers are some of the best in the world," I said.

"Got that right! And you said your grandfather kayaked in Colombia a long time ago."

"That's true," I replied, smiling. "People still know who he is around these parts?"

"*Um*, actually I hadn't heard of him before you and I exchanged e-mails." Jock looked a little sheepish.

"Oh." I was dumbfounded. "But he did quite a few first descents in South America, even tried for one here in Colombia."

"That's what you said."

"He'd have finished it, but he claims he got run off by the locals."

"I see."

He isn't even going to ask which river? Fine. "How far from here to where you run your operation?"

"More than a four-hour drive, unfortunately. Our roads are pretty potholed." He lifted my pack into the back of the truck. "We'll get there well before dark."

I shed my jacket and hopped into the front. "Sounds good. I read it's not all that safe to drive after dark here. Is that true?"

"No way!" Jock answered so fast that I felt a little suspicious. "Colombia's all cleaned up from the bad old days. It's totally safe now, an awesome place for tourists to come. Almost all my clients are from Britain, the United States, or Canada."

"Guess that's why your English is so good. My Spanish is lousy."

"No problem. You can practice it with me if you want to."

"Nah, I'm good with English. So, is this a new business for you?" I sniffed the orange scent of the air freshener hanging from his rearview mirror. The inside of his cab looked freshly vacuumed.

"Absolutely. I started as a kayaker, then guided for a raft outfitter, then started this business last year. You three will be just about the first to paddle the new kayaks I just bought." We were winding our way through Neiva traffic. Half-choking on the vehicle fumes, I rolled up my window.

"What kind of kayaking do you do?" I asked.

"Whitewater. Mostly on the Magdalena."

"*Mmm*, ever done a first descent?" I ventured.

"I'm not into that. Sounds like you are, judging from your letter to the Colombia Tourism Board."

"I kayak the heaviest whitewater I can find. Colombia has the same international scale, Class I to VI, right?"

Jock grinned. "Yes, same scale. Well, the Magdalena section we do downstream from my shop is Class II to III. Good fun and safe for my clients. Safe is good for a new business."

I sighed. Safe meant boring, but never mind. Henrique, Tiago, and I hadn't specified where we hoped to paddle after the Magdalena, for fear Jock might try to scoop us. He just knew we were going to "check out the possibility" of a first descent.

He certainly wasn't kidding about the potholes. As we headed out of Neiva, we bumped and wound along the two-lane highway, sometimes sharing it with donkeys carrying heavy loads. We passed girls in tight dresses with spaghetti straps, dusty guys peeing in the grass by the roadside, and scooters overloaded with helmetless riders. Every few yards, stands with corrugated tin roofs featured vendors selling juice, fruit, cheese, and pastry in plastic bags. Plus baskets, pots, and cell phone minutes.

Must've been the long flight or the humidity, but I nodded off till Jock's pickup truck lurched and came to a halt. I lifted my head, saw a sign identifying some kind of battalion, and soldiers with machine guns. The soldiers were scattering large pieces of truck tires all over the road.

"Now there's a different way to make speed bumps," I said. "Is this a police roadblock or something?" I shivered in the cooler mountain air.

"It's the Colombian Army looking for paramilitaries or guerillas. Don't speak unless you have to," Jock warned in a low voice.

A soldier poked his head through Jock's rolled-down window and demanded photo identification. When I handed over my passport, he glared at me, then wandered off to hold a roadside conference with other soldiers. Just as I was worrying whether I was going to get my passport back, he dropped it through the truck window and waved us on with his gun.

"Are we going to get stopped very often?" I asked. Privately, I was thinking it was a good thing the national army was around and so thorough. Made me feel safer.

Jock's smile seemed forced. "No, the Colombian Army doesn't go much farther up this mountain."

For a moment, I felt unsettled. *But what do I know about how things work around here?* The embassies hadn't warned me off, and Jock himself had been pretty keen for me to come. So I didn't ask more questions and slept for most of the ride.

———

"We're here," Jock finally announced. I sprang out of the truck and walked briskly to the river. It smelled fresh, the scent of pine and eucalyptus in the air. I had to admit how pretty it was — maybe even one of the most beautiful places I'd been — and neither Montana nor Alberta are shabby in the natural-beauty department. The river was big, moving at well over 3,500 cubic feet per second. Fun and safe-looking, like Jock had said. Downstream I glimpsed midriver boulders, but not much that would worry a skilled kayaker or a big rubber raft. Upstream was even tamer, swift-moving water for as far as I could see.

I stretched my stiff body, turning 360 degrees to take in the surrounding mountain range. The mighty Andes, Gramps' playground when he was young. The upper stretches looked like they might hold steep mountain creeks for "real" kayaking. I couldn't wait to get the show on the road.

I followed Jock to the basic concrete-block building with tin roof that served as his headquarters. Its single window and door faced the river. My eyes passed over the stack of inflated rubber rafts in an attached shed and focused on a small rack of new-looking plastic kayaks in army camouflage pattern. *Excellent.*

"So, you rent out kayaks often?" I asked Jock.

"No. They're mostly for my guides."

"And you've kayaked some rivers higher up in the mountains?"

Jock hesitated. "No. I don't know much about the rivers farther up."

"Why not? Can't we take the truck up there and you can join Henrique, Tiago, and me?"

He turned and stared at me. I couldn't read his expression. Finally, he said, "Not many roads up there. So, no, that's not an option. If you want a first descent, there's one creek close by I was going to recommend. . . ."

"No, we're set on the Furioso," I informed him, taking satisfaction in the way his eyebrows shot up. "So how else would we get up there? Tractor? Mule?" I smiled at the image of kayaks balanced on a mule's back. I knew there were trails up there. I hadn't been able to get topographical maps, but Gramps had told me. Back in his day, he and his expedition mates had used lightweight, fold-up canvas kayaks, carried them up in big backpacks, then put them together like a tent with tent poles. Those were the days before sturdy plastic kayaks, like Jock had. None of us — my Brazilian friends and me — were old enough to rent a car, so we had to figure out a way to get to the Furioso. I'd been hoping for a ride from Jock.

Jock's hands moved to his hips. "Rex, the Furioso is out of the question. Even if it were runnable, which I doubt, it's on *indígena* land, *resguardos*. Like your Indian reservations. Basically, no one goes up there except the local priest and soldiers." The last word came out kind of tense.

"*Indígena.*" I stumbled over the pronunciation and pictured the barefoot, felt-hatted Indians of my grandfather's journal. I smiled. They'd know the rivers up there, might help me out for a little money. *Or an avocado sandwich?* I stifled a chuckle. Oh, yeah, and I was supposed to look up the family my grandfather had gotten the necklace from.

"Ever met any? Do they come down the mountain some-times?" I tried to keep my voice nonchalant.

"Yeah, at the market here in town. You should check it out this afternoon. Good for souvenirs. Plus, buying things from the *indígenas* helps support their community," he added tentatively, like he wasn't sure that would concern me.

"Sounds good, and the Magdalena looks fun," I said politely, even though it looked a little boring. I'd push for more information about rivers up the mountains tomor-row, after my teammates arrived.

Jock smiled. "Yeah, you'll enjoy the market. I'll drop you off at your hotel now and pick you up at eleven in the morning, just after your friends get here."

"Okay."

Set back from the main street's uneven dirt road, the slightly dilapidated Magdalena Hotel, I noticed, was under renovation where it shared a wall with the police station, which also seemed to be undergoing repairs.

"Hey, next to the police station. Can't get safer than that!"

Jock gave me a strange look, but didn't say anything. Three machine-gun-toting policemen in front of the station searched me with their eyes as Jock lifted my pack out. They looked all of eighteen. *Don't they know it's rude to stare?*

Jock helped me check in. "The market closes in an hour. It's down the main street, then turn left."

"Gotcha."

———

I left my stuff in the ordinary-looking room and headed for the market. When I rounded the corner, I smiled. Music blared from dusty boom boxes; people in stalls shouted out their wares; and crowds moved up and down the flagstone plaza. The tons of natives didn't look so different from ours, except for their ankle-length skirts, ponchos, and funny felt hats. The men's skirts were long and straight, and their ponchos were sleeveless. They wore their black hair short. The women's fuller skirts had lines of trim, and their ponchos covered their arms. All the women had long braids, and many carried babies in bright sashes.

I approached an older woman. "Calambás *familia?*" I asked, gesturing around the market. Gramps had made me memorize the name.

She looked at me and held up a tray of cookies.

"*Cuánto?*" I asked, fishing into my jeans pocket for change.

"*Dos miles pesos.*" Two thousand pesos.

Dead cheap, but I handed her half of what she asked for, just like Gramps had advised.

Her dark eyes turned resentful, but she passed me the cookies. I bit into one. *Not bad.*

"*Gracias,*" I said.

I worked my way through the market for more than an hour, asking lots of people if they knew the Calambás *familia.* Growing frustrated and impatient, I was about to give up and head back to my hotel when, finally, someone pointed me to an elderly, barefoot woman. She was seated across the plaza on a blanket in dusty grass, selling bundles of herbs. I headed over. She was turned the other way. A long braid extended from below her hat to her tiny waist. Even from the side, I could see that whiskers poked out above her upper lip. *Gross.* She looked way too old to be selling stuff in a noisy, dirty marketplace.

"*Cuánto de las hierbas?*" How much for the herbs?

She turned and stared.

"*Cuánto?*"

She looked briefly at the herbs in her lap, then returned to studying my face. Finally, she seemed to pull herself together and named a price. This time, I gave her the full amount. She pressed a big bundle of herbs into my hands and smiled a toothless smile. Then I remembered to ask, "Calambás *familia?*"

"*Sí.*" Yes.

"Rex Scruggs," I said, extending my hand. Her hands flew to her face. *Okay, why am I freaking her out?* Next thing I knew, she rose on those tiny, frail-looking legs and clasped both my hands in her dark bony ones. I barely stopped myself from yanking my hands away. The top of her hat came to my shoulders, but that uplifted face, whiskers and all, glowed. She radiated welcome.

I started to babble in broken Spanish about my grandfather meeting someone from her family ages ago and about me wanting to hire a guide to kayak the river near her village.

She didn't seem to understand, and I couldn't figure out a word of her response. Plus I felt my face redden as she refused to release my hands. I'd pretty much decided she was crazy when a shadow fell over us. I turned to see a tall, skinny native boy, a little older than me, glaring. The old woman dropped my hands and started talking at the boy, calling him Alberto and gesturing wildly.

He listened to her for a moment, surveyed me coldly, then walked to a stand where a girl was selling embroidered tablecloths. He spoke to her briefly and then led her back to us.

The girl was lighter skinned and way better looking than any of the other *indígenas* I'd seen. She reminded me of the long-legged beauty at Milltown High I'd been rude to. But this one wasn't friendly. She looked at me with suspicion, then held an animated conversation with the herb lady, not a word of it in Spanish.

"I'm Myriam," she finally said, extending her hand reluctantly while the boy beside her hovered.

"You speak English!"

"My grandmother thinks you look like someone she met when she was young. But all white people look alike to us," she added. "What is it you're trying to tell her?"

I felt tongue-tied for a second. *All white people look alike? Who does this girl think she is? And why does the guy beside her remind me of a bouncer about to throw me out?* I had half a mind to whirl around and head back to my hotel.

Instead, I drew myself up to my full height. "My grandfather, who's a famous explorer, traveled here sixty years ago. And he met the Calambás family near the Furioso River. He told me to ask around for them."

She didn't reply at first. She just looked me up and down like she'd taken a sudden dislike to me. The boyfriend, if that's what he was, was watching her every expression. The old woman was speaking excitedly in her language.

"I'm Myriam Calambás," the girl finally said.

"Hey, that's great," I enthused. "My name's Rex Scruggs, and I'm looking to hire someone who knows the Furioso. I'm going to kayak it with two friends."

A half-smile played on Myriam's lips. But just as I thought we'd gotten somewhere, she turned and spoke to the boy, Alberto, beside her. He laughed, called out to others, and pointed at me. In no time, he'd drawn a small crowd, who pressed around him to listen. The only word I understood was *"El Furioso."*

I looked from the crazy woman, who was staring at me, to Myriam, who just stood there with crossed arms. *Of course*, I thought. *They don't know what kayaks are. Or they don't think it's possible to kayak the river, since they know nothing about the sport.* That wasn't the right way to start.

I pulled out my wallet and tugged some bills from it. "This is what I'll pay you for a week of guiding," I told Myriam. "All you have to do is answer some questions about the river and hike along it with me and my friends for a ways. Maybe not even an entire week."

It had the intended effect. People stopped laughing and fixed their eyes on my money. Myriam uncrossed her arms and looked from the wallet to me. And the crazy woman started talking to the girl. I got the sense the crazy woman was on my side, but Myriam shook her head.

"Twice that," she stated, meeting my eyes with firm resolve.

My mouth dropped open. *What should I do?* Gramps would walk away, for sure. And give her an earful. But, hey, she was a member of the family he'd told me about, she spoke English, and she was extremely cute. *And so what if she's a tough little negotiator?* Clearly the natives had learned a thing or two since Gramps' time. Though it would cut into my spending money big-time, I could do it. There wouldn't be many other expenses, after all.

"Okay," I said, half-regretting it as murmurs of admiration for Myriam rose all around. Admiration from everyone but her bouncer, that is.

Did I detect a flash of amazement on Myriam's face before she smiled? Man, she was more than cute; she was drop-dead gorgeous. And I'd finally impressed her. She stuck out her hand out for me to shake.

"How will you get your kayaks up to our village?" she asked.

I shrugged. "Does someone in your village have a four-wheel drive?"

She smiled in a way that made me feel stupid. "Tractor or mules. I'd recommend the mules. And that will be extra because it takes it away from planting and moving our crops and materials for a day."

I sucked in my breath and felt very tired suddenly. Okay, I was getting taken to the cleaners by Myriam Calambás. But I convinced myself it would all work out.

Over the next half hour, we agreed that the hostile bouncer – Alberto – would show up at Jock's place with two mules in three days and guide me, Henrique, and Tiago up to their village. For this, I had to pay Myriam half the guiding fee up front. But it was almost worth it to see her face light up again.

I then found myself buying three embroidered table-cloths without even bargaining, I guess because I was sure my mom would like them. By now, the market was rapidly disappearing, with stalls being taken down and goods going into the burlap bags everyone seemed to carry.

"Thanks for everything," I said, holding my hand out once more to Myriam as I ignored the frown this put on Alberto's face.

"You're welcome. See you Tuesday," she said, shaking it briefly with a hand that wasn't half as warm or moist as mine.

Rex, get a grip, I told myself as I headed back to the hotel. *She'll fall for you soon enough. Play hard to get until then. And remember, you're the boss.*

CHAPTER SIX

I t was Monday, two days after market day. Myriam
watched the schoolchildren crest the hill and tear ahead
of Rosita. Rosita and some of her girl cousins lowered
the smaller children they were carrying so they could race
into their mothers' arms with happy cries. Myriam's eyes
remained on Rosita. She felt her heart turn over as her
sister fished an envelope out of her skirt pocket.

"What does it say?" Rosita asked as Myriam tore it open.

Myriam took a very deep breath to keep from shouting
for joy, using all her self-control to force a serious expression
onto her face. *Should I tell Rosita, swear her to secrecy?* she wondered. *No, not yet. There are still plans to make and money to collect
from the ignorant white boy. The one I might persuade to deliver me
to the bus for university, if I actually have the nerve to go through
with this.*

"It's from my teacher. It's the exam I have to take and
send back. And she says she enjoyed teaching me and best
of luck." Myriam allowed herself a sad smile.

Rosita shrugged and strode over to Mamá.

"Myriam," Mamá called, releasing the twins so they could hug Rosita and jostling to calm the baby on her back.

"Yes?" Myriam responded, stuffing the acceptance letter – accepting her on condition she pass her final exam, which of course she would – deep into her skirt pocket and walking to her mother with the twins on her arm.

"Abuelita's feeling poorly. She's begging for a coca leaf."

"She doesn't remember that the soldiers destroyed our garden?" Myriam asked.

"No," Mamá said with a sigh. "Coca plants were always around when our elders were young. They won't accept anything else for aches and pains."

"Should we fetch a doctor?"

"You know we can't afford one. Abuelita's the closest thing to a doctor we have. And as stubborn as a mule," Mamá added.

Myriam nodded. Between farmers growing coca for illegal, high-paying cocaine operations and the government set on destroying those fields, the cost of the leaves had risen more than tenfold within Abuela's lifetime. The elders just couldn't understand that it was impossible to get any outside of the community's garden.

"What are you asking, Mamá?" Myriam's stomach tightened.

"See if you can pick some," Mamá pleaded. "Ask Alberto to help you."

Myriam felt her own sharp intake of breath. "You can't ask us to do that, Mamá. Please, Mamá, don't."

But Mamá merely hugged Rosita and the twins close,

fastening her eyes on the ground. Myriam's throat felt dry and scratchy, and she knew she couldn't argue further.

"Be careful," Mamá said as she leaned over to kiss Myriam's cheek.

Before supper, Myriam and Alberto climbed on their bicycles and rode up a series of bumpy trails.

"We ditch the bikes here," Alberto said in a low voice, pointing to a field surrounded by a barbed-wire fence.

"Is the fence electric?" Myriam asked.

"No, that would draw too much attention," Alberto replied. "See how they mix potatoes, corn, and plantain in with the coca plants? So military helicopters can't tell it's a coca plantation."

"And they have labs for turning the coca leaves into cocaine?"

"Somewhere," he said uneasily.

"And the money goes to pay for soldiers' food and uniforms and guns and grenades. . . ."

"The paramilitaries," Alberto said forcefully. "Only the paras live off drug money. Not the guerillas."

"That's right. The guerillas kidnap people instead," Myriam said sarcastically, knowing full well that some guerilla units ran on drug money as well. "I've also heard that both paras and guerillas torture soldiers who disobey commands. Even the little-kid soldiers."

"Shut up, Myriam. You don't know anything about it, and if someone's listening, you'll get us killed."

"It's Abuelita getting us killed. For a handful of coca leaves."

"Because our garden got hacked up," Alberto said, spitting into the dirt. "You know I should join the guerillas. You have to face up to it one of these days. Now stop talking."

I'll never encourage that, but I'll shut up for now, Myriam thought wearily. She didn't want to fight anyway. Alberto was a good man, as fiercely loyal to family and the community as she was. Just not the right match for her anymore — not since he'd quit school. She tried to shrug off the guilt she felt for refusing to marry him.

He crept up to the fence, pressed the bottom wire down with his shoe, and held the other up high. "Quick," he whispered.

Myriam bent low and stepped through the opening, then crouched and looked around. Little birds hopped about on the ground between the rows of plants. Larger birds sang to the gentle swish of bushes in the breeze. It was peaceful here. She crept stealthily through the field to some head-high coca plants. Inspecting their straight branches, she ran her fingers along the opaque, oval leaves. Among the *indígenas*, picking coca leaves is a sacred act, one that only women and children perform. Myriam had to select, pluck, and stash the leaves in her fiber bag, and Alberto had to stand guard. It would take a few hours to ferment and dry the leaves back home. Then she'd place them on low-burning wood coals in a big clay pot, moving them about just so to make sure they didn't burn.

Her ancestors had been doing this for thousands of years — for medicine, nutrition, and ceremonies. *Why should narcotics agents from other countries suddenly make it so difficult?*

Something is not right about this field, Myriam thought as she walked the corridors between the plants, searching for leaves that were ready. *Something is different about the leaves.*

A distant dog's bark jerked her head up. She looked back and saw Alberto waving frantically at her. Bending lower, she plucked, walked, and plucked her way back towards him. *Do I have enough yet? Just a few more.*

The dog's bark was louder, and Myriam thought she heard a shout. She was close enough now to see Alberto silently mouthing "hurry." She closed her fiber bag and started running, flying past the potatoes, corn, plantain, and yucca root planted around the coca.

The dog's bark sounded alarmingly close now. The dog came tearing down the dirt corridor straight for her. For a second Myriam froze in fear, then sprinted for Alberto. Small rocks cut into her bare feet. Branches slapped her face. Roots threatened to trip her. A man was shouting somewhere behind the dog, which was only a few bounds away now. Alberto's worn shoes were firmly holding down the lowest wire. One long arm held the next wire as high as it would go, and the other reached for her hand. Their fingers met as the dog sank its teeth into the back of her ankle. Alberto's palms clenched hers as she started to fall headlong. Then he caught and pulled her through. Pain shot up her leg as the movement ripped her skin from the dog's teeth.

"Run!" Alberto insisted as he turned to throw stones at the dog.

She heard the dog yelp and, seconds later, heard its owner fire gunshots. But, by then, she and Alberto were sprinting in a wild zigzag pattern for the heavy brush by the river. They mounted their bikes and tore down the trail, Myriam's ankle throbbing and her precious fiber bag of leaves dangling from her handlebars.

Suddenly, she knew what was wrong with the field. "Alberto!" she called as he came abreast for a moment. "The coca leaves – they were trimmed!"

His face went pale. He understood what that meant.

CHAPTER SEVEN

Jock's kayak bobbed through the sunlit whitewater ahead. I yawned as I saw his signal from the eddy below this, our second rapid of the day on the Magdalena River. I patted the pocket of my paddling jacket, which held the special necklace. Beside me, in his kayak, sat Tom, a bearded young backpacker from Texas who'd dropped into Jock's shop and signed on for this afternoon's trip. Henrique and Tiago, fresh off a plane and bus this morning, were nearby.

Henrique was just like I remembered him: an ever-serious face beneath a generous mop of dark curly hair, complemented by a "soul patch" of hair on his chin. He was as short and powerfully built as his "shadow," the much quieter Tiago, whose more relaxed face was framed by straight black hair pulled into a ponytail. I remembered that ponytail hanging loosely from under his helmet as he negotiated slalom poles with impressive ease at the last whitewater slalom world championships.

"How's this compare with the Brazilian rivers you guys do?" I asked Henrique.

He gave me a sardonic smile. "More action at home than this one."

"This one's got more than enough action for me," Tom cut in, stretching his neck to glimpse Jock's kayak pulling into an eddy at the bottom of the rapid. "Does it look okay down there?"

"It's fine," Henrique responded, winking at me as Tiago rolled his eyes. We all found it a pain to have a novice along on our afternoon trip.

"Looks easy," I told Tom while grinning at Lina, the cute young female reporter Jock had arranged to shoot the Brazilians and me. She was squatting onshore, aiming her camera at us.

"Great, thanks," Lina said in Spanish as Tom beat Henrique and Tiago in translating her words for me. Henrique and Tiago spoke decent Spanish and English as well as their native Portuguese, but already we'd noticed that Tom was the best of our group when it came to Spanish.

"See you at the end of the river run," Lina added. Her smile sparkled. Her tank top showed off her tanned shoulders beautifully. I pretended not to notice my Latino teammates staring at her appreciatively.

"She's a hot one, huh?" Henrique said when she was out of earshot. "I think she and Jock are an item."

"They are," Tom confirmed.

"Oh," I said, vaguely disappointed. *Oh, well.* I waved good-bye to Lina. "You're next, Tom. Go for it."

Tom wiped sweat from his forehead and fiddled with

the buckle of his helmet. "Jock went left after the big rock, didn't he? I couldn't see. You sure it's okay?"

Henrique and Tiago smiled as I failed to stifle a chuckle. Poor Tom had paddled only a few times before, and he'd warned us he didn't know how to roll if he capsized. Which meant Jock, the Brazilians, and I would be rescuing him if he flipped. The river was fast-moving, but this rapid was only Class II, so he'd have to be pretty incompetent or unlucky to go over.

"Relax, Tom," I reassured him. "Jock's ahead and the three of us are right behind. We'll be there if you get into trouble. Just go with the flow and lean a little downstream."

"Gotcha." Still, he put off leaving the security of our eddy. "So all three of you have paddled in the world championships?"

"That's right," Henrique spoke up.

"Well, that makes me feel better. And, Rex, your grandfather was a famous expedition paddler?"

"He was, and he taught me how to kayak."

"Wow, guess it's in your blood. Well, let me know what I'm doing wrong today, okay?"

"Tom, you're doing fantastic," I said.

"Go for it," Tiago added.

Tom slowly pushed out of the eddy, his paddle clawing awkwardly at the water. He floated sideways towards the "V" that generally marks the best route, hips rocking the boat as he attempted to achieve a downstream angle. Then his kayak hit the whitewater, and he cranked his paddle like a windmill about to come off its moorings. I winced as he bounced off a rock. Henrique shook his head as Tom spun and slid down a section backwards. All three of us cheered him when he slap-braced upright from a near tip-over.

The river, perhaps out of pity, eventually delivered him to Jock's eddy at the bottom of the rapid.

Jock signaled me to come down next. I plunged my paddle in and shot out into the current, heading for the "V." I sized up the rock that Tom had hit and decided to do a fancy S-turn around it. I could feel Jock's and the Brazilians' eyes on me as I traced a series of perfect S's while I was at it. Pausing to play on the largest wave, I surfed it back and forth until I'd all but worn it out. Then I spun around and slalomed around every rock that remained between me and Jock and Tom, pretending I was negotiating an Olympic slalom course.

I slid into the eddy between Tom and Jock. But the funny thing was, as I exchanged high fives with them, the boulder in front of me appeared to tilt and spin for a microsecond. I placed my hands on their boats to steady myself, then quickly removed them so no one would notice.

Jock nodded at me in an approving way, as if accepting me as a fellow expert. Henrique and Tiago whipped into the rapid almost nose to tail, negotiating the waves and rocks like a well-practiced team. Jock and I grinned at them, me proud I'd persuaded such solid paddlers to join me on my Colombian expedition.

"What's up, Tom?" Henrique asked as he stuffed his bow neatly into our eddy. I turned to see that Tom had pushed his boat up to the riverbank and was climbing out of it. Not chickening out after two easy rapids, I hoped.

"Hey, guys, sorry, but I gotta take a leak," he said, and scurried up into the brush. Something frightened by his sudden appearance came bounding out of the bushes.

"Look," Jock said, pointing to the creature. "A *pudú* – a miniature deer."

I looked at its tail flicking as it bounded down the riverbank and into some acacia. "That's cool," I said, pleased to see some local wildlife.

"We don't have those in Brazil," Tiago said.

"Jock," I said, grabbing the opportunity for our threesome to talk to him without Tom around, "Henrique, Tiago, and I have made definite arrangements to kayak the Furioso this week." I didn't bother adding that my Brazilian friends had taken lots of convincing at first, preferring to do the creek lower down the mountain that Jock had recommended.

"You have?" Jock asked, looking startled.

"Yeah, the one on the Indian reservation."

"*Resguardos indígena*," Henrique corrected me.

"Right. Anyway, a girl I met at the market is going to tell us about the river rapids."

"A girl named Myriam?" Jock asked.

"Yeah, you know her?"

"I've met her. I know where she lives. She's probably the only one up there who speaks English. But I seriously doubt *El Furioso* is runnable."

I ignored Henrique's frown and the way he exchanged glances with Tiago.

"Do you have any topo maps of it? Do you know anyone who's looked at it or tried it?" I asked.

"No. Just a guess based on Myriam's descriptions and how steep the slopes are. All I know is, it's maybe half the volume of the Magdalena."

"Any army trouble?" Henrique asked Jock, if I understood his Spanish.

Jock shrugged and avoided our eyes, so I spoke up. "Well, her family is sending down two mules to carry our kayaks up tomorrow – the kayaks you're renting us for a week."

"Two mules." Jock didn't even crack a smile. "Good thing I got a deposit on your kayaks."

"And we were wondering if you'd join us," I continued. "Safer with four of us, or more if you have other guides up to it, and you'd get a first-descent credit with us."

"A what? Rex, you guys can't kayak up there." He leaned back in his boat, which still sat in the wide eddy.

"Why not?" I asked.

Henrique sat up straight in his kayak, and Tiago pulled his boat closer to Henrique's.

Just then, Tom reappeared and climbed into his boat.

"These three think they're going to kayak the Furioso," Jock informed Tom.

Tom laughed, like he and Jock knew something the rest of us didn't.

"Listen, guys, you have no idea what's up there," Jock declared.

I spoke quickly, before my Brazilian friends could: "Or maybe I do, since my grandfather has been up there and given me inside information. So would you consider joining us?" It was an offer of a lifetime, if he'd just see it that way.

Jock shook his head and rolled his eyes at Tom, who smirked back, which I thought was pretty rude, especially since Tom wasn't even from around here. Henrique and Tiago looked worried, and I was getting pissed off.

"Not a chance I'll join you, buddy," Jock said. "And I think you have no idea what you're planning. Your famous grandfather's information is sixty years old. As in, before the civil war."

The sarcasm annoyed me. "The Colombia Tourism Board said it was fine. The embassy agreed and said it wasn't dangerous, politically."

"We made a bunch of calls and got the all clear on the political situation too," Tiago inserted. "Are you saying not to trust that information?"

"I'm saying —" Jock began.

"So what if my info is sixty years old?" I interrupted. "Rivers don't change. What if I pay you to join us?" *Man, this is getting to be expensive.* I hoped Gramps was good for wiring me some more money. As to the political risk, I figured we were already here. And I reasoned the tourism board and embassy knew more than Jock.

Henrique and Tiago started mumbling to each another in Portuguese. Jock exchanged looks with Tom again and tapped his fingers on his kayak. He seemed totally uninterested in the money offer, and I feared he was ready to lecture me. Then his fingers stop tapping. He took a moment to collect his thoughts.

"If the mule handler's bringing two mules, we'll load them up with five kayaks and have him drop off two of them where *El Furioso* runs into the Magdalena. That's right where *El Furioso*'s canyon section ends. For $100.00 plus a deposit on those extra two boats, another guide and I will meet you there and paddle down the Magdalena to the door of my shop. The boat deposits are fully refundable as long as the boats don't disappear before I get there. But the hundred bucks is nonrefundable, even if you don't show at the prearranged time."

"Awesome!" I enthused, ignoring the negativity. *Note to self — the Furioso has a canyon section.*

"Now you're saying the Furioso is okay?" Henrique asked Jock, studying him closely.

"Go for it," Jock said, keeping his eyes on the water just downstream of us.

"So if Rex, Henrique, and I do the Furioso, you'll join us near the bottom," Tiago pondered aloud. He was studying Jock's face.

I was resenting how quickly Jock had named his price. But it soothed my teammates' nerves, I reasoned, and Gramps would front the extra money.

"Hey, now that you wheeler-dealers are done planning your next trip, can we get on with this one?" Tom interrupted. "I really want to know, do the rapids get any harder than what we just did?"

"Only one of them," Jock informed him. "It's nice, slow-moving water until that one."

"Wake me up if I doze off," I joked. *Or was it a joke?* I felt unreasonably fatigued for someone who'd had a pretty good night's sleep.

We paddled out of the eddy and floated, me feeling curiously light-headed. "Here we are in the world's coffee capital, and I forget to grab some this morning," I complained.

Tom guffawed. "World's drug capital, you mean."

I noticed Jock throw him a disapproving look. "Not anymore," he asserted.

"Yeah, right," Tom said, stroking his beard below a grin. "Try telling me cocaine's not still your top export."

"Maybe in the Seventies," Jock said firmly. "Tourism's one of our biggest industries now. Anyway, Tom, where are you staying?"

"Camping outside of town with friends," Tom replied. "What about you, Rex?"

"I'm at the Magdalena Hotel. So are my friends, as of tonight."

"No way – the place that got hit when guerillas attacked the police station last week?" Tom exclaimed.

"Huh?" I asked. He was joking, I decided.

"Rapids coming up, guys. Let's concentrate," Jock said.

I glanced up. Nothing remotely resembling a rapid was within sight, but Tom straightened his shoulders, positioned his paddle, and turned himself downstream. "What class will these be?" he asked.

"Class I for a little while," Jock said, winking at Henrique, Tiago, and me. "Then a Class III, which is as hard as it gets."

Class III, still easy for me and my first-descent mates. I looked at the hint of whitewater well ahead. Strangely, the calm river seemed to be surging up and down. *Or is that my head?* I squeezed my eyes shut and opened them again.

We fell into our agreed order: Jock, Tom, me, and the Brazilians. Tom snagged on a rock. I had to come up behind and push his kayak off it. The effort seemed to drain me. I sat in an eddy with my neck craned to make sure that Tom, slow and nervous, stayed ahead.

Finally, we hit a series of riffles. Easy stuff. *So why do I capsize halfway through, and take two tries to roll?*

"Nice roll," Tom said. Jock just looked at me. I didn't turn to assess my teammates' reaction.

"I needed to wake myself up," I said.

As if to punish me for lying, my head started pounding and my stomach felt like it was going to upchuck.

A little while later, Tom flipped. I watched him swim out from his overturned boat, and I paddled over to rescue him. I shook my head in frustration when he let go of both his boat and paddle, which headed downstream.

"I've got him!" I called to Jock up ahead. "You chase his gear."

"Okay," he called back, scooping up Tom's floating paddle and maneuvering towards the runaway boat.

I did have Tom, I really did — at first. He clutched my stern, and I turned my kayak towards shore to haul him in. There was a rapid coming up downstream, the Class III. Plenty of time to get him out before then, even if the Brazilians didn't sprint to catch up and help.

As my kayak shuddered and rocked, I realized Tom was panicking. *No! What an idiot! He's climbing up my stern!* I sucked in a quick breath as I tipped into the drink, upside down, knees still gripping my kayak, holding my breath. *I will roll as soon as Tom gets off the bottom of my overturned boat. One, two, three. . . .* Reaching my paddle upward, I flashed it across the surface above me, flicking my hips.

What? I didn't even rise far enough to catch a breath! Heavy, heavy feeling. *Tom must still be lying on my boat.* I set up again, tried again. *Please get off my boat, Tom.* I tried rolling three times. *My lungs, my lungs!* I must do what I never, ever do. I reached forward, grabbed the loop on my spraydeck, and pulled to eject. *I need to breathe.* I surfaced and sucked blessed air into my bursting lungs.

Shame enveloped me. Now Jock, Henrique, and Tiago would have to rescue two swimmers. I saw them click into action.

Jock threw Tom's paddle to shore and abandoned trying to push Tom's boat there. "Help Rex!" I heard him shout to Henrique and Tiago as he raced over to Tom.

Water slapped my face as I glimpsed Tom grab Jock's stern. *Get him to shore, Jock, before we hit the Class III rapid.*

My fingers clung to my boat as I angled my body. *At least I'm not dumb enough to let go of my kayak, like Tom.* Water flew skywards as I kicked towards shore. My chest strained with the effort. As Henrique and Tiago headed toward me, I kicked harder. *Must show them I can get to shore by myself.* I saw Jock reach shore and Tom scrabble up the riverbank. Jock swiveled his head to make sure the rest of us were okay, then tore after Tom's runaway boat again.

"Are you okay?" Henrique asked as he and Tiago pressed their kayak bows against my boat and began to push us.

"Uh-huh." But I felt weak, like I was swimming in molasses. I couldn't seem to move my limbs as my buddies stroked hard towards shore. *Almost there. No!* Bigger waves engulfed me; stronger currents tore us away into the fast-moving Class III. My rescuers abandoned me to look out for themselves. They'd descend on me again at the end of the rapid.

Must get out. Must self-rescue. No, still in the rapid. Fog seemed to have enveloped my mind. *Okay, maybe here.* I lowered my legs and tried to stand. Only my chest was above water. *Wham!* Rocks grabbed my right foot like I'd stepped in an animal trap. *Whoosh!* The current nabbed my body and plunged me face-first into the water, stretching me between the rock anchoring my foot and the waterlogged kayak on which my hands held a death grip.

I had to do it. The guys would have to forgive me. I released my kayak. Still I flailed for a breath, the hurtling current refusing to free my foot from the river bottom. Water pushed up my nostrils as, facedown, I slapped and slapped to lift my mouth above the turbulent surface. I simply couldn't do it; there was no air to be had. At the same time, I kicked, pulled, and yanked to free my ankle, which only caused the entrapping rocks to further gouge the skin around it.

This is it? I screamed silently. *Foot entrapment on a measly Class III rapid is how I'm going to die?* My thoughts slowed down, even as the pain and pressure in my lungs built up. *Stay calm!* I told myself. Then I visualized the good-luck necklace I always carried. It was in my paddling jacket pocket. *I'm not going to drown!*

I felt someone's hands on my ankle. Someone's strong hands tearing at the rocks around it to free it so I could rise above the surface and breathe, breathe, breathe. *I'm free!* I gasped, coughed, and tried to take an arm stroke.

"Roll onto your back and keep your feet up!" Henrique

shouted as his arm went around my chest in a lifeguard's grip. He was out of his boat. He must've beached it lightning-fast, run ashore, and leapt in to save me. We floated down the rapid as one unit, Henrique using his strong free arm and leg kicks to maneuver us ever closer to shore. There, Jock, Tom, and Tiago – who'd run upriver from the bank where they'd deposited the two rescued boats and paddles – helped Henrique haul me to dry ground. I rolled my head to one side and puked. The Colombian sky swirled in Technicolor.

The guys sat waiting.

"Thank you," I finally managed. My eyes focused on Henrique and Jock, their heads bent over mine.

"What happened?" Jock asked. It sounded like an accusation.

"Tom wouldn't get off my boat. I couldn't roll with him on it."

"Tom let go of your boat the second you flipped," Jock corrected me. "And I rescued him. Henrique hung back after you let go of your boat, but it's still amazing he managed to beach his boat and get to you in time. And Tiago rescued your boat. Couldn't you tell you were mid-river when you tried to stand up?"

I heard the underlying message: *What are you, a beginner?*

"I was feeling dizzy and weird."

"You didn't say anything." Jock was more polite than Gramps would've been, but he had the same way of letting me know I was a failure.

"Altitude sickness," I realized. "I haven't gotten used to the elevation here yet."

I could read Jock's expression: *Yeah, right*. Henrique and Tiago knew my paddling abilities and believed me, I knew, but in Jock's mind, I'd been demoted to a novice.

Tom and I emptied our kayaks and sheepishly climbed back into them for the final leg of the trip. Jock kept a sharp watch on both of us, while conversing only with Henrique and Tiago. Wet and disillusioned, I finally sighted Lina's car. *Please, Jock*, I thought, *don't tell that reporter what happened or it'll get back to Gramps. And don't tell Alberto when he shows up with the mules tomorrow.*

Both of which Jock did, of course.

CHAPTER EIGHT

I woke up with a head-throbbing hangover the next morning, thanks to Henrique and Tiago, who'd decided I needed a cheer-me-up after the river episode. Their idea was to haul me around bars that didn't seem to care we were all underage.

I made it to Jock's shop looking pretty rough – rougher than my Brazilian buddies – even though we'd stopped at an Internet café to glug coffee. There, I'd notified Gramps and Mom that I was fine, had met up with my teammates, had hired a guide, and needed more money.

Alberto, waiting with the mules, took one look at my sorry state and sneered at me. He said something to Jock that made Jock, Henrique, and Tiago smile. Alberto's dark eyes took obvious pleasure in noting that I, alone, didn't understand their exchange in Spanish. Hopefully he wouldn't try to use Spanish to drive a wedge between my buddies and me, and hopefully he wouldn't tell Myriam I was a drunk.

Jock carried the first kayak across the grass and, skirting the mule's hind legs, set it gently on her back.

"I told Alberto about your episode yesterday," he said, "only in hopes he'd talk you out of this idea before you get yourself killed."

"Thanks a lot," I said. As Alberto held the kayak, I followed Jock back to the boat shed to help him, Henrique, and Tiago with the other four kayaks. He'd stashed break-apart paddles in each of them, as we'd arranged.

Alberto was pretty adept at tying our load securely. He was also pretty surly when I insisted on taking a photo for Gramps and Mom. After the click, he stared at my digital camera, which made me tuck it deep into one of the pockets of my backpack. He gestured at our backpacks, offering to hoist them atop the poor mules. Henrique and Tiago happily handed theirs over, but I shook my head. *Not with my camera inside.*

"I'm good at carrying heavy loads," I said in broken Spanish. It was so broken, Henrique felt a need to translate for me.

Alberto turned away and patted the mules to urge them forward, leaving the three of us to follow.

"Good luck," Jock said, standing on his shop's doorstep, frowning.

"See you next week," I replied with confidence. When I return, I wanted to assure him, we three would have the dream of a lifetime in our hands: a first descent on the Furioso River.

We adjusted our pace to that of Alberto and the heavily loaded mules. For the first two hours, Alberto said nothing and rarely glanced behind, ignoring Henrique's questions. He also ignored the Brazilians' conversations in Portuguese, but when they broke into English to include me, he turned to deliver such a glare that soon we abandoned all conversation.

During those first hours, the four of us traveled along a dirt road and were passed now and then by colorful old buses, with music blaring and people hanging on to the back doors and roof racks. I dug out my camera to take a picture for Mom. The shot showed everyone on the buses staring openmouthed at us, like they'd never seen mules carrying kayaks before.

Eventually, Alberto left the road and climbed a steep trail. I examined him from behind: tall, straight-backed, dark, wearing a felt bowler-type hat, old dirty jeans instead of the "skirt" a lot of the *indígena* men wore, a T-shirt, and a hooded sweatshirt he would no doubt shed as the morning sun rose higher. His high-top basketball shoes were one stitch away from falling apart, and two holes in their soles blinked at me with every footstep. But that certainly didn't slow him down over the increasingly rough trail.

Long grass tickled my calves where it managed to poke up inside my jeans.

"Any snakes around here?" I finally asked Alberto, in an attempt at conversation.

"*Sí.*" That meant he could understand my Spanish sometimes.

"Poisonous ones?"

"*Sí.*" The chill in his voice made me feel like he wished one would strike me on the way. *What is it? Jealousy of my equipment and money, or hatred of whites in general? Or is he Myriam's boyfriend, who has picked up on my interest in her?*

"Is Myriam your girlfriend?" I asked, ignoring the startled look that put on Henrique's and Tiago's faces. *Might as well get that question over with*, I thought.

He whirled around and narrowed his eyes at me. "My fiancée," he pronounced, slowly and deliberately.

"That's nice," I said. Judging from the cold-shoulder way she'd treated him during our previous encounter, I doubted it. But at least our mule-guide and I were having a conversation.

"How many mules do you have?" Henrique asked in Spanish, expanding on my attempt to draw out our guide.

"Two." He added something about needing them for harvesting crops. In other words, we were decadent idiots compromising his entire community's harvesting efforts for the day.

I figured they must be pretty poor to have only two mules and not be able to take a day off. But the pay Myriam had demanded was obviously enough to make up for it, or he wouldn't have been sent down. And it wasn't like I expected Alberto to understand what I was up to. Otherwise he or one of his friends would've taken a kayak down their local river long ago. Instead, Fate had saved this first descent for me so I could outdo, and maybe even impress, Gramps.

As I opened my mouth for more conversation, Alberto stopped abruptly and stripped off his hooded sweatshirt. I wrinkled my nose and turned away from the ripe body odor, then shook my head politely when he offered me the shirt.

That's when he put his hands on his hips and pointed at me. "Put it on," he ordered in Spanish. Henrique translated.

"*No, gracias.*"

"Soldiers, maybe," he said in Spanish, pointing to the stubby pine trees up the hill.

I saw Henrique's eyes widen. Squinting against the bright sun, I saw nothing and wondered if Alberto was just trying to scare us.

"Now," he barked, then said something else to Henrique and Tiago.

"He says neither he nor the mules are taking another step until you shed your backpack and pull his hoodie on. Guess you'd better do it," Henrique said sympathetically.

"I'm too hot," I objected.

"Just do it," Tiago said quietly.

I sighed and reached for the sweatshirt in Alberto's outstretched hand. Hardly had my head appeared through the top than he reached forward and yanked the drawstring of the hood tight, as if trying to hide my face. Then he removed his felt hat and perched it on my head, tilted to shadow my face, and grabbed my hands to stick them into the ratty sweatshirt's pockets.

Henrique and Tiago failed to smother smiles. I definitely didn't want a felt hat on my sweaty, now-hooded head in the noonday sun. Again, Alberto pointed to the trees, which instantly dissolved my buddies' smirks. *Right, I get the message.* He was trying to dress me like an *indígena* to cover any white skin. He wasn't worried about Henrique or Tiago because my skin was whiter than theirs.

I was pissed, but I tried telling myself it made some sense. Maybe now we wouldn't get delayed by soldiers wanting to question us. *Fair enough*. I'd go along with the little charade, if only so we could keep moving towards the cooler temperatures farther up the mountain. Not that I could imagine soldiers being the least bit interested in two dusty mules, whose loads resembled green wings, and four young men, one overdressed and carrying a heavy backpack.

We continued on up the ever-steepening trail for what seemed like hours. The smell of the mules assaulted my nostrils. It was worse when one paused to defecate and I stepped in the mess.

"Good one!" Henrique teased.

Only once did we head downhill, towards a grove of trees that I sensed hid the place where the two rivers joined. My heart quickened as I heard roaring whitewater.

"The Furioso and Magdalena?" Tiago asked.

Alberto nodded. When we got to the convergence itself, Henrique, Tiago, and I rushed forward to look at the impressive volume of water spilling out between tall, pink granite walls that seemed to march upstream forever.

"Sweet," Henrique murmured, stroking his soul patch.

"Class V," Tiago said.

Upstream, the canyon walls squeezed the river into nonstop rapids that made my mouth water, too. Downstream, the rapids joined the fast-moving, much larger Magdalena River.

When I looked around, Alberto was unlashing one of

the kayaks. Like most people who'd never kayaked, he hoisted it atop his head instead of hanging it from his shoulder. He marched it over to thick brush on the riverbank, near the foot of the canyon walls, and dumped it there. Henrique and Tiago hurried to help him with the second kayak while I gathered some branches to cover them with, even though their camouflage coloring made them hard to spot already.

"Are you sure Jock will find them here?" I asked.

Alberto kicked the kayaks another few inches under cover and strode back to the mules as if to say he couldn't care less whether Jock or anyone else ever found them.

Within minutes, we were back on our difficult trail, the mules down to three kayaks. I paused now and then to drink from my water bottle, as did the rest of the group. Even with the heavy pack, I made sure to keep up with the other three, step for step. Despite occasional shortness of breath, I could tell that after forty-eight hours in the Colombian Andes, I was getting used to the elevation.

When we ran out of water, we stopped at a stream to refill our bottles. Henrique, Tiago, and I added purifying tablets, which Alberto watched with a mix of curiosity and disdain. He let the mules lap up their fill and checked the straps on the remaining kayaks. Again, he offered to strap my backpack to a mule. Again, I said, "I'm good at carrying heavy loads."

Henrique and I tried to start up conversation. I suggested he ask Alberto about the Furioso. But Alberto placed a finger over his lips and pointed at the surrounding forest, like the trees might have ears.

That prompted Henrique to whisper a question to Alberto in Spanish, which Alberto ignored. *He doesn't like to talk and is tired of our accented Spanish*, I concluded. I could understand that.

It was well past noon by the time we trudged into a dirt-caked plaza with an outdoor clay oven beside a group of rundown buildings. The biggest was a former *hacienda*. Half-naked children with runny noses ran around, chasing hens. Wrinkled old women sat spinning on simple, ancient looms or preparing food. They looked up and stared, unabashed. They must have been expecting us, but we were an exotic sight anyway.

Alberto lost no time pulling the Brazilians' backpacks off the mules and throwing them at Henrique and Tiago. Then he unloaded the kayaks and tossed them roughly into a corner of the plaza, which made me wince, even if they were indestructible plastic. He motioned for me to return his sweatshirt and hat, which I did happily.

Then his entire demeanor changed. He turned his back on us, laughed and joked with the old women, and picked up some children to tickle and tease. He stole some food off a baking tray one woman was preparing and popped it into his mouth with a smile as she, also smiling, shook a wooden spoon at him. He filled his water bottle from a pipe that ran down a hill and dripped into a pile of rocks – from the river, I guessed. That made my parched throat long for a swig.

Then he led the mules off towards a lean-to without so much as a backward glance at his three paddler-clients.

Henrique and Tiago promptly sat down on a bench in the shade, stroking a dog while chatting to each other in their own language, as if they dropped into Andean villages all the time. I stood there with my backpack in the center of a square teeming with honking geese, cackling hens, barking dogs, a cat nursing kittens, drooling children, and barefoot old women with long skirts, shawls, and felt hats on their heads. Everyone carried on with their tasks as they looked me up and down with their dark leathery faces.

I burned with discomfort. Sweat trickled down my face, even in the cool mountain air. I'd never felt so foreign or alone. Just as I was about to utter the question "Myriam?", the old lady who'd been selling herbs in the market shuffled out of the largest building with her cane. Her face radiated a warm welcome. But she seemed less steady than when I'd last seen her. In fact, her face looked a little pinched and her eyes a little glassy.

"Rex Scruggs," she said, patting my hands as Henrique and Tiago glanced up. She was so tiny. "Hungry? Thirsty?"

I was so relieved to hear two Spanish words I knew, and I straightened as Henrique and Tiago looked at us. Nodding at Myriam's grandmother like she was an old friend, I eased my backpack off, then introduced her to Henrique and Tiago. She greeted them in turn, then spoke to one of the older children, who brought us something that looked like a patty of cornbread. I said *gracias* and munched on mine slowly. It was delicious.

The old lady shuffled back into the building, then reappeared with a plastic chair like my mom has on Gramps' deck at home. It was outfitted with an embroidered pillow.

Mom would be amused at that, I knew, but I resisted pulling out my camera. She insisted I sit in the chair as Henrique and Tiago retreated to their bench and played with the dog that had befriended them.

As Myriam's grandmother issued orders around, I got the sense she was an important elder. Soon I had a cup of coffee in my hands, and it tasted incredibly good. Then someone brought me a chipped ceramic plate with a sandwich on it. I peeked inside: a fat slice of avocado. I was about to offer pieces of it to my buddies when two more sandwiches appeared.

Someone fetched the old lady a plastic chair, and she pulled it up to mine like we were best buddies on a camping trip, all but ignoring the Brazilians. Again, as I looked at her closely, I got the sense she wasn't all that well. Children chasing about the plaza gradually began to circle me, then came closer to sit cross-legged on flagstones as the old lady started talking to me. Henrique and Tiago didn't seem to care; they were engrossed in their own conversation.

"I'm Myriam's grandmother," she began, reaching forward to pat my hands again. Her palms felt clammy, like she had a fever. "You may call me Abuela."

Spanish for "grandmother" — at least I could remember some words. I bit into the sandwich. It tasted so good, I could've downed it in two bites.

"How are you related to Malcolm Scruggs?" she asked.

My eyebrows went up. "He's my grandfather."

It seemed like she'd been expecting this. "You look like him."

Not many people say that, but I was okay with it. "You met him many years ago when he kayaked here?"

She nodded, her tired eyes struggling to focus. She was younger than Gramps, I decided, but not by that much. She started speaking faster, hands gesturing, like she was telling me a story. I caught a phrase here or there. "Your grandfather was very ill" was one of them. *Not true*, I thought. *Neither his journal nor the stories he'd told me ever indicated that.* Then something about a necklace. *The one her family has given Gramps?* I wondered. *The one in my paddling jacket pocket right now?* I decided not to pull it out, in case they might try to claim it back.

I glanced about the square as she spoke and could tell from their gazes that the older women didn't understand Spanish, but the younger ones did. One girl around twelve years old, embroidering a tablecloth while chewing on her braid, was watching me intently.

"Abuelita" came Myriam's voice just then, and I felt immense relief as she strode into the plaza. But her eyes weren't focused on me. She placed a hand on her grandmother's forehead and frowned. Calling for someone to bring some water, she motioned to me. "Help me get her back into the community center. She should be resting."

"No problem, but, Myriam, these are my friends, Henrique and Tiago, from Brazil. They're going to kayak with me."

She turned around briefly, shook hands with the two kayakers when they rose, then motioned me to place an arm under Abuela's shoulder. Abuela, I judged, weighed as much as one of the goose feathers scattered about in the dirt. She sagged into Myriam's and my arms as if she'd spent all her energy being my welcoming committee.

Myriam lowered her onto a thin mattress atop box springs in the community center and pulled an embroidered blanket up to her chin. Then she took the cup of water from the girl who'd been embroidering.

"Thanks, Rosita." They lifted Abuela's head gently to help her drink. Myriam fetched a leaf from a bottle on a nearby shelf that was crowded with bottles of leaves, oils, and flowers. She placed the leaf in a clay cup and fetched some hot water from the stove in the plaza to pour on top of it.

Abuela looked like she needed a doctor more than a leaf-tea. *Do doctors even come up here?* Jock had said only a priest and soldiers ventured this high.

I looked around the room. Concrete walls, half the floor concrete, the other half dirt. Plastic chairs scattered around and one filthy window, whose sill was filled with candles. Wooden weaving frames crowded the room. There were dried herbs hanging from the ceiling and boxes of magazines and newspapers around the floor. A radio sat in a place of honor on a rough wooden table. This village was very poor, for sure. I almost felt guilty for accepting the coffee and avocado sandwich.

"Thanks," Myriam finally addressed me. "She's not well. Let's move outside."

Abuela seemed to have fallen asleep already. The girl named Rosita hovered over her.

Myriam and I sat in the plastic chairs still in the plaza, Henrique and Tiago still conversed nearby, and I pretended that it wasn't full of dark-skinned women and children staring at us.

"Hey, guys, want to join us?" I asked my friends, trying to quash a sense of foreboding about the way they were sitting out of earshot and speaking in near whispers.

"Later," Henrique replied with a forced smile before he and Tiago started in again – in Portuguese, of course.

"Did anything go wrong on your trip up with Alberto?" Myriam asked me, one eye on my buddies.

I shook my head, wondering what she meant.

"I only just got back from guard duty. Do you need something to eat?"

I wanted to ask her what she meant by guard duty, but not now. "Abuela gave us sandwiches," I said, "along with a story I couldn't follow."

A small smile tugged at Myriam's lips. "The avocado sandwich story."

I raised my eyebrows. "The what?"

"When she was my age, Abuelita was wandering in a field when she met a white man who traded her an avocado sandwich for her necklace." The smile was gone; resentment had taken its place. "It was a necklace that had been passed down in our family for generations. She should never have given it away. It would be worth a fortune now."

I swallowed. Heat flared in my cheeks. "So why did she?"

Myriam's face grew colder. "She was starving, like all our people were."

"Oh."

"Then the man fell ill, and his companions left him. Abuelita is a healer, so she brought him medicinal herbs where he was camping. And then he disappeared. End of story."

End of story? But we've only just got started.

"That was my grandfather," I said in a voice that started to crack. "He was trying to kayak your river, the Furioso. But not all her story is right."

She looked at me, then turned her eyes to the kayaks lying where Alberto had dumped them. That's when I noticed that, while we'd been talking, the children had pulled them out from the wall and were climbing all over them, fighting over who could sit in the cockpits. I grinned, walked over, and squatted down to their level. Henrique and Tiago stopped talking to watch me. I wriggled the kayaks a little to make the kids' rides more exciting. A few scrambled off and ran crying to their mothers. But the rest rollicked and laughed and motioned me to make the ride rougher and faster, especially a toddler with a red knit hat who was sitting in the cockpit of my boat. Like a coin-operated ride in an arcade, this was a new toy for him. Come to think of it, I'd seen no toys in the plaza at all. So I rocked the kayaks for the children, and even pulled the collapsible paddle out of my backpack. I put it together and showed them how to play-paddle. A long line soon formed to take turns captaining the boats.

When the children waved to someone behind me, I swiveled my head. What I saw was a row of astonished-looking men and boys in skirts and sleeveless ponchos, most barefoot, some holding hoes and machetes. And beautiful Myriam, failing in her effort to not smile.

CHAPTER NINE

The next day, morning sunshine sparkled on the Furioso River as Henrique, Tiago, and I paddled the last rapids between us and the clearing where Myriam had agreed to meet us for lunch. *"Whoo-hoo!"* we shouted with big grins. The water was refreshingly cool, nothing like the cold I was used to at home. We'd just paddled a series of challenging but fun rapids, none of them hair-raisingly dangerous. Just like Gramps' journal had promised.

Ah, fresh mountain air, peaceful woods, and vaguely interesting rapids. Delighted to finally have embarked on our endeavor. My companions seem nervous, I have no idea about what. Me, I'm almost bored with this trivial whitewater so far. On the other hand, this river section allows me to evaluate my men, whom I consider lacking in some pertinent skills. But off the water, they have responded well to my orders to bargain vigorously with the primitive indigenous villagers. Since these damned boats are heavy enough in the skimpy currents, it is unfortunately necessary to buy some of our food en route. — Malcolm Scruggs

Gramps' observations sure made me appreciate my little plastic kayak and the way it spun and played in the waves. I was psyched to finally be tracing his footsteps and determined to show him I was up to finishing what he'd started.

"Nice rapids," Henrique said as he paddled close by.

"Yeah, a good warm-up for the canyon," Tiago agreed. "But do you think it'll be a day or two before we hit this canyon?"

"That's what I think," I said.

"That's a day or two more of exposure to soldiers up here," Henrique said with a long face. "Tiago and I are worried about that. We think you should be too. We grilled some of Myriam's people last night, and there's more going on up here than the government reports let on. Politics and unrest, you know."

A bolt of panic hit my chest, but I stifled it fast. "Politics? What are you talking about?" I asked, making sure to look exasperated. We'd come this far; we were so close. I refused to let anything get in my way. "I'm not into politics. I'm into paddling. I thought that's what you came here for, too."

I didn't like the way that made them exchange glances. Before they could say anything else, I sprinted ahead, determined to ignore what they were trying to say. I relaxed only when I caught sight of Myriam on the riverbank. The sun was shining on her lovely face, her white blouse, and her long, dark braid. She was wearing jeans today, which were much more flattering than the shin-length wool skirts the older women wore and that I'd always seen her in until now. She was playing on the riverbank with her little brother and sister. They were cute, especially the boy in a red knit hat, Freddy, who'd taken to sitting in my kayak when it was onshore. The bike Myriam had ridden up the river trail — with one twin in her sash, the other on the handlebars — was lying in the grass nearby. Too bad Myriam and I weren't alone up here, but I needed my two buddies in order to paddle the river, and I guess she had to do double duty while her mom worked a loom back at the community center and her younger sister Rosita went to school.

"Why don't you go to school?" I asked Myriam as I pulled into the eddy beside her and flicked water at the twins to make them giggle. Henrique and Tiago paused to play on a wave above.

She pursed her lips. She specialized in resentful looks, but not half as much as Alberto. "I just left school last week."

"Now that you're finished school, are you going to marry Alberto?"

Her eyes widened and her hands moved to her hips. "Did he say that?"

"He did."

She chewed her lip as if deciding how to respond. "It's not decided," she finally said. "I want to go to university to be a reporter, but that's not what *indígena* girls do, I've been told."

"Well, I think you *should* go to university. *Indígena* girls in the United States and Canada do."

Her face turned my way with a glow of something like hope. "Very many of them?"

"Sure," I said. "If they want to go and don't have much money, sometimes they can get scholarships."

I was only a foot from where she sat cross-legged beside the water, but I remained in my boat, reluctant to end my morning's session and happy to let my paddling partners play upstream till they got that political nonsense out of their heads.

"And their parents let them?" Myriam asked.

"Why wouldn't their parents let them?"

Flora and Freddy, free of their sister's hold, stuck their bare feet into the water and touched my boat.

"Hey, Flora and Freddy. Want to see me roll?" I asked.

They turned their eyes to me because I'd said their names. I paddled to the river's center, capsized, and hung upside down, counting to three just to worry them a little. Then I rolled back up and waved, watching their eyes grow big.

Henrique and Tiago pulled up, smiling. They'd seen me entertain the twins.

"What happens if you don't roll up?" Myriam asked as she took the twins' hands in hers.

"I always roll," I said, refraining from looking at the Brazilians.

"That's not what Jock told Alberto."

My face reddened. "Except when I'm straight off a plane and have altitude sickness."

"How are you three going to get under that bridge?" she asked, pointing to a little footbridge downstream. The water lapped just inches under the bridge. There was no clearance for my head and body even if I ducked.

I winked at Henrique and Tiago. "Watch this."

I paddled to the bridge. Just as the bow of my boat reached it, I purposely flipped and counted to twelve as the current continued to move my upside-down boat and me downstream. By the time I rolled back up, my boat was downstream of the bridge. I spun the kayak around and paddled back upstream to the bridge, then leapt out to walk back up to my companions.

Freddy and Flora were clapping. Myriam offered a faint smile. Henrique and Tiago repeated the performance to more clapping.

"I'm going to show the twins one more trick," I told Myriam as they pressed themselves against their big sister.

Myriam shrugged and said something to the twins, who sat still and clasped their hands as if waiting for a new show.

Getting back in my boat, I maneuvered it to the deepest part of the quiet eddy and capsized. I ejected from the boat, but instead of coming to the surface to grab a breath, I came up directly underneath the over-turned boat, my face now in the little air pocket beneath the kayak's seat. I hung there underwater for a good few minutes, until the air in the air pocket was plenty stale. Then I ducked out from under the boat, surfaced, and waved at the twins, who were crying, and Myriam, who was looking concerned. The Brazilians, well aware of what I'd been up to, were starting to look bored. Henrique released his spraydeck and stepped onto shore, heading for the picnic blanket.

"You can hold your breath a long time," Myriam observed, clearly relieved I hadn't drowned. She rocked the twins to quiet them as they looked at me warily.

"Anyone else hungry?" Tiago asked, exiting his boat and joining Henrique.

I lifted my kayak out of the water and also headed to where Miriam had spread a blanket on the grass. Setting my boat down, I emptied it of water. "I was hiding under the boat, breathing in the air pocket beneath the seat," I explained to Myriam. "I used to drive my grandfather crazy after he made the mistake of teaching me that trick."

She smiled wanly, turning to the twins on the picnic blanket and opening her small burlap bag. "I didn't bring much food," she apologized as the twins eagerly grabbed for the corn patties she handed them.

"No problem. We have lots in the waterproof storage bags in our kayaks," I said.

Henrique, Tiago, and I produced guavas, tangerines, cheese, sausages, crackers, and an avocado. Myriam and the twins stared at the food like it represented a feast.

"Help yourselves," I said to the three of them. "There's lots more where that came from. We bought supplies in town before we came up."

"That's why your backpacks were so heavy?"

"Partly, but our sleeping bags and paddling gear add up to a lot of weight, too. It's no big deal. I'm used to walking with a forty-pound boat on my shoulder."

This morning my friends and I had woken in the dusty, windowless hut beside the Calambás family's hut that Papá had insisted we stay in. There, I'd unrolled my sleeping bag and tucked Gramps' journal under the bundled-up clothing I used as a pillow. Long after my buddies were snoring, I read the journal by flashlight, my heart beating fast to know that I was no longer a small boy reading it on the sly after lights-out, but a grown-up expedition member in a Colombian hut beside the legendary Furioso.

"No camping near the river," Papá had objected to my suggestion before we'd moved into the hut. "Safer near us." Maybe he wanted to keep an eye on us, though I didn't see why. It's not like there was anything to steal. I hurriedly dismissed the notion that he might be worried about soldiers. We hadn't seen any, after all.

They'd spared a boy and the mules long enough for the animals to carry our boats from the village to where Gramps had described starting his journey with two expedition mates. We'd walked alongside the mules. But I'd arranged that, beginning tomorrow, we'd use bikes borrowed from Myriam's village to get to the start of each paddling section. Then, at the end of each day, we'd hide our kayaks where we finished paddling, walk back to the day's starting point, and retrieve the bikes to cycle back to the community for the night. Lots of walking and biking, but good for our lower-body fitness. The other option – carrying food and sleeping gear in our kayaks – would add weight that might compromise our paddling performance. Not to mention that everyone kept insisting it was dangerous for us to camp – advice that didn't sit well with Henrique and Tiago. I'd have to keep reassuring them – and talk Myriam into telling her villagers to stop scaring them with talk about soldiers being up here. Even if they existed, they had no cause to hassle us. We weren't hurting anyone. We were just paddling a river.

I smiled as I watched the twins tear into the food once Myriam had given them permission. They ate like they hadn't eaten in a while. Myriam held herself back until Henrique, Tiago, and I told her several times she was welcome to it. Then she demonstrated one heck of a voracious appetite for a slim girl, all but polishing off the cheese. Not that I minded.

"So what's downstream from here?" Henrique asked.

"Trout tanks. They're a ten-minute walk from our village."

"I mean for rapids."

I waited for her answer, wanting to see if her description matched Gramps', as it had this morning.

"Bigger. More white waves. And there are no breaks in the rapids between here and our trout tanks. Then it is calm for a stretch."

"No waterfalls or mazes of boulders?" Tiago asked.

"There's nothing like that between here and the trout tanks."

I fished out Gramps' journal and ran my finger along his entry.

Continuous Class III rapids until shortly before an Indian village. Had my men sweating a little, but delightful level of challenge in my opinion. We startled a cougar as we came around one river bend. If only I'd had a gun on me! Just now, we've paused to pick some berries and check our kayaks for damage. – Malcolm Scruggs

"Class III till the village, he agrees," I reported. "Not that we'll take his or Myriam's word for it entirely." We would stop, get out, and walk down the riverbank to explore anything we couldn't see from an eddy. Kayakers call that scouting. And I was beginning to trust Myriam's knowledge of the river. *Her river*, I thought with a grin. *Hers and ours.*

"You'll meet us at the calm section?"

"Yes," she said, lifting Flora into the sash that the *indígena* women carry babies and toddlers in. She picked up her bike and repositioned Freddy on the handlebars. "And I'll show you our trout tanks."

"Okay. Sounds interesting. Race you there," I said with a wink at my buddies. She'd beat us, of course, even with two children along.

We waved as she took off on the riverside trail.

"Nice girl," Henrique said, watching her.

"Hands off. She's mine," I joked, which prompted laughs.

We stopped regularly to scout, play on the waves, and look around. She'd warned us not to walk into the fields on the far side of the river, claiming it was planted with land mines. I figured she just didn't want us to trespass on private property.

The rapids were more continuous now, but no more difficult. I tried to imagine Gramps here as a young man, paddling with his teammates in their canvas kayaks, so much less maneuverable and durable among these rocks. I was thrilled he'd allowed me – even sponsored me – to come finish what he'd abandoned. I only wished he'd been more specific on what had made him give up the run. I couldn't imagine my grandfather being intimidated by locals who wanted to run him off. Not for long, anyway.

I despise taking time out from paddling to enter the smelly villages up here in our ever-present quest for additional food. At least they have given us no trouble. They're shy, quiet, industrious people, even if appallingly backward. – Malcolm Scruggs

———

Less than an hour later, the river took us towards something giant and manmade on the left bank. As we drew closer, I counted a bunch of enormous, concrete-edged holding tanks. After lifting our boats from the water, we saw the tanks were filled with flitting trout.

"Eight trout tanks," Tiago observed.

"This is where we meet her, right?" Henrique asked.

"Yeah," I responded. "Can you imagine all the work it took to build these tanks?"

"Especially without concrete mixers or bulldozers," Tiago agreed.

We pulled off our paddling jackets and settled onto the grassy bank to sunbathe when we heard the giggle of toddlers.

"Hi, kids," I said as Myriam and the twins appeared with fistfuls of figs they'd clearly been picking in the woods. I dug into the waterproof storage bag in my kayak for a chocolate bar they could share. The kids mobbed me and soon chocolate covered their hands and ran down their chins. Myriam, Henrique, and Tiago chuckled as we watched them.

Henrique pointed at the tanks. "This is a serious operation. Are the fish for eating or selling?"

"Both," Myriam said with pride. "Our community spent days building them. They will earn us much money soon."

"I believe it," I said.

She dipped a cloth into the river and used it to clean the twins' hands and faces. Then she pulled some pellets from a woven shoulder bag and poured some into the children's outstretched palms. I lifted my own palms towards her with a kidlike smile, and she rewarded me with a handful. Henrique and Tiago shrugged off an offer to join us, but watched as we leaned over the wire fence that surrounded the concrete tanks and let the feed drift down from our palms.

We were observing the feeding frenzy when a plane's engine sounded. I lifted my head and squinted into the clear blue sky, framed by forest branches.

"It smells so fresh and clean up here," I murmured, trying to sight the plane.

Myriam looked up, one hand shading her eyes. As the engine's noise grew closer, a small plane came into view – a white single-engine turboprop, flying low. Just as I was thinking that the twins might like to see a plane, Myriam picked up Freddy, shoved him into my arms, scooped up Flora, and started running.

"Follow me!" she screamed.

Myriam was my guide, so I followed her upriver, off the path, as Freddy stiffened in my arms. I glanced back once, astonished to see Henrique and Tiago sprinting in the opposite direction, toward the village. As Myriam, the twins, and I ran, trying not to stumble, I looked up once to see the little plane eject lines of cloudy white smoke, like a giant comb with thin teeth dispersing gently through the air. I'd seen planes spray crops on farms near home. I'd also seen planes spray fancy colored smoke at air shows. This was nothing worth worrying about, I reassured myself, as some of the white smoke drifted down on us.

We came to a rock wall, with steps gouged into its side. I followed Myriam up the steps. Not ducking low enough,

I banged my head at the entrance to a nifty little cave with a bird's-eye view of the river and surrounding landscape.

"Where are Henrique and Tiago?" she asked, breathing hard.

"They headed to the village."

"Oh. It's a little farther, but that's okay." She looked downriver for a moment, then lay on the cave floor and gathered the twins to her. I spread myself full length on the hard rock beside her, waiting for an explanation. Flora started to cry. Freddy moved closer to his big sister.

"Anti-narcotic police," she said, still panting.

"Huh?"

"They spray the illegal coca fields up here – and don't care if it hits us too."

"What's coming out the back of the plane?" I asked.

"Poisons that make the coca plants shrivel up and die."

"Oh." I looked at Flora and patted her head awkwardly as she sobbed. "What does it do to people?"

"Nothing, according to the officials," Myriam said, placing gentle hands on Flora's tear-streamed face and leaning close to examine the little girl's eyes. That's when my own eyes started itching.

I was still bare-chested from when I'd been sunning along the riverbank. Looking down, I brushed white powdery residue off my arms and chest. Within seconds, I felt a rash forming on my skin. I looked at Freddy, who was rubbing reddened eyes, and at Myriam, who was wiping the twins' faces with water from her water bottle.

"Get it off you," she urged, dabbing water on her own face after she'd treated her siblings.

"I'm glad you and the twins have long sleeves on," I said, pointing to where my arms and chest were turning patchy red.

She nodded vaguely and watched me brush more white dust off my skin. "We have to get back to the village."

"But . . ." I started, then held my tongue. There wasn't going to be any more paddling today if this was some kind of emergency. Watching us kayak more rapids or advising us what was downstream was the last thing on Myriam's mind.

I made my way down the steps on the rock wall gingerly, Freddy's arms wrapped around my neck. Then I lifted a hand to help Myriam, who was carrying Flora down the last few steps. I kept my grip just a second longer than I needed to. Myriam didn't seem to notice.

We walked silently to the trout tanks, where Myriam paused. I looked over the tanks' fence. "What the heck?" I said.

The fish were jumping like crazy and swimming erratically in circles. I watched some big ones all but throw themselves against the sides of the holding tank, as if desperate to escape.

"Look, the ones at the top are dropping like pebbles to the bottom," I observed.

"Chocolate," Freddy said, pointing at fish in the tank beside the one Myriam and I were examining. Myriam and I brushed shoulders as we leaned over to look where he was pointing.

"They weren't that color before, were they?" I asked. It was as if the blood vessels of the translucent fish had turned chocolate brown. *Eerie. They don't look one bit appetizing*, I thought.

"They're poisoned," Myriam cried. "We'll lose them!"

She looked so despondent that I slipped an arm over her shoulders. "Maybe it's just temporary," I said. "Maybe it'll be okay."

She shook my arm off and stared coolly at me. "What do you know about it? We'll starve without those fish." With that, she picked up her bike, loaded up the twins, and rode off. I was left standing there, feeling stupid. It wasn't my fault a plane had sprayed their mountaintop.

I turned to look at the three kayaks, all lightly powdered. The village was only a few minutes' walk and I knew the way, so I picked up the three kayaks, rinsed them in the river, and stashed them in some brush. Then I headed briskly back to the village.

The men were gathered in a circle around the fire pit, talking fast. I was relieved to see Henrique and Tiago there with them, but less pleased to see my friends directing a stream of questions at the villagers. The women and children, some crying, were sprinkling water on the leaves of the plants in their garden. Myriam was with them, ignoring me. I looked towards the men, where I caught Alberto's eye. He pointed at me and said something to the men. *Great, what now?* But this time, his look wasn't unfriendly. He strode over to Myriam, reached for her hand, and spoke to her while pointing to me, then to the Brazilians.

She pulled her hand away, but followed him over to me. "You said you and your kayakers have lots of food in your backpacks," she said, not quite meeting my eyes. "Alberto thought —"

"Of course we can share it," I said, relieved that no one was going to kick us out of the village.

"Most of our garden crops will die now. Maybe the trout too. People will go hungry," she explained.

"They don't need to go hungry. We have —"

"Alberto and I saw coca leaves being trimmed on a plantation near here. We knew that meant the owners were expecting a spraying, so we covered some plants in our garden. Otherwise things would be worse."

"What can I do, Myriam? What can I do to help besides donate some food?"

"Alberto says you're good at carrying a heavy pack."

I turned to look at Alberto. *He said something positive about me?* Of course, I had boasted about that to him. "You need me to carry something?"

She looked at me uncertainly. "Alberto would like you and your friends to go down to town, buy some food with money Papá gives you, and bring it back in your packs."

"On our own? No mules?" I regretted the words the minute they were out of my mouth.

"We need the mules and all the men to save the crops," she said. "Alberto thinks you'll remember the way."

I stood there staring at her. It had taken Alberto and us kayakers half a day to get up here. It might go faster without the mules, but we'd lose an entire day of paddling, not even counting the time it would take to buy stuff in the market. At least my buddies' better grasp of Spanish would help that. And carrying up heavy packs would be a total drag, and we might get lost. . . . I looked at Freddy and Flora, realizing for the first time how skinny they were. All the kids here, adults too, were skinny. Starving, almost. And the plane had just poisoned most of what food they had.

"Sure," I said.

Myriam relayed my answer to Alberto, who passed it on to the men.

"No problem," Henrique said as Tiago nodded beside him.

Myriam's father, who seemed like some kind of leader here, laid a light hand on my shoulder. He handed me a pitiful number of coins for buying food and explained what they especially needed. I shook my head, calculating that Gramps would have wired me more money by now.

"*Gracias,*" he said.

"No problem," I answered, echoed by my friends.

Alberto hovered near Myriam, smiling at her like she was some kind of hero for putting me and the Brazilians up to this. Henrique, Tiago, and I moved towards our backpacks and started handing out the food we'd counted on to get us down the Furioso. Elderly women lined up barefoot and somber to collect it, their eyes thanking us.

CHAPTER TEN

Miles below the calm stretch that moves past the village, the river picks up again. Big challenging rapids for several miles. We had to have our wits about us. Finally we approached a sharp bend, beyond which I thought I could hear a thundering waterfall. Tomorrow we will find out, but tonight I returned to camp exhausted and feverish. Once we get past the waterfall, I anticipate a half day of very challenging paddling to reach the point where the Furioso joins the Magdalena. Must sleep now, feeling a little off.
— Malcolm Scruggs

"Feeling a little off?" I echoed. "Exhausted and feverish?" But the next entry said nothing about being ill, or about his companions abandoning him. I double-checked the next entry's date: It was for the following day. I'd read the next paragraphs a hundred times because they were so exciting — his account of being chased away by angry villagers, being forced to abandon his kayak, and deciding to return home.

But Abuela had never mentioned a chase, and she was clearly mistaken about him being ill for a long time. *She's old*, I reminded myself, *probably forgetful. And it was a long time ago. . . .*

"Was it a waterfall?" I had asked Gramps back at home.

"I never found out," he'd said, eyes full of regret. "Those savages never gave me a chance."

"You couldn't sneak back and finish the river, Gramps?"

"It was time, Rex. Time to come home. We'd been in South America for four months, had accomplished numerous first descents, and your grandmother was expecting your mother anytime."

"Oh." I liked that he'd wanted to get home to be with his family. But I knew him well enough to not fully trust the answer. For the first time, I wondered if Gramps had lied in his journal. *Had the river served up too many impossible rapids? Is the Furioso River truly runnable? But if he knows it isn't, he wouldn't have let me come, right?*

So the illness Abuela claimed he'd had might have been one evening's fever. *Then what? Had he and his teammates fought and separated, or had some Indians really threatened them? Or had he and his team racked up so many first descents that they could afford to leave one?* The journal entry after the chase scene merely documented his trip home. Then the diary ended – no more helpful information about the river and its rapids.

Once the guys and I finished our grocery-buying spree and got back up to the Furioso, then we'd be relying on Myriam, our instincts, and whatever scouting we could do.

I lifted my empty backpack onto my shoulders and was waiting outside our hut for Henrique and Tiago, when they appeared with sleeping bags tied to the bottom of what looked to be fully loaded packs.

"Hey, we're supposed to hike down with empty packs to collect the food," I said as my stomach tightened.

"Rex, we're not coming back up," Henrique said, fixing his eyes on me and standing firmly in the doorway. "We're quitting. We think you should, too."

"What? I thought you were having fun. The river's been fine. We'll have it knocked off in no time."

"It's nothing to do with the river. We just think it's too dangerous around here — you know, the land mines and soldiers and all."

My mouth went dry. I should've been expecting this, but I'd been ignoring the signs.

"Bullshit. You flew all the way here. You agreed. A deal's a deal, and you know I wouldn't have come without backup."

"Rex —"

"We haven't seen any trouble. You're letting a bunch of ignorant villagers scare you!"

"Ignorant?" Henrique's face took on a dark look. "You're the one who doesn't speak Spanish, and you won't listen even when we translate for you."

"Myriam didn't say it's unsafe. And Jock encouraged us."

"You're paying them, you idiot," Tiago spoke up. "What else would they say?"

I felt my face drain of color. My pulse quickened. They were right about that. I'd never let myself admit it. *Am I being stupid? Naïve? Are we really in danger?* But even if we were, we were already here. *So why not finish it? Why not get out of here by river instead of by hiking alone, without Alberto or anyone else to protect us?*

My jaw tightened. I had to fight for this trip – my dream, my only chance to conquer the Furioso. And, anyway, like Gramps said, it was a small window of opportunity. Some other kayaker would come scoop it up if we didn't do it now. I couldn't return to Gramps and Mom as a failure. And I needed these two for safety on the river.

It took me only a split second to decide on a different tactic. "You're chickening out of the canyon. You don't think you can handle the Class V." That sounded childish, even to me.

"I told you he wouldn't listen," Tiago addressed Henrique.

Henrique directed a long, hostile glare at me. "We'll walk down with you," he finally said. "And we've left money with Alberto to return our kayaks by mule when he can. I'm sorry, Rex, I really am. But we agreed based on outdated government information. If the Furioso were in a safe area, we'd stay, honest."

I felt my entire body sag.

"Don't try paddling it by yourself, Rex," Tiago added, studying me to assess whether I was crazy enough to do that.

"Like you've left me any choice," I said bitterly. "I'm not quitting." I drew myself up and spun around so my back was to them. "Besides, I just promised to bring them back some food. Something you two assholes don't even care about. Let's go."

We were a sorry threesome that morning, a silent column almost the entire trip down. I made some stabs at trying to change their minds. They exaggerated the information they'd supposedly gotten from Myriam's people to try bullying me out of carrying on. They didn't know me, or my family history, well enough.

We made it down the mountain in record time. The minute I caught sight of the road where the buses ran, I snatched Alberto's hat off my head and stuffed it into my empty pack. Myriam had made me promise to wear it until we got to the road. She'd said soldiers were more likely to hassle a white boy than a Latino. *Hassle, schmassle. I can handle myself.*

"Internet café, then the market?" I suggested.

"Sure," the guys said stiffly.

We ducked into the Internet café, where I was relieved to find that Gramps had wired me more money. Not as much as I'd requested, but enough to cover the second shopping trip with some to spare.

"You need to bargain harder with those locals, Rex," his e-mail read. "Don't be a wimp; don't go spending my hard-earned money foolishly; and don't expect any more."

I thanked him and assured Mom I was fine and that my teammates and I were enjoying the river, which hadn't been difficult at all so far. While Henrique and Tiago were finishing up, I scooted over to the money-wiring place. Then the guys joined me at the market and bargained ruthlessly to help me collect the supplies. They even donated a bunch of money toward the stuff. Clearly they were suffering some guilt for not carrying food back up. *Should I really abandon my first descent?* I could decide after hauling the food up. I would not decide before then.

"Thanks for helping me out with the shopping," I addressed Henrique when my pack was so full it resembled something Mt. Everest-bound. We stood awkwardly at the edge of the marketplace.

"Least we can do," he said, his voice tinged with sadness.

"Please don't talk to Jock or any reporters or my family till I decide what to do, eh?" I wanted to make sure the two of them wouldn't say anything that might get back to my mom or Gramps – who, after all, had allowed me to come only on condition it would be a team effort. *If I carry on, it's a new team,* I thought. *Myriam as my shore crew and me, myself, and I.*

The guys nodded, clearly relieved that I seemed to be backing down.

"No hard feelings?" Tiago asked as we prepared to part near the bus station.

"It was fun doing a few rapids together," I allowed, trying not to grit my teeth. "It would've been good to do the whole thing, but you may be right."

"Take care, then," Henrique said, and punched me lightly on the shoulder, his dark eyes trying to read mine. "See you at the next worlds or something."

"Or something," I agreed and turned away, feeling empty and vastly alone, even as I held my head high. I forced my feet in the direction of Jock's shop, easing my heavy pack off my back and setting it beside the counter, whose glass top displayed *Expediciones del Río* T-shirts.

Jock entered when I rang the little bell on the counter. "Rex! I didn't expect to see you back down here so fast, or in one piece. Does that mean it was a super-fast ride or that you got smart and gave it up?"

"I came down on an errand for Myriam," I said sheepishly, not wanting to explain about the plane poisoning. "We've done some of the rapids and will start again the day after tomorrow. Are you okay for joining us where the two rivers meet later than we agreed on?"

"Absolutely. Are Henrique and Tiago with you?"

"Doing their own thing at the moment. Myriam's working out great, by the way."

"Super. You're lucky. Pretty much nobody else up there speaks English, far as I know. And the rapids are okay?"

"Just fun stuff so far," I said.

"Perfect. Tom's still around, you know. Another guide and I took him on the Magdalena again yesterday."

"Bet that was fun."

"He made it down without coming out of his boat."

"That's good." I reddened as I flashed back to my own humiliating swim.

"Tom's outside now, jabbering with one of my guides. Then he's going ziplining. You should go with him. It's a blast."

"You mean, hanging off a T-bar thing on a pulley while you zip down a steel cable at high speed?"

"Exactly. A friend of mine just started it up as a business catering to, you know, the English-speaking market."

"Sounds fun, but I have to get back up the mountain by dark." Not to mention I was running out of money.

"It only takes an hour, and the truck ride is partway up the mountain. It'll save you nearly an hour of walking." He named a price – less than what I'd pay for a CD at home. I drummed my fingers on the counter, tempted. I was feeling abandoned and downhearted, even a little unsure of my decision to head back up. *Maybe this will be a nice pick-me-up?*

"It's fun and totally safe, and you can see the country-side all around. It even goes across a mountain creek at one point."

Hmm, I thought. *Good for scouting rapids and the terrain if I decide to knock off another river instead of the Furioso.*

"Better decide fast. That's the truck pulling up now."

"Sure, sounds sweet. I'm in."

He was a good businessman, Jock. Probably got commission for sending customers over to his ziplining buddy. *Oh, well. I'm here to have fun, aren't I?*

"Hey, Tom," I said as I lugged my backpack out Jock's front door.

"Rex! You're the man! Back from bagging a mountain creek already? Buddies gone home to Brazil? And you're going ziplining with me?"

"Something like that." We climbed into the rear of the dusty pickup truck. I used my pack as a backrest. The driver came around and collected money, his smile showing yellowed teeth.

Tom and I coughed as the truck took off in a cloud of dust.

———

"I can't believe you walked up and paddled a river and walked down again without getting shot at or kidnapped," Tom said. "You're a crazy kid, you know that?"

"I'm not a kid, and we didn't even see any soldiers," I said, offended.

He laughed as the truck lurched around potholes. "It doesn't mean they didn't see you."

"I thought the Colombian Army pretty much had things under control." *Everything except some paranoia up in Myriam's village that scared my buddies away*, I thought.

Tom laughed harder. "Yeah, sure. Totally under control. Only 'pockets of resistance,' the media likes to say. Any reporter who sniffs around for more info than that gets murdered."

I stared at him. "Well, we didn't see any trouble."

"That's good, Rex, 'cause that's one helluva pocket of resistance up there. Guerillas and paras and coca fields and what have you. The Colombian Army won't go near the place, except to fly over in planes."

And dump poisons on innocent indígenas' *gardens*, I thought.

"What's the difference between guerillas and paramilitaries?" I asked. Gramps might have explained it, but I hadn't much listened then.

"Originally, the guerillas were fighting to make life better for poor people. The Colombian Army couldn't beat the guerillas, especially in the countryside, so landowners and businessmen started hiring private soldiers — paramilitaries — to protect themselves from the guerillas."

"Sounds reasonable," I said.

"Yeah, but these days, both the guerillas and paras are bad news and out of control – like big-city street gangs always trying to get more territory and members. Unfortunately, the Colombian Army isn't big enough to stop either."

"Oh."

"Jock wasn't about to tell you directly, Rex, 'cause he's all about business. But you made it back down the mountain, so it's all good."

I thought about Alberto insisting I pull the hood around my face and wear his hat, and about Myriam warning me not to step into the fields across the river. I thought about Jock and Tom trying to tell me my grandfather's information was out of date. I wondered if Henrique and Tiago had just done the right thing.

"We have a guide," I said, straightening my shoulders and deciding Tom just enjoyed exaggerating. "We stay in the guide's village. They're hosting us. Looking out for us."

"An *indígena* community," Tom said, shaking his head incredulously. "Looking out for you? I don't think so. They can't even look out for themselves."

"What do you mean?" I demanded. His superior attitude was starting to bug me.

He shook his head again. "Rex, you're a babe in the woods. You need to expand your knowledge, kid. The *indígena* communities are getting massacred left and right by people – including guerillas and paras – who want *indígena* land to grow coca fields for cocaine, to mine or drill for oil, or just to keep their soldiers' camps on. The Colombian Army and most Colombian people couldn't care less about *indígenas*, so they're pretty much on their own up there."

"On their own." I repeated the words numbly, not willing to believe him. "Massacred?"

"Massacred, Rex. Some people use the word 'genocide.'"

"That's when someone tries to wipe out a whole group of people? Like the Jews in World War II?"

"Good, Rex. You're not as dumb as I thought. Sorry to be the one to bring you into the real world, kid, but this is Colombia, not Disneyland."

"What're you here for?" I asked, determined to change the subject.

Tom scratched his ear where an earring decorated it. He grinned. "Adventure. Money goes a long way here for us gringos, and I'm all about seeing the world."

I nodded. That was something we could agree on. I pulled a chocolate bar out of my backpack and offered him half.

"Thanks," he said, devouring it almost as quickly as Flora and Freddy had.

He offered me some time on his iPod in return. The music helped me banish his comments from my mind, and I rocked my body a little to the tunes from home.

"So, Rex," he interrupted me after a while, "how does a first descent work, anyway? Does it count as a first descent if you have to portage around some rapids?"

"Of course."

"What if you did, say, a couple of rapids and then portaged the other ninety percent of the river?"

"There's the odd kayaker who might try to claim that, but not an honest one." Gramps' group did the Furioso to the canyon, then left. *They never tried to claim it*, I reminded myself. I hadn't even done as many rapids as they had yet.

"And did you guys make it down this Furioso to where it joins the Magdalena?"

"No, I just interrupted our run to come down for more food. I head back this afternoon."

Tom sat up straight. "You're returning, alone, today?"

"That's right."

"Nutso, dude. It's been nice knowing you."

I turned up the volume on the music and tried to focus my thoughts: *Scruggs family legacy. Finish what Gramps started. Make Gramps proud.*

A larger thought formed, loomed, then crowded out everything else: *Myriam's people need the food I picked up, and they need the second half of the guiding fee more than ever. I'll deliver the food and pay Myriam that, even if I decide to stop paddling.*

The truck pulled up beside a strong-looking steel cable that stretched across a narrow valley.

"Cool," Tom said.

"Got that right," I responded.

We jumped out, and I asked permission to store my pack in the hut. Then someone emerged from the hut to hand us harnesses, gloves, and helmets. Oval metal clips called carabiners jangled off me as I ascended a platform with Tom and got a safety briefing. The heavy gloves had plastic grooves where my fingers would curl over the cable.

"Use your gloves to keep yourselves in an upright position and to slow yourselves down when you get a signal from the guide on the platform at the other end," our guide said. "If you slow down too fast, you'll end up stopped in the middle of the cable, and we'll have to rescue you."

"What if we forget to slow down?" Tom asked.

"We have a safety mechanism at the end to keep you from crashing into the platform on the far side. Don't worry. You'll get the hang of it after the first ride."

I had butterflies in my stomach as the guide clipped my harness to the overhead cable and said, "Ready?"

Then I was flying through the air, my gloves barely touching the cable, my feet dangling two hundred feet over a thousand shades of green as orchids, ferns, trees, and grass waved up at me. Above the greenery rose a joyful array of mountains backdropped by a pure blue sky.

"*Yahoo!*" I screamed, slowing myself just in time for a smooth landing on the far platform.

Tom was next, and much rowdier in his screams of delight. After getting unhitched from the cable, we followed our guide up a well-worn path to the next platform and repeated our performance over a wider, deeper valley. This time, I was more relaxed – so relaxed that I accidentally lost my grip on the cable and tipped sideways as I flew along it. Someone at the far tower pulled on a safety cord that slowed me down before I reached the platform.

"Hold that grip next time," the guide scolded me lightly.

Before embarking on a third ride, I stood on the platform squinting down into a deep canyon, with a stream running along the bottom. Its flowing water winked at me in the sunlight. I followed the stream as far as I could with my naked eye to where it disappeared. Then it reappeared around the next bend.

"Anyone have binoculars?" I asked.

The guide shook his head. "At the speed we go, binoculars are useless anyway."

True enough. But I love scouting creeks.

Tom went first this time, whisking fast and furiously away from me, high over the stream. I let the guide clip me to the cable next and adjusted my helmet.

"This is a long cable without the same decline as the last one, so make sure you keep your speed up," he advised.

"Gotcha." I hung my full weight from the wire and off I slid, my eyes locked on the stream. The cable moved me faster and faster towards it, until I was approaching the place where the river disappeared from view. I pressed hard on the cable to slow myself down and stared. A *pudú* was wading into the stream below me. *Wow! Love those miniature deer*, I thought. *Too bad I'm moving too fast to take a photo.*

Then the deer stumbled. I craned my neck to watch the little creature fall into the stream and get caught by the current, desperately hoof-paddling to get out of it. As I approached the midpoint of the cable, I slowed myself to a near stop, so focused was I on the drama below me. *Hey!* If my eyes were not playing tricks on me, the stream completely disappeared into the ground directly below and reappeared a ways on! And the deer was going to get washed into that underground tunnel and drown, poor thing.

I hung there, wishing I could eject and parachute down to rescue the unfortunate *pudú*. My mouth fell open as the deer struggled harder, then got sucked into the subterranean passage.

Oops! I was nearly at a standstill on the cable. The tension of watching had made me grip it too hard. I eased off and slid further, high over the dry land under which that stream was hurtling, towards where it burst out of the ground and carried on. Curious to see the deer wash out, I gripped again, ignoring the far side guide's frantic waving.

Okay, I was at a dead stop now, hanging hundreds of feet above the underground river. I tried to jiggle myself forward, but there wasn't enough slope on the steel cable. The guide shouted at me from the platform, but I glanced up only long enough to see him clip his harness to the wire and use a device to jimmy himself along the cable towards me.

I was going to be rescued, pulled to the far end, and told off. *Oh, well.* Meanwhile, I could stare at this fascinating phenomenon: a stream that dove underground. I'd heard of such rivers, but had never seen one. I'd even heard of kayakers who set up strobe lights to paddle an underground whitewater river. There had to be porous rock to allow such a feature, but I was no geologist. I'd better knock this stream off my list, anyway.

I glanced up again. The guide was making his way towards me, his face beaded in sweat as he used raw muscle to slide his device in jerks along the cable. When he was two feet away, I looked down and shouted, "The *pudú*! It washed through! It's still alive!"

The guide narrowed his eyes. "Concentrate," he ordered, reaching forward to pull my harness towards him.

He smelled of sweat, and his grizzly face was making a poor effort to disguise his annoyance. I was a paying customer, but I was a pain in the neck. I cooperated, doing a hand-over-hand maneuver to help slide us along. He nodded like he approved of my muscle power. If you have to have a customer who gets stuck, preferably have one who's strong enough to help with his own rescue.

It took ten minutes of hot sweaty work to get ourselves to the far platform.

"Way to go, Rex," Tom teased, high-fiving my grooved glove as the guide unclipped me and signaled for the guide on the far side to join us. That guide whizzed down to us so fast that I was startled when he dropped lightly onto the platform.

"That's how fast you should've been going," Tom whispered. "It's more fun seeing how much speed you can get up."

"Okay," I said, and made sure that for the last half hour of ziplining, I was a perfect customer.

By climbing up steep hills between each zipline segment, we managed to do a full circle and still land back at our first platform beside the hut. I checked my watch and panicked.

"I've gotta get back up before dark!" I said, grabbing my heavy pack from the hut and pumping one of the guides for directions. "Nice to see you again, Tom. Good luck. Thanks for the ziplining, everyone. It was awesome."

CHAPTER ELEVEN

Myriam's tears dripped into the corn she was grinding, but she kept her head low so no one could tell. The men were gathered around the fire pit, discussing Alberto's defection. The women, as always, were tending to the children and chores.

"He has been wanting to join the guerillas for a long time," Papá was saying, shaking his head sadly. "The spraying that caused this food shortage was the last straw for him. He thinks the money he can send us will help."

No! Myriam wanted to scream. *It's my fault because I refused to marry him.* The two of them had argued about his desire to join up numerous times. She'd always stopped him by promising to break up if he did. Then she'd refused his proposal. That had angered and humiliated him — and left him no reason not to join. *What will be his fate now? He'll be killed in some battle. I'll never see him again. Even if I don't want to marry him, I care about him. We've grown up together. This is all my fault, and no one even knows it.*

"His joining will keep the guerillas from returning to ask us for a *vacuna*," she overheard one elder say.

"But it will anger the paramilitaries if they hear about it," another replied. "They might use it as an excuse to take our land for a coca field."

"But that's illegal," a young boy piped up. The others looked at him. Their silence was his answer.

The fire crackled as dark closed in. "We need to double the number on guard duty," Papá ruled in a deep voice.

"We'll never get our crops cleaned, fertilized, and watered if we do that," an equally deep voice protested.

"Maybe someone can sneak into the guerilla camp and tell Alberto to come back?" the young boy suggested.

There were only grunts from around the fire.

"When are the kayakers returning?" someone asked softly, trying to ensure Myriam wouldn't overhear.

"Rex will return tonight, if he doesn't change his mind or get lost or attacked on the way," Papá replied. "The Brazilians said their thank-yous and farewells. Their packs were full. They won't be returning."

Myriam turned her head just enough to see Papá peer at the sky, watching darkness descend. She'd worried all day about Rex's safety, about Alberto sending him and his friends on such a dangerous errand, but she didn't dare say anything. She'd noticed the sleeping bags strapped onto Henrique's and Tiago's packs and heard them tell her father good-bye. But Rex's had been empty. *So he plans to return — doesn't he?*

"Tell Myriam to charge the white boy more money," someone suggested.

"She has already negotiated a very high price. Leave her be," Papá said.

Myriam hung her head. Yes, she'd negotiated a high price. The villagers had been impressed. But she hadn't told anyone that a second payment was coming when he finished the river. She was toying with the idea of keeping that for herself, for her bus trip to campus. Now guilt enveloped her. She doubted she could go through with leaving her beloved village or defying her elders.

"Are they likely to kidnap the white boy when he's with Myriam?" someone asked.

"Less likely," Papá replied.

"Is Myriam in danger if they do try?" someone else asked.

"She is fast on her feet and knows the terrain well," Papá said, failing to hide a note of concern. "They'll let her escape."

"*Shhh,*" another said. "Here he comes. Alone."

The men looked over at Myriam. She turned, rose, and rushed to Rex, remembering to slow down at the last minute to not look too enthusiastic. There were many in her community who didn't like her associating with a foreign white boy, whether it brought much-needed money for the community or not.

"Myriam," Rex greeted her, his smile broad in the shadows, his body poised as if to hug her. She shrank back.

"I'm glad you found your way," she said as he slid the pack off his shoulders and began unzipping it. "The others?"

"They quit. I'll carry on alone."

She didn't know what to feel. Relief about the money, or worry about his safety. *Didn't he tell me it was risky for kayakers to paddle solo?*

Both the men and the women stepped forward to inspect what he'd hauled up the mountain. There were nods of admiration from the men, who'd said earlier a white boy couldn't carry much, and grunts of approval from the women, who were already pushing forward to sort the bags of fruit, vegetables, canned beans and corn, and powdered milk Papá had requested.

When Freddy and Flora ran to Rex, he squatted down and pulled out a chocolate bar. "They'll share it with the other kids, won't they?" he asked Myriam.

She quickly translated for the twins, who gave Rex big smiles and ran to share their prize with their playmates.

When the backpack was empty, except for a packet he'd reserved for himself, Rex nodded at the villagers, then at Myriam, and began walking to his hut.

"Good night, Myriam," he said, turning to wink at her in such a way that no one else could possibly see.

She drew in her breath, burning with resentment. *How dare he!* But she could feel a half-smile hiding behind her frown.

The next morning, Myriam's mother offered to look after Flora, so Myriam had only Freddy to bike with. She followed Rex as he biked up to the trout tanks, where he'd hidden his boat and paddle two days before. She watched him stash the bike, then pick up his kayak and perch it on his broad, naked shoulder. He was wearing tight black rubberlike shorts, boots of the same material, and nothing

else. He had his paddling jacket tied around his trim waist
and a small waterproof pouch in his hand. She'd never seen
a kayak or a kayaker, except in pictures, before Rex and his
friends had shown up. Now she felt like she knew quite a
bit about kayaking gear and how kayakers maneuvered
their little boats around river boulders and through waves.

She still thought it was ludicrous that someone would
fly halfway around the world to paddle a river. It reeked of
money, arrogance, and stupidity. But she couldn't help
admiring the way Rex made his little boat work the rapids.
He seemed to read invisible routes through the water the
way birds read air currents.

In all her years of watching the *El Furioso* tumble by,
she'd never imagined a vessel that could dance down it as
if at play. However strange she found Rex and his motivations, she recognized in him the same fascination for river
currents she'd always held. *Is it possible a stranger can appreciate my river as I do?*

Rex set his kayak down on the riverbank and fished out
his life jacket, paddle, helmet, and spraydeck. He flipped
the boat over to inspect minor scratches, then turned and
smiled at Myriam with a warmth that distracted her from
the guilt and misery Alberto's departure had invoked.

"It's calm here," he said, seating himself on a rock,
drawing his feet up to his knees, and staring at the peaceful water flowing by. She parked her bike and seated herself
on a stump near him, studying his features as he watched
the river. Morning sun shone on his white face, so full of
both determination and gentleness. The scent of eucalyptus drifted on the breeze. Birdsong floated down from the

softly drooping acacia tree branches, harmonized by the gurgling river.

Myriam lowered Freddy to the ground. Immediately, he crawled up onto Rex's overturned boat, positioned his legs like he was riding the community's mule, and made *cluck-cluck* sounds like Papá did to urge the mule on.

Rex chuckled. "Ride 'em cowboy, Freddy." Then he turned to Myriam. "What's after this calm section, Myriam?"

She straightened her poncho over her jeans and shifted on the tree stump. *Why doesn't he just ask me to draw a map of the whole river and let me get back to my duties in the village?* Then again, she loved the freedom of hanging out by the river all day and watching him muscle his boat around. She didn't even miss Henrique and Tiago, who asked too many questions. Difficult political questions. But there was another reason Myriam was okay with continuing to come to the river with Rex. She was aware that her presence – specifically her ability to bring *indígena* guards running to her aid – discouraged any guerillas or paras who were eyeing him. Not that she could be certain they wouldn't try something anyway.

Beyond all that, though, since last night she'd been wrestling with how and when to ask Rex for the other half of the payment.

"Myriam?" He interrupted her thoughts. "What's after this calm section?"

"Rex, I'd like to have the second payment before I tell you." She couldn't believe she'd actually said it. *Hopefully not too abruptly? I need to collect it before the river kills you or the soldiers take you,* she thought darkly. "You can trust me to keep guiding after the payment, you know."

He smiled, rose, and walked over to sit beside her on her stump. She stiffened. "I trust you, Myriam. But the deal was, I pay you when I reach the Magdalena."

Should I tell him now or wait for him to find out for himself? *El Furioso* would never, ever allow him to reach the Magdalena by kayak. And even if he did make it there, he shouldn't hike back up through paramilitary territory to pay her. Never mind that he'd managed to return to her village the day the Brazilians had abandoned him.

"I need the money now," she insisted. "Our community needs it now," she corrected herself with a stab of guilt. "I promise to guide until you give up."

"I'll never give up!" he said.

"Why? Do you get money if you kayak to the Magdalena? Do you get your name in the newspapers? Do you become a celebrity?" She tried not to let sarcasm and bitterness creep into her voice, but she couldn't get past that he was using her river for shallow purposes.

He shrugged. "Yes, but I don't care about any of that."

He met her eyes with a steadiness no liar would have been able to maintain. "Then why?" she asked again.

He sighed, moving his hand near where hers rested, but refraining from touching her. "My grandfather tried to kayak the Furioso and gave up. I have to do it to prove myself to him."

Myriam gazed across the river, towards where Alberto was probably being initiated, this very moment, into a guerilla band he mistakenly thought would cure their people's problems. *Alberto is trying to prove himself to our village*, she thought miserably, *even though the paras might punish us for him joining up. That and to hurt me or get away from me.*

"That's not a good enough reason," she said aloud. "If your grandfather doesn't love you, maybe nothing will change that."

Rex looked startled. He crossed his arms and surveyed her.

"*El Furioso* isn't going to take you to the Magdalena," Myriam declared, then panicked that she'd said it. "Especially if you don't have a better reason than that."

Rex stood and walked to his boat. He gently lifted Freddy from it and eased the boy into her arms, then turned his boat right-side-up.

I've blown it, she thought. *He's going to slide into the river without paying me and without asking me again what's below. If he dies, it will be all my fault, just like it's my fault that Alberto is going to die.* "Rex?"

"I'm paying you," he said gruffly, handing her a wad of money he'd pulled from his waterproof pouch.

She counted it – the precise amount they'd agreed on for the final payment. She blushed and mumbled thank you.

He backed away and sat down on the rock again, eyes not leaving her. Freddy gazed at the cash and poked a grubby finger at it.

The money – enough to get to campus *or* to seriously help her community – felt like it was burning her hands. Her heart pumped double time. A big decision lay before her, but first things first.

"When the rapids start again," she said, "they're very

big. There are at least five of them, each broken by a small calm section. Then the river plunges over a waterfall."

He jumped up. "How tall?"

"Like five of those trees, one on top of another." She pointed to a nearby pine tree.

"Fifty feet," he calculated aloud. "Rocks or logs piled up below it?"

She hesitated. "I don't think so."

"Easy to walk around?"

"Impossible to walk around. It's the start of a canyon with high walls."

"And what is the whitewater like between those walls?"

"Crazy. And not possible to kayak. You will have to stop at the falls."

Instead of declaring that he'd give up now, as she expected, he announced, "That is where you and I will part, then. But I will carry on. I figure it's only half a day's paddle from there to where the Furioso runs into the Magdalena."

She was about to protest when he pulled a nylon bag out from inside his kayak. A loop of rope stuck out of the bag.

"This is called a throw bag. It's for rescues."

She nodded, waiting.

"Between now and the falls, if I get in a situation that forces me to come out of my kayak, and you are onshore, you could save my life."

Her eyes grew large. So Rex was finally admitting he could come out of his boat in the river and that doing so could kill him. *Because Henrique and Tiago are no longer here to help.*

"How?" she asked.

He stood and placed a hand through the rope's loop. Then he loosened the drawstring on the bag. Inside, she saw that the loop was one end of a long rope that filled the entire bag. The other end was securely attached to the bottom of the bag. With one swift move, he threw the bag towards the center of the river. The rope unwound quickly until just the empty bag, still anchored to the far end of the rope, hit the water and started floating downstream.

"If I were in the river, I would grab that, and you would reel me in, hand over hand, standing like this." He bent his knees and straightened his back, hauling in the rope as if it had something heavy on its end.

She looked serious, pulling Freddy close.

"We need to practice it, Myriam."

"Okay."

First, he coached her in throwing the rope. She tossed, watched it unravel in the air, watched him pull it in and drop the coils of rope back into the bag each time.

"You're a quick learner," he finally said, satisfied. "I'm going to get in my boat now, tip over, and come out of it."

He paddled to the middle of the river, capsized, and ejected, just like the time he'd done so before, hiding under the boat to amuse the twins. She gripped the rescue rope's end loop and tossed the bag through the air. The bag, empty of rope by the time it reached the kayak, landed on the overturned boat with a thud. Rex grabbed it. She braced herself to haul him in, which was no easy task, given that he had hold of his boat and paddle, and the current had hold of him. Still, she managed to pull him and his gear to shore.

Freddy clapped as Rex emerged, dripping wet, and went out to do it again. After several practice rescues, Rex seemed satisfied. He tugged off his paddling jacket and life jacket and stood in the sun's warmth, naked from the waist up again.

"But what if I'm not there when you need rescue?" she asked, failing to avert her eyes as he stood beside her.

His wet shoulder muscles glistened in the sunlight. Droplets worked their way down his chest hair and over his flat stomach. He was powerfully built, more like Papá than the mostly scrawny men in her village. His smile was as wide as his helmet strap. He smelled of clean wet hair.

"You will be. If I come to a rapid I think could separate me from my boat, I'll position you at the bottom before I run it."

"Oh." *But that won't work in the canyon*, she wanted to say. *You'll be on your own there. And you'll drown.*

"Myriam, is it safe for you to hike along the river while I'm paddling? Are there soldiers?"

Myriam straightened herself in surprise. *So he isn't as naïve as I'd thought. And Henrique's and Tiago's departure has to make him wonder.* She shrugged and tussled Freddy's hair. "Maybe. But this is our land."

Rex moved closer to her, too close, and looked into her eyes. "You're the bravest girl I've ever met."

She stepped back, shaking a little. Suddenly, she was less scared of soldiers than of him. Then anger surged. *I'm not brave; I have no choice. My people have no choice!* And he'd forced her into this position by offering her money that her community couldn't afford to turn down.

She lifted the whistle that dangled around her neck. "If I'm in danger, I blow on this, and those on guard duty will come running. We take turns being on guard duty, strung out within hearing distance of one another's whistles." She let the whistle drop back to her neck.

He studied her face, then reached forward to touch the whistle. Her neck grew hot where it rested against her skin.

"Will you blow it if I kiss you?"

Panic seized her. She took two long steps backward and raised the whistle like it was a shield. "Get into your boat," she ordered him. "You are here to kayak."

"No problem," he said, shrugging his shoulders in a maddeningly unperturbed way. "I'll paddle to where the next rapids start. I'll wait for you there." He pulled his paddling jacket and life jacket back on.

She gathered up Freddy to secure him on her back and moved towards her bicycle. "Rex," she said, hesitating.

He turned.

"If I call the *indígena* guards, they will come and protect me. But they may not be able to protect you."

He stood there for a long time. "You suggest I hide?"

"Yes," she replied, not willing to tell him there was no place a white boy who didn't know this terrain could possibly hide. And he didn't even speak Spanish. *What is he doing here, anyway? And why should I care if they come for him, now that I have my money?*

He climbed in his boat, snapped the spraydeck around

his cockpit, and launched himself into the current. She watched her client disappear around the bend, paddling in such a relaxed, easy fashion that she wondered if he'd registered any of their conversation.

CHAPTER TWELVE

Just as Gramps' journal and Myriam had said, the calm section stretched for more than a mile. For the first time, however, my mind was not on the river and its features. Instead, it was torn between my growing attraction for the girl I'd just left on the bank and shadows I was beginning to sense along the shore. I kept glancing at the brush, onshore boulders, and trees that flashed by. Everywhere I looked, I imagined soldiers watching me.

Why didn't Gramps warn me it was dangerous up here? Because he had no way of knowing, I reminded myself. He couldn't even get a topographical map, let alone know the exact whereabouts of ever-moving "pockets of resistance." He'd assessed it the best he could. Henrique and Tiago had also thought it was okay till they got here.

Reporters who try to determine what soldiers get up to on *indígena* land get murdered, Tom had said. So most people outside of Colombia wouldn't have any way of knowing. *But what about* indígena *reporters?* Hey, that's what Myriam said she wanted to go to university to become. But her family won't let her. Bummer for her.

I pivoted around a rock and sat bobbing in the eddy for a moment. A wind had picked up, and it felt like someone breathing on me. *Pull yourself together, Rex,* I told myself. *You're doing a first descent. You'll have it nailed in two days, then you'll be out of here. There's nothing you can do about trouble that has been going on here for half a century. Just go with the flow, do what you're good at, and finish what you came here for.*

I leaned out from my eddy, stuck my paddle into the current, and let it whip me out in an arc. A rock I hadn't seen just under the surface broadsided my boat before my bow had fully swung to a downstream position. I had to throw in a slap brace to keep from going over. No biggie, but I heard Gramps' voice nonetheless: "Sloppy, boy. Gotta keep your eyes open better than that."

I glanced up and saw Gramps standing onshore, pointing an accusing finger at me.

"But I didn't go over, Gramps, because my reactions are fast and I don't panic. How about that, Gramps? But you never say anything positive, do you?"

"Just keeping you on your toes, boy. Don't forget I taught you everything you know."

"Not true. I'm not a kid anymore. I've had lots of coaches, and they were way better than you."

"Watch how you talk, boy! And where are your teammates?"

I paddled faster to try to get away from him. But he appeared around every corner, shouting insults at me and insisting I wasn't allowed to do it solo. *It has to be just trees bending and the wind whistling, but why can't I shake him?*

"You don't really want me to finish this river, do you, Gramps?" I finally shouted. "Because it'll make you look bad. You don't really want me carrying on *your* legacy. You only let me come 'cause Mom pressured you into it. Or because you want me to fail."

He turned away then, mumbling, "Guilt is a terrible thing to live with," before vanishing.

It was just me and my little boat and this dark river rushing towards the last rapids Gramps had paddled. His diary said he'd heard but not seen the waterfall. He hadn't paddled the canyon below it. *What will he say when I do? And why do I care?*

The wind blew up the river, skimmed droplets from wave tops, and flung them at my face. Serious rapids ahead. *Slow down*, I told myself. *Give Myriam time to position herself.*

I paused frequently to surf waves back and forth across the river, trying not to miss the companionship of Henrique and Tiago. *Deserters. Chickenshits.* I listened to the moos of cows in a nearby pasture, smelled smoke, and heard the distant voices of men as they burned a field.

Half an hour later, I caught a glimpse of Myriam's people cleaning and watering their crops with buckets and hoses. I sensed the river picking up and strained my ears for the sound of rapids. What I heard instead as I paddled around a river bend was Myriam's whistle, blasting in three shrill calls.

I spotted her and Freddy on the riverbank, trembling beside her bike, which she'd let drop to the grass. As I sprinted towards her — ready to protect her and Freddy at any cost — I saw her eyes widen and her arms wave frantically at me.

When the bow of my kayak touched shore, I heard the thunder of boots running. Since most of Myriam's people worked barefoot, they had to be soldiers' boots! There was no time to sprint away, no time to jump out of my kayak and find a tree to hide behind.

"Get away from here!" Myriam hissed, misery written in every pore of her face.

So I did what any sensible kayaker in my situation would do. I capsized in the deep dark eddy, ejected, and surfaced underneath my boat.

From the air pocket under my seat, all sounds were muffled. I tensed as I heard shouting and Freddy start to cry. Cringing, I expected the end of a machine gun to poke through the water and into my face, flip the boat back upright, and expose me.

I couldn't follow Spanish at the best of times, never mind the Spanish of soldiers threatening a girl alone by the river with her baby brother and an overturned kayak. Nor could I understand the Spanish of the villagers on guard duty as they arrived to aid Myriam. Distorted by the thick shell of my boat, the arguments meant nothing to me. But the tone rattled me to my very core.

Suspended in the lukewarm water up to my neck, I felt terror in every limb. As I tried to still the thumping of my heart, I began to worry how long they'd argue. With every jagged breath, I was converting a limited supply of oxygen into something unbreathable.

How long before gunfire will erupt? Can a handful of unarmed indígena *farmers scare off a unit of armed soldiers? How long before a bullet will penetrate plastic to hit my skull? How many minutes of breathing does a kayak cockpit offer?* In all my childhood days of playing tricks on Gramps, I'd never measured that last one. I never imagined it would someday be a matter of life or death.

After a while, my face went clammy and my breathing felt labored. I would pass out soon. But better to pass out than come to the surface. Better to suffocate than be shot, especially if my very presence posed any danger to Myriam and Freddy.

The air grew ever more stale, and I felt my dry throat begin to close up, like someone was strangling me. I allowed my right hand to rise slowly from my hip to the paddling jacket pocket where Gramps' necklace lived. The item on which I'd pinned foolish superstitions for so long was failing me. *Maybe Gramps should have paid far more than an avocado sandwich for it . . . should not have taken advantage of a starving woman. Maybe she'd had no right to sell it, which means I have no right to own it. Maybe I should give it up to Myriam. Why didn't that occur to me before? Maybe, for this oversight, I'm going to die.*

As my tiny space spun in circles, I felt myself falling into darkness. Suddenly the boat lifted and brilliant light blinded me. Myriam's father reached into the water. His strong arms grabbed me under my armpits. I felt myself flopped onto the riverbank.

"Myriam," I mumbled, trying to focus on a circle of concerned *indígena* faces above me.

"They're gone," she said.

CHAPTER THIRTEEN

Have I mentioned that the indigenous men here wear skirts, usually go barefoot, and carry the most rudimentary tools? I've seen only one or two alluring specimens among the undernourished females, who do all the cooking over open fires. They're mostly kept away from us and speak no Spanish, as far as I can tell. — Malcolm Scruggs

They let me hang out around the cook fire that night, sipping a thin broth the women had prepared. The soup only made me hungry for real calories after kayaking all day, but I wasn't about to complain, knowing they'd all been doing such hard physical labor since sunrise. I sure could've used some of those fried cornbread patties they'd served me that first day, but I knew without asking what had happened to most of the corn in their fields. At least not all the trout had died, they informed me.

We were sitting on wooden benches against the outside of the community center, kerosene lanterns flickering around the plaza, everyone in hats and wool ponchos except me. I'd just jogged down the hill from my little guest hut, wearing jeans, T-shirt, and fleece jacket. When it gets dark, it can get plenty cool at fifteen thousand feet elevation, even on the equator.

I leaned casually against the adobe *hacienda* wall, just like all the leathery-faced, mostly toothless men around me. I even extended my running shoes out in front of me, the same way they splayed their bare feet in the courtyard's dirt beneath those calf-length skirts.

Next time I'm at that market, I'll buy a sleeveless poncho to fit in better around here, I thought. It would be an interesting souvenir.

I wanted to sit next to Myriam, but she'd led me to the bench her papá shared with half a dozen men and motioned for me to sit beside him. Like the other women – even her elderly abuela – she hardly ever sat down during a meal. It seemed like the women served the food, ate, chased children, and embroidered all at the same time.

"Eat well," Papá said to me in Spanish, with a booming voice and a big grin, as he scraped his own clay bowl with his spoon. "Today you were the fish too clever to be caught."

I smiled wanly, wondering what he meant, exactly. *And how can he joke about a life-threatening experience?*

Secretly, I'd nicknamed him the big friendly giant. He was tall, confident, happy, and generally at the center of any cluster of men. Every time I saw him, he was either working at the rate of several men or waving a large hand while answering questions and directing others. I could see where Myriam got her energy and assertiveness from.

"Papá!" cried the twins, toddling over and trying to

clamber up his long legs. He lifted the kids effortlessly into his lap while beaming at Myriam's mother across the courtyard. Flora sat contentedly on his knees, but Freddy raised his chubby little hands and swiped Papá's hat, reaching over to place it on my head.

"*Gracias*, Freddy!" I joked as Papá broke into a barrel laugh.

If I couldn't sit beside Myriam, I didn't mind being beside Papá. He was the only man there I felt comfortable around. His powerful build, angular jaw, and sharp eyes reminded me of Gramps. He even had the same self-assured, leaderlike personality. But where Gramps was impatient and sarcastic, Myriam's father struck me as a study in patience and contentment. Which made no sense, considering the poverty and stress of this place.

"Bunch of dirty Indians," I imagined Gramps saying if he found himself dropped into this scene.

"And how much of our river did you kayak today?" Papá asked me. His eyes communicated genuine interest, and he delivered his Spanish so slowly and clearly that I could understand him.

"From the trout tanks to where you found me," I said. "Myriam has been very helpful. She knows the river well."

"Of course," he said, smiling. "She has lived on it all her life."

I nodded and shifted on the hard bench. I could tell the villagers were watching me, but it didn't feel as uncomfortable as when I'd arrived a few days earlier.

A kitten rubbed up against my leg. When I picked it up, Myriam's mutt, Capitán, barked at the little furry ball as if jealous.

"Was I in danger of being killed this afternoon?" I addressed Papá, hoping he'd understand my poor Spanish.

Papá studied me before answering. I got the sense he approved of my directness. "You're worth more alive than dead," he replied, looking me in the eyes. "Because you're white."

I took a deep breath and let it out slowly. Of the many feelings that statement evoked, I decided to focus on my appreciation for his honesty. The kitten on my lap purred and leaned into my stroking hand as if to reassure me.

"And Myriam?" I asked. The cat blinked up at me.

Papá studied his calloused hands this time. "She's not in danger of being kidnapped," he said. "Killed, maybe. All of us are in danger."

I felt someone standing beside me and looked up to see Myriam.

"Especially leaders," she added, looking at her papá, who didn't flinch.

"They don't kidnap *indígenas*, only kill them," she elaborated. "They would kidnap kids to make them soldiers, except there are enough *indígenas* who volunteer for that."

Bitterness crept into her voice. I wondered if she was referring to Alberto. Earlier, when she'd told me about him joining up, I could tell she was unhappy, but I was half-glad to be rid of him.

"Kids volunteer because they're desperate for food," she continued. "Or because they believe the lies the soldier recruiters tell them. Both the paras and the guerillas take in children as young as eight, not that you'll ever hear the leaders admit it." Again, there was barely restrained anger in her voice.

"Eight?" I half-choked as I looked towards Rosita's younger cousins, who were helping her wash dishes under the pipe that led from the river. "What good is an eight-year-old soldier?"

Myriam's eyes were cool as she surveyed me. "The little ones are assigned to guard the camps. If they fall asleep, they're tortured or killed while the others are forced to watch."

My breath left me. Thin as my soup had been, it churned uncomfortably in my stomach. "That's illegal." I felt stupid the moment I said it. The kitten leapt from my arms. "And any of you could be killed at any time?"

Myriam shrugged. "Yes, but there is safety in numbers and in not carrying weapons." She drew herself up tall, then repeated our conversation for her father's sake.

He nodded.

"Why?" I asked.

"Occasional murders aren't noticed," Myriam replied. "Massacres of unarmed *indígenas* have a chance of making the news. And that's bad publicity, even by the twisted standards of paras and guerillas."

"Oh. How do you live with it?" I asked.

Myriam translated that to Papá.

"We have no choice. We are used to it. And this is our land," he said. "Besides, they can't kill all *indígenas*, and someday we will be left in peace. We will even regain more of our land, like the indigenous of North America. This is our goal."

I wasn't much good at history, but I had the vague feeling that Native North Americans had been through this. *Didn't Canada's prime minister formally apologize to them a few years ago? Aren't Native American land claims a big thing in the courts nowadays?*

"And your goal," Papá continued, "is to paddle *El Furioso* to *La Magdalena?*"

I stared at the ground, even though I detected no trace of irony or resentment in his voice – no sense he was contrasting my goal with his, which was helping his people survive.

"How many more days?" he asked, releasing the twins as they squirmed out of his lap and ran to their mother.

"Two, maybe three," I replied.

"Are you finished with Myriam yet?"

I hung my head. I needed her only that first day to describe the river. I knew it was selfish to keep asking her to meet up with me, but I craved her company more each day. I was helplessly attracted to her, even if she seemed uninterested in me.

My hesitation prompted him to speak again. "Because tomorrow we are having a *minga*, a work party to restock and repair the trout holding tanks on the river. We need all the men who can help. The women make the food."

I looked about and saw the women cutting and piling up firewood. They were putting what was left of their maize – the corn – in the ashes. That was to soften it and clear its rind, Myriam explained to me earlier.

I raised my eyes and made a quick decision. "I can help," I said. "I can take a day off from kayaking. My river experience might even be helpful."

As Myriam translated, I swear I heard pride in her voice. And Papá's eyes settled on me in an approving way.

"I accept," he said.

The next morning, I found Myriam working feverishly with the other women and girls. They were boiling chicken, kidney beans, onions, plantain, and some kind of root that looked like a cross between a carrot and celery in giant pots on the fire. Much of the food came from the load I'd fetched.

"Smells delicious," I said, breathing deeply as I paused by the oven in the center of the plaza.

Myriam smiled. "The men will be hungry after working on the trout tanks."

"I'm a little worried about how helpful I can be up there without much Spanish," I said, glancing at the path to the river.

"I know. Papá said I could come for half an hour as you get started, to help with explanations. They have been there since dawn. You slept in," she teased. "Then I'll come back here."

"Super," I said, a little sheepish that they'd let me sleep in.

She tapped her stirring spoon on the edge of her clay pot and said something to a stout, middle-aged woman beside her. The woman nodded without glancing at me, adjusted her poncho and hat, and took over, but not before I caught her disapproving look. I half-smiled as I interpreted her body language: Men shouldn't linger in the kitchen and women shouldn't visit the *minga* site. Myriam beckoned me, and we set off up the path.

"I just need to make a quick stop on the way," she said.

Curious, I followed her as she walked briskly up the trail. When she detoured to the cave's steps, I pursued her all the way to the top and watched her pull the money I'd paid her from her skirt pocket and stash it under a rock in the cave.

We heard the men laughing and talking before we came upon ten of them working in the sun by the river. With boards, plastic sheeting, and rags, they'd begun repairs on some of the rims of the trout tanks. They also had a pitiful number of buckets with new trout stock.

Papá greeted me with a warm smile. He even rested his hand on my shoulder. "Our whitewater expert," he said, introducing me to the men, some of whom had come from a nearby village. "You have helped repair such tanks before?" Papá asked.

"Yes, in Montana. A summer job."

"*Aha*, good boy. Your papá taught you, perhaps?"

I lowered my eyes. "I don't have a papá. Just a grandfather."

A million times I'd wondered who my father was, what he was like. It hadn't helped one bit, thinking about it or asking Mom.

Papá looked at me curiously. "And your grandfather is your hero, yes?"

I shook my head, then caught Papá's disbelieving look. "He used to be, when I was growing up." Even as I said it, I had a sneaking suspicion that Papá wouldn't think much of Gramps.

He chuckled. "I will be your papá for today. And you will be our hero if you can unplug the water intake."

"No problem," I said, with a rush of warmth for Papá and the way he encouraged the community to accept me. Through Myriam, he explained that the gravity-fed water intake unit had a screen on it to keep debris and animals out of the tanks. Every few months, it plugged up. To unplug it, someone had to pull themselves underwater against the dangerous current, remove and clean it, then pop it back on.

"It's much harder than it sounds," he said. "It's too easy to run out of breath, get washed downstream, or be pulled and held against the concrete, which can scrape your skin raw. Most men here are frightened of the job. Especially since some cannot swim. The man who always did it drowned last year."

I looked at him respectfully. "It's the perfect job for me. Paddlers spend a lot of time reading and outwitting currents. We learn early on to stay calm underwater."

We chatted some more through Myriam. Papá explained that high water and time worked to erode the concrete structure, undercutting it. Since the trout were a major source of food and income, nearby communities held *mingas* to repair them at least once a year.

"I'm honored," I said.

Myriam left. I shed my jeans, under which I was wearing my neoprene shorts. The men – some wearing skirts and felt hats and others wearing jeans and baseball caps – stared. *Well, what else would they do? Wouldn't I stare at them if they showed up in their skirts, felt hats, wool ponchos, and bright red scarves in Montana or Alberta?* Here, most of them worked barefoot. And none of those who shed their ponchos and

T-shirts had chest hair, I noticed. No wonder they were staring at mine.

The men pointed toward where I was supposed to work – the far side of the trout tanks. I walked along the narrow concrete wall like a gymnast on a balance beam, appreciating that my neoprene boots offered good traction. The men looked at my boots curiously.

I lay down on the end of the concrete wall and peered into the water. The men talked fast in their native language, which I was starting to like the sound of, as they tried to instruct me. Realizing, of course, that I couldn't understand them, they began to pantomime what I should do, perhaps unaware that Myriam and Papá had already explained it. I smiled and eased myself halfway into the rushing water, keeping a tight grip on the wall's edge.

The men's leathery faces looked concerned. Me, I was appreciating how mountain rivers in the Colombian Andes are nowhere near as cold as what I am used to. Still gripping the wall, I took a deep breath, lowered my head, and opened my eyes underwater. Reaching forward to run my hand over the gunked-up screen, I realized it was a foot or so farther than it looked. *Okay.*

I popped to the surface, took a very deep breath, went back under, and let the water slam me against the tank. Ignoring the pressure and danger, I wrestled the screen off, wiped it clean, wrestled it back on. Then I clawed my way to the edge of the unit and unplastered myself from the concrete to let the current sweep me downstream. My knee caught on the cement before I floated free, but no big deal.

I surfaced, took a quick look at what was downstream,

then flipped onto my stomach and did a strong breast stroke into the nearest eddy. I knew exactly how to flop my entire body over the eddyline and let the eddy's countercurrents shove me to shore.

As I stood and made my way back to the structure, the men were watching me, clearly pleased I'd done the job in one go.

I lapped up their praise, even if I understood few of the words, then set my ego aside and worked hard the rest of the day, taking pantomime instruction on everything from pouring concrete to replacing some of the chicken wire.

The way they worked, I sensed a pride that surpassed any community project I'd ever seen in the United States or Canada. It brushed off on me in short order, making me labor as hard and fast as ever. Even those I'd sensed didn't like me, didn't want me here, seemed to give me grudging respect.

Numerous times, Papá called "good work" over to me in Spanish. And I found myself shyly practicing my Spanish on the younger men and boys, one of whom fetched me a felt hat after pointing to the bright sun, shaking his head at the crazy sunburned white man.

Cool, I decided. *A gringo in neoprene shorts and felt hat. If only Myriam were here, trying to hide that sweet, sweet smile of hers.*

We finished before dark, and I found myself in the middle of the pack, pretending to know the words of the songs they were singing as we headed down the trail for the promised feast.

Before lining up with a plate that a little girl shoved into my hands, I dashed back to the hut to stuff some gear into my sleeping bag and bring it to the plaza to give away: my jeans, T-shirt, fleece, first-aid kit, running shoes, baseball cap. I held nothing back but my paddling gear, some food, my waterproof headlamp, emergency space blanket, camera, passport, wallet, Gramps' journal, and one pair of shorts. And the necklace, which I'd present privately to Myriam later. I'd left the embroidered tablecloths I'd bought from Myriam at Jock's shop. I wanted as little weight in my kayak as possible through the canyon, and I didn't want to have to come back up for my belongings. Plus, I figured Myriam's people might be able to use some of the stuff.

After supper, as the women washed up and some of the men who were sitting around the fire produced flutes and guitars, I shook the belongings out of my sleeping bag and had Myriam explain that I was giving them away. The sleeping bag, I added, would be available in the morning. Tomorrow night, I planned to sleep beside the falls in my neoprene shorts and boots, wrapped in my space blanket. I'd buy sandals and a T-shirt before boarding the plane home.

Freddy, whether he knew what was going on or not, toddled forward to pick up my baseball cap, which sent a ripple of laughter through the crowd.

Some looked unimpressed; others nodded in appreciation, their smiles lifting my heart. Abuela herself claimed the first-aid kit, though she clucked her tongue as she went through it, as if disappointed at Western medical knowledge.

It started to rain. Papá loaned me a poncho and felt hat. They felt warm and comfortable. Speaking through Myriam, I said good-byes and thank-you's to everyone, and even felt my eyes mist a little as Papá gave me a bear hug. Looking into his kind green eyes, I found words tumbling out: "You're the papá I always wanted."

He squeezed my shoulder as Abuela looked on, a mist in her own eyes.

Suddenly the rain turned into a downpour, tat-tat-tattering on the corrugated tin roofs. I ran to my hut, my hand holding the borrowed felt hat on my head.

CHAPTER FOURTEEN

"Today will be the best day of the trip," I announced to Myriam with a wink as she approached my hut the next morning, wheeling her bicycle. The rain had beaten down all night and showed no sign of letting up now. I was leaning casually against the wall of my accommodation, wearing nothing but my neoprene shorts. Freddy grinned up at me. Flora peered at me from where she was secured to Myriam's back, a floppy hat on her head to divert the rain's dribble.

"Why is that?" Myriam asked as she leaned the bike against the far end of my hut.

"Because according to Gramps' diary and your descriptions, I'm tackling Class IV today."

We're into heavy rapids now, engaging in life-or-death battles with rock-strewn watery routes. One of my men overturned this morning and would have lost his boat or drowned had I not rescued him promptly, at great risk and effort. Happily, his gear and supplies were well lashed in. With no appreciable breaks between torrential sections, we run the constant danger of boat damage and capsizing. But we are a strong, determined team and, so far, we've suffered no disasters. Just as well, since we have a long way still to go. — Malcolm Scruggs

"Class IV. That means dangerous, right?" Her eyebrows knit together.

"Yes," I said as I gave her a reassuring smile. I liked that she worried about me. It meant she liked me. *She'll like me even more when I surprise her with the gift of the necklace*, I told myself. I hadn't given it to her yet because I couldn't get her alone. *Sometime today, hopefully.*

"Especially dangerous after a hard rain like this," I explained, "which can raise the river level. So today is the day I'll need you most, on rescue rope duty."

"And tomorrow?"

"I'm expecting we'll reach the waterfall by the end of today. That's where I'll say good-bye."

"You're still insisting on camping by the falls tonight? And in the rain? We've told you it's not safe to camp around here."

"I'll jump or use my rope to get myself and my kayak down into the canyon. I'll camp there beside the falls."

"With no sleeping bag or blanket? And where?"

"With my space blanket. On a rock or in a wall crevice . . . somewhere," I assured her with more confidence than I felt. It would be a miserable night if the rain didn't stop, but that just comes with expedition kayaking. "That way I'll be safe and get an early start tomorrow on the finale."

"What does 'finale' mean?"

"The end of my performance, the final section of the Furioso. That means the canyon. Beyond the canyon is just fast-moving water on the Magdalena before I reach Jock's place. I think it'll be less than a full day's paddling from the waterfall to Jock's."

"But you don't know what the water is like in the canyon! Nobody in our community has ever been down there and come back alive. That's why we call it Dead Man's Canyon."

"What a wonderful name! You didn't tell me that before. Gives it special appeal to kayakers like me. It probably means solid Class IV and V, which I love." I reached down and yanked Freddy's red hat over his eyes, which made him giggle and hide behind Myriam's legs.

Myriam placed her hands on her hips and stamped her bare feet in the rain-soaked grass. "You hired me as guide, and I've ordered you to walk the trail between the water-fall and where *El Furioso* joins *La Magdalena*."

"Ordered!" I laughed, daring to move closer and place my hand on her shoulder. "Advised, yes. And I've taken that advice into consideration."

Her face flushed and she flung my hand off. *I mustn't touch her when people are around!* But I was burning to do so later today — our last day together. No Henrique or Tiago around. If only she could ditch the twins.

"Is it not a 'first descent' if you portage the canyon?" she demanded.

"Yes and no," I replied. "Yes, technically, but no by my grandfather's and my standards."

"Well, it won't be a first descent if you die."

"That's true. But I've paddled many outrageous canyons in my career, Myriam. I know how to scout what's coming up while I sit in safe eddies. I know how to free-climb along a vertical wall with my kayak on a rope, if I have to get past something that's impossible."

"*You* are impossible," she declared, pointing a finger at me the same way I'd seen Abuela scold children in the community.

"And you are beautiful this morning, as always," I said, running my eyes appreciatively down her wet blouse and jeans. "Especially when your eyes are flashing."

The finger withdrew. The lips went into a deeper frown. My eyes lingered on those lips. *Later*, I dared hope.

I glanced at her bike. "Each day has been a longer and longer bike ride for you," I pointed out. "Maybe it's too far to bike with the twins today, especially in this downpour." It also went without saying that since we'd be parting at the end of the day, I couldn't borrow a bike; I'd have no way of getting it back to her. That meant a very long jog beside her.

"I know. But Rosita is home from school today with a cold, so she's taking the twins. I'll drop them off to her and be with you in a minute. You can pedal. I'll ride on the handlebars." She smiled shyly.

"Perfect!" I said, elated.

For the next hour, we giggled and sang as I pumped the bike through the rain down the trail. I dared to rest my chin on her damp, clean-smelling hair every time a bump in the trail threw her near me. Eventually, she relaxed and allowed her shoulders to rest against my bare chest. Her buttocks perched on my handlebars, her toes extended far ahead, and her braid swayed and occasionally caressed my face as we sped along.

I pedaled carefully, not only to keep her aboard, but because a part of me didn't want the ride to end. I finally slowed, and she jumped off when we reached the bush where I'd stashed my kayak. I donned my paddling jacket slowly, to make sure her eyes would watch my body. The warm rain felt kind of good up here in the mountains and made everything smell fresh.

"You might need the rescue rope today," I reminded her, lifting it from my kayak and placing it in her palms. I folded my hands over hers as if to make sure she didn't drop it. She pulled away, but not as fast as usual. She put the rescue bag in her sash to secure it to her body.

"A kiss for good luck?" I asked playfully.

Smiling, she backed away and blew me a kiss. A wet strand of hair, which had worked its way out of her braid, hung from her forehead, over her breast to her trim waist.

"You're a tease," I said, running a hand over my paddling jacket pocket to ensure that the necklace was still there.

"You do that every time you're about to paddle," she observed. "Is that a good luck thing?"

I stiffened for a moment, then forced a smile. "Yes."

I couldn't give her the necklace before I paddled the canyon, I suddenly realized. I just couldn't. I'd have to leave it with Jock to give her. She'd said it was worth a fortune, so maybe she'd use it to help her community. It was going to be hard to say good-bye to her today, to know I'd never see her again. *Did Gramps feel that way when he left Colombia? Did the beauty of this place grow on him, captivate him despite the dangers? Did the kindness of the people affect him?* Not likely. He was too single-minded. Maybe that's why he's a legend.

Tightening my life jacket, I climbed in my boat and prepared for takeoff. I noticed that the river was running higher and faster today after last night's volume of rain. It would be much safer to paddle it with other experts. For a split second, I wished Henrique and Tiago hadn't left me in the lurch. My teammates' defection was a problem, I admitted, but surely a challenge I could overcome.

"*Adiós,*" Myriam said, worry lines reappearing on her forehead. "See you in the calm pools between rapids."

"*Perfecto* and *adiós,*" I replied, tearing away in a muscled sprint that Gramps would have approved of.

Right away, I felt like I was in a different league. The Furioso took its name seriously here. Waves rose, tossed, and battered against boulders. With my senses on full alert, I let my kayak rise and fall with the giant whitecaps. I'd dig in for a pivot here, sprint down the wave full-force there. Every time I crested, my eyes did a fast scan of everything downstream, as far as the veil of rain allowed, so that I could veer away from writhing patches of foam and the gray topsides of rocks. The dark green tongues of water guided me to safety like lights on an airport runway.

Except that the runway down this first Class IV dodged from left to right like a skittish animal. But that's what I love about whitewater kayaks. They're made to spin on a dime and give chase to any line the pilot chooses.

I darted, spun, sprinted, and rested. Anywhere I could find a calm eddy, I'd whirl into it and wait, chest heaving, until I was ready to enter the fray again. I'd done hundreds of challenging rapids in my career, but never alone. Solo whitewater kayaking at any level is neither safe nor sensible. Soloing heavy whitewater kayaking is insane – unless you find yourself without mates on a river that's begging to be written up as a first descent, and you're willing to risk your life to claim it.

Whoa! A massive boulder in the middle of the next rapid rose like a thin granite tower leaning at a slight angle. It divided the river as neatly as a comb, forming a part in free-flowing hair. *Should I opt for the left or right chute?* Rain ran down my face and off my chin as I considered. Wise kayakers go where the most flow heads, but something about the way the fuller chute on the left acted farther downstream gave me pause. On instinct, I opted for the right channel.

Bang! I cursed as my boat smacked against a rock just under the surface. It turned me sideways as I hurtled towards an ominous wave gully followed by a rearing wave crest. I threw in a hard left sweep stroke to give myself the punch I needed to shoot through the watery half-pipe, then reached, reached, reached my right paddle blade to find and cling to a patch of water moving downstream. The "keeper" tube wanted me, strained to keep me captive, but as my heart beat double-time, my blade's stubborn hold on the far side gradually lifted and pulled me over.

I shook water from my head to clear my eyes, spotted an eddy, and stuffed my kayak's bow into it. *Whew!* Now I could look upstream and see what I'd missed. *Holy!* The innocent-looking chute I'd rejected poured straight onto a downed tree, hiding treacherously just below the surface and sending the current into a wicked reversal at the bottom. I might have been able to fight my way out of that back-current, but then again, it might have taken me all day and the strength of ten men. *Thank you, Furioso, for sending me a vibe.*

The river calmed itself for a minute, as if needing time to contemplate what to throw at me next. I floated through an all-too-brief, rain-dimpled pool, staring down at its green depths. It was the clear green of Papá's eyes, so wise and calm and patient that I felt my pulse slow a little.

One big rapid down, several to go. I thrilled to the pounding aggression of the current. Today's rapids would be a perfect warm-up for the canyon, which I was guessing might be more difficult. In Class V, even a minor mistake can mean death. These are the kinds of stakes I like.

The next rapid was bouncy and mean, but so rich in eddies that I was able to work my way down it in a neat zigzag pattern. Seeing Myriam at the bottom, standing with the rescue bag at the ready, reassured me. I doubted I'd need her today, but if I did, the skill of her toss might get fully tested.

"I'll play here for a while," I called out to her, meaning I'd give her enough time to position herself at the bottom of the next rapid before I committed myself to its foam-laced entrance tongue.

I found myself an excellent play wave and carved back and forth, as content as I'd ever been. The rain cooled my sweat. The Furioso was my friend. The trip was going smoothly. Late tomorrow, I'd be phoning in my victory to Gramps. Finally he'd see me for who I was: a man. And, finally, I'd usher myself into what I regarded as a secret society of first-descent champs.

Myriam was winded from biking the trail. Rex seemed in too big a hurry, overdetermined to reach the falls today. He was like – she smiled – a mule plodding home who'd just caught sight of its shed.

Since the trail only rarely afforded a glimpse of the river on this section, she was getting sore legs from dropping her bike at intervals and running down the bank, especially where the rain had turned things muddy. But she had to keep track of what the river did, where it calmed down. In those places, she had to locate a piece of level ground from which she could toss the rope if he needed it, which she fervently hoped he never would. From these spots, she would turn upstream and search the upper horizon of tumbling water, so she wouldn't miss his performance coming down the whitewater.

Even after days of being with him, she found it a thrill to witness the way he tackled impossible-looking rapids. But she feared for his life in the canyon and felt desperate to talk him out of paddling it. Not because she wanted to escape with him – no, she'd given up that idea. She didn't have the guts to pursue a university education, after all. She wanted him to portage the canyon because she was sure it would kill him. Then again, the rapids he was paddling right now looked to her like they should kill a kayaker, so maybe the canyon was possible.

She found a level patch, where a broad eucalyptus tree sheltered her from the rain, and stood there enjoying a moment of being dry. Rex was obviously taking his time playing upstream, giving her more time than she needed to get into position. She loosened the rescue bag's drawstring and readied it for a throw. While she waited, she listened to the drumming of rain on the ground, breathed in the forest scent, and gazed at the pretty wildflowers on the far river-bank. No one lived near the river over there, she knew. It wasn't far upstream from where people said the guerillas had their secret headquarters, and it was probably littered with land mines. She scanned the trees out of habit and froze as she saw something move.

The soldier came into full view, his gun pointed to the ground, his eyes locked on her.

"Alberto!" she almost cried out, but he was holding a finger to his lips. He wouldn't be alone, she realized, as goose bumps formed on her arms. His unit would never allow him to wander far from his fellow guerillas. She should retreat; she should warn Rex. But just as Alberto refused to budge, so did she. It was the sadness of his face and the slump of his shoulders that kept her rooted to the spot and made her heart sink to a depth she hadn't known. Neither one dared call out to the other, but she could read volumes from the way he stood and watched her. He was homesick; he was unhappy; he was depressed.

A shout from the forest behind Alberto made him jerk back to attention. He mouthed something to her, spun around, and disappeared. She was sure he was trying to protect her from being sighted and hassled.

Myriam sank to the ground and struggled to keep tears from spilling. He'd mouthed "I love you."

Her head was still down when Rex pulled up.

"Myriam, are you okay?"

"Yes," she whispered, leaping up. "Don't stop here. Keep going."

He looked at her with concern. He was a kind boy, and she was more than aware that he was attracted to her. Occasionally she even felt tempted to give in. But the rules in her community were very, very strict: Dating a non-*indígena* was forbidden. And, anyway, he was leaving today.

She ran back up the bank to find the trail, her hands wiping the tears from her face. *It was a mistake to join the guerillas, Alberto. Papá tried to tell you. I tried to tell you. And when the paramilitaries figure it out, they'll punish our community. And . . . and I miss you.*

She found her bike, jumped on it, and dashed down the trail, her head twitching right, wishing that whoever had built the trail had put it within view of the river. She needed to be ahead of Rex to get into position. In one of the few places she could see *El Furioso*, she slowed down as she spotted him.

Rex was paddling very slowly. Then she noticed he wasn't moving at all. *No! His boat must be stuck on a rock just below the water's surface.* She watched him try to bounce his kayak off the snag. It didn't work. She watched him lay his paddle down on his boat so he could place his big hands on the rocks on either side of the boat to free himself without climbing out.

Oh-oh! He came off the rock and capsized! And his paddle,

which slid off the boat as he went over, was floating ahead of him. *He has no paddle to roll up with!* Both the paddle and Rex, in his upside-down boat, were headed down the rapid. *He'll drown, he'll drown!* But no, he rolled up with his hands – an amazing trick he'd never told her about – only to find himself heading down the rapid with no paddle.

Pedal, Myriam! she told herself. As soon as she was well ahead of Rex and his runaway paddle, she dropped her bike and sprinted for the river. Throwing off her hat, she reached for the paddle as it floated towards her near the bank. Seeing she was going to miss it, she stepped into the river and extended her arm and body as far as she could. *There! I've got it!* Abruptly, the current pulled her off her feet and swept her downstream.

The water wasn't cold, but she was fully doused head to toe as she bobbed and flailed to the surface. She wasn't a good swimmer and she wasn't wearing a life jacket, but she had an iron hold on Rex's paddle, which afforded a bit of flotation. As the river flung her towards a midstream rock, sticking half a foot out of the water, she lunged for it. Grabbing hold, she struggled until she could pull herself up on it.

Shaking, she spun around on her wet stomach and saw that Rex was still upright, but battling for control by hand-paddling and pushing himself away from rocks as he slithered past them. It was only a matter of time before he'd tip over again.

"Rex!" she shouted, standing up on her rock and waving his paddle.

"Yes! Throw it to me!" he called. She aimed the paddle like a spear and threw it through the rain, drumming down harder by the minute.

The paddle flew through the air. He caught it and slap-braced with it as a wave tried to knock him over. Then he dug its blades into the water and powered himself to the riverbank across from her rock. He leapt out of his kayak, cupped his hands, and shouted, "Are you okay?"

"I'm fine," she called back, loosening her sash and holding the rescue bag in her hands.

"Yes, toss it to me the way we practiced."

She tossed it, holding on to the end loop. It unwound as it flew through the air. He caught the bag.

"Wait until I say," Rex directed, drawing in the slack rope until the length between them was taut. "Now slip into the water and hold on to that loop. Don't let go!"

I'm not about to, she thought as she sat down on the rock, shivered, then lowered herself into the churning water.

The current was strong, but so was his hold on the rope. Just as she'd done for him in practice, he pulled her neatly towards shore. Water splashed up her nose; rocks bruised her hips and tailbone as she was dragged halfway across the river. When she found herself in an eddy she could stand up in, she reached up to grab his extended hand.

Hardly had she regained her feet than he wrapped his arms around her and led her to higher ground. He sat her down on a rock and fetched her hat.

It wasn't all that cold, but she found herself shivering uncontrollably. That's when he leaned in, hugged and kissed her. His chest and lips were warm. She forgot to protest.

Sitting back on his heels, he smiled sheepishly. His voice was husky. "I can't believe you kept a hold on my paddle, Myriam. That was heroic."

"*Mmm,*" she said, glancing across the river to make sure there had been no witnesses to their embrace. "I-I-I . . ."

"You're still shivering," he said. He pulled his paddling jacket off and wrapped it around her. Even though it was wet, it kept the breeze off, so she pulled it around her tighter. He kissed her again, longer this time. They looked at one another. He reached into his kayak and pulled his camera out of his waterproof bag. After he snapped a photograph, he sat down beside her, holding the camera at arm's length and taking a photo of the two of them. Then he handed her the camera and said, "Take a few of me as I go down the river, okay?"

She stuffed it into her jeans pocket and smiled. "When I first met you," Myriam began, squeezing water from her braid, "I thought you were a jerk."

"Me? A jerk?" he teased.

"Then I was hoping to run away with you."

Rex's eyes grew large, and an astonished look appeared.

"I don't mean romantically," she said hurriedly. "It's just that . . . I've been accepted at university, and I had no way to get there without someone's help. *Indígena* girls don't travel alone."

"But," Rex looked confused, "how can I help you when I'm in a kayak about to go into a canyon and you're . . . ?"

"I know. It never made any sense. Anyway, I can't do it. I can't disobey my family and leave my community. I don't know why I ever thought I could. And I don't know why I'm telling you this."

"Because you want to escape Colombia and go to Canada with me?" he asked, moving closer. "We could meet at the market when I finish the canyon. My grandfather will be shocked, but he doesn't run my life anymore."

She stiffened. She'd given him the wrong idea altogether. "No! Why would I ever leave Colombia?"

He looked hurt.

"I mean, I didn't like you at first, and now I do, but not in that way." His hurt look deepened, and she felt a stab of guilt. She also felt irritation at herself – and at him. *I only kissed him because I'd been thinking of Alberto, right?*

"Rex, forget what I just said. I had this stupid idea about running away to university so I could be a reporter and tell the world about . . . just forget it, okay? I'm sorry."

He slowly turned away and stared for a split second at his kayak, which the wind had blown from a riverbank rock down into the eddy below it. Rex leapt up to rescue it before it headed downstream.

The rising wind blew against her as the rain continued to pelt down. Myriam pulled his paddling jacket around her more tightly. She felt an uncomfortable bulge in it against her neck. Without thinking, she ran her hand upwards, squeezed the lump, and slipped her fingers into the pocket to pull out whatever was in there.

Her mouth dropped open as the necklace of her grandmother's stories spilled out. She'd know it anywhere, even if she'd never laid eyes on it. It was a necklace that should have been hers. He'd had it all along. He'd never said a word. Rage shook her.

"Myriam? Myriam, I can explain," he said, his rain-spattered face pale.

CHAPTER FIFTEEN

Myriam rose, flung Rex's paddling jacket away from her, and ran up the riverbank towards the bike. She had to get away from him. Had to think. Had to do something with all that anger.

"Myriam!" he called, chasing her.

"Leave me alone!" she shouted, doubling her pace, splashing through puddles.

"I was going to give it to you!" he wailed.

She left the trail to lose him, running as fast as she could in the pouring rain even as sharp, wet stones cut into her bare feet. His neoprene boots slapped against the ground, gaining on her; she'd have to hide. Spotting a tree trunk that had blown half over, she ducked beneath it and sat on the ground, her head pressed up against the trunk's inner arc of rotting wood, appreciating the momentary shelter from the rain. A spider crept down her forehead. She brushed it off and felt a small sting as it dropped onto her ankle. She flicked it into the wet grass. Sitting tucked up with her hands around her ankles, she listened to the rain and for the sound of Rex's footsteps.

As her rapid breathing subsided, she examined the reddening patch on her ankle from the spider bite. That's when Rex appeared. He was panting, his face so flushed it almost frightened her. His eyes went to her ankle.

"Myriam! You've hurt yourself?"

"Spider bite." As she said it, she became aware of a hot throbbing sensation, which distracted her from being angry. He sat down beside her under the fallen trunk, reached gently for her foot, and inspected it.

"*Ow!*"

"Sorry. Wish I had my first-aid kit."

"I'm fine. Do you have any water? I'm thirsty."

"I'll just run back to the boat to get my water bottle."

He leapt up and left her before she could object. She tilted her head and looked warily into the empty spider-web above her. *Why did I try to run and hide from him? Because he has a necklace that Abuela had given his grandfather years ago? It's not mine to demand back.*

As he disappeared towards the trail, Myriam stayed where she was. She didn't like being alone here, in the woods. And though she was out of the rain for the moment, she was utterly soaked. She shivered as treetops swayed in the wind and rain. For most of the past week, she'd been close enough to her people to whistle or radio if in danger. But she and Rex were beyond that region now, just across the river from guerilla territory and not far from where her people had been approached by paramilitaries — a few weeks ago, on their way to market. She startled as something moved in the bushes behind her. Her throat dry, she twisted around to look.

A tiny bird hopped out and peered at her, cocking its beak as if concerned.

She sighed and stood up to stretch. Her ankle was swelling. *Will I still be able to help Rex this afternoon and bike home afterwards?* A minute ago, she'd been too angry to carry on helping him, but somehow — remembering that this was his last day — she felt the anger drain away. She walked a few steps to test the foot. It hurt, but she was mobile. She sat back down and tried to ignore the throb.

It seemed a long time before Rex returned. As she strained to see or hear any sign of him, what was left of her anger entirely evaporated. She stood eagerly as he jogged towards her, water bottle and waterproof pouch with lunch in hand.

He handed her the water bottle. She drank eagerly. "Hungry too?" he asked. He held open his pouch. She took a small piece of cheese. They ate their lunch in silence.

"I really *am* going to give you the necklace at the end of this trip," he finally said. "I was putting it off because . . . it's just that, well, I'm kind of superstitious about it. I have this feeling it keeps me safe." He lifted his eyes to hers as if pleading for understanding.

She stiffened. "Let's not talk about the necklace."

He looked so pained that she wondered for a moment if he really had planned to give it to her. *But superstitious? How dare a white boy think that an ancient* indígena *necklace all but stolen from my people has any power to protect him?*

"Ready to go back to the river?" he asked after a long period of silence.

"Yes." Her ankle was throbbing like crazy, and she could feel the poison making it swell, but he didn't have to know that. If only she'd accepted her abuela's offer to learn herbal medicine, she could find something right here in these woods that would stop it from getting worse. Instead, she'd just have to bite her tongue and get herself through the day. Abuela would treat it once she returned to their village.

She followed Rex back to the trail, frowning. The rainstorm was starting to get to her. Once he was in his kayak, she mounted the bike and rotated the pedal with her good foot, avoiding any pressure with the other. This worked fine for downhill sections. Where the trail flattened for any length, she got off the bike and pushed it, leaning on it heavily as she limped along.

After several rounds of duty below rapids, she waved him over.

"You okay?" he asked.

"No," she admitted.

He stepped out of his kayak and studied her ankle. "Whoa. It's all swollen. Must've been a poisonous spider."

She sank down on a rock beside the river and let him touch the red, angry-looking mound on her ankle, which was pulsing with a beat that seemed to extend all the way to her head.

"Why didn't you say something? And why, why, why did I give away my first-aid kit?"

"It's okay. I just need Abuela to put something on it."

"You need it treated right away, Myriam," he urged. "I'll hide the kayak and bike you home."

She wanted to protest, but couldn't. She'd watched a

bite like this nearly kill a cousin a few years ago. Abuela said that the cousin hadn't come to her in time.

She limped to the bike and waited for him. When he'd positioned himself on it, she lifted herself up to the handlebars, crying out when her ankle brushed against the front wheel.

For hours, then, Rex labored to pedal the two of them, mostly uphill, towards the village as Myriam slumped on the handlebars, wiping rain from her brow. They were still three miles from the community when the front tire went flat.

"Never mind!" Rex said, easing her down. "You sit here, and I'll fetch Abuela." Myriam sank to the ground and sat cross-legged on a wet rock beside the discarded bicycle. He sprinted away.

A long time passed before he came walking back, Abuela shuffling along beside him with her cane, wearing a plastic poncho.

"Abuelita, it was too far for you to walk," Myriam greeted her grandmother as a sense of relief washed over her.

"Nonsense," Abuela said, kneeling beside her granddaughter and opening her fiber bag of herbs. Rex produced the first-aid kit he'd carried for Abuela from the village, but she ignored it.

Myriam held her ankle out to her grandmother. While it didn't surprise her that Abuela had found the strength to make the long walk to help her, Myriam knew the old woman would suffer tomorrow.

Rex hovered and Myriam stayed sitting as Abuela shook her head, checked her bag of herbs, and clucked her tongue. She swiveled her head left and right to scan the forest floor.

"Wait a minute," she ordered Myriam in their language, ambling towards the river, her cane helping her over the uneven ground.

"What's she doing?" Rex asked.

"I think she needs a plant that grows by the river."

"Oh. Should I follow her?"

"No. She knows what she's doing."

Rex sat down beside Myriam as Abuela disappeared from their sight. He lifted a hand to feel her forehead. Then, without warning, he took her in his arms. "Myriam, Myriam," he said, rocking her and kissing her brow.

A shout prompted them to pull apart. Myriam shuddered as she saw Abuela standing stock-still just down the bank, freshly picked plants in her hand, her face livid.

"No, no, no, no!" she screamed, walking towards them with her cane pointed accusingly.

Rex leaped up and moved a short distance away, where he stared at the ground. Myriam, still sitting, felt sweat break out on her forehead and drip down her face. Thunder sounded as the rain intensified.

Abuela moved towards them, her face a study in fury. Her eyes were locked on Myriam with such vehemence that Myriam found herself cowering. *Abuela has never hit me, but is it possible she's considering it now?*

Abuela walked right to Myriam, towering over her seated granddaughter. "How long has this been going on?" she demanded.

Myriam, aware that Rex couldn't understand a word they were saying, responded, "Nothing is going on, Abuelita. Please believe me."

Abuela's eyes flashed fire; her fists clenched. Then she seemed to waver and all but collapse at Myriam's feet. Myriam, not sure whether to cower or help her, watched Abuela rise on all fours. Then she mumbled incoherently as her eyes began leaking tears.

"Abuelita?" Myriam said, alarmed.

"No, no, no, no!" Abuela said in a weaker voice, staring again at Myriam. She lifted a hand to wipe the wetness from her cheeks, then stuffed the plants she'd brought from the river into her mouth. She began chewing vigorously.

"Is she okay?" Rex asked.

"Yes, she's chewing the plants to make the medicine my ankle needs," Myriam replied in a tight voice, not daring to look at Rex. "They have to mix with her saliva."

Rex, still hanging well back, didn't reply as Abuela spit the mess into her hand and applied it to Myriam's spider bite. Then she found a clean portion of sash and bound the foot – far tighter than necessary, Myriam thought. The old woman took a long swig of water from her water bottle, then passed it to Myriam, urging her to drink far more than Myriam wanted. Abuela was rocking back and forth in a way that frightened Myriam and coo-cooing at her like she was a child.

Finally, Abuela motioned for Rex to sit down.

"Translate," she ordered Myriam, who nodded numbly.

I found myself all but shaking as I sat down on the hard, wet ground with Myriam and her grandmother, who seemed a little crazed. I'd never seen Myriam look frightened of her before. Worse, Abuela had now pinned her eyes on me and was jabbing a finger at my chest while speaking rapidly.

"I forbid Myriam from helping you further," she declared through her trembling translator.

"But —" I started to argue, panicked at the thought of parting with Myriam in this way.

"All contact with each other ends here, now, this moment."

I felt defeat. This was all my fault. *What had Gramps warned me?* "Leave it at the looking, if you know what I mean. We're not meant to mix with Indians."

But Gramps was wrong. Abuela was wrong, I dared to think. I listened dully as Myriam tried to plead with Abuela. I needed no translation to see the old woman wasn't buying it.

"You are meant for Alberto," Abuela told Myriam sternly. I figured that out, since Myriam didn't bother to translate it. Then Abuela turned to me.

"Your grandfather," she said in an accusatory tone, "he came here to kayak *El Furioso*. He and his friends paddled to the waterfall. Then he became ill. His teammates left him. He got a parasite from drinking bad water. He was ill for two months."

"Two months?" I echoed. "Not true. I have his journal to prove it!" Unfortunately, the journal was in my water-proof bag back in my kayak.

"He might have died if my village hadn't allowed me to tend to him. They didn't trust him, but they pitied him, even though he gave us no money in return for the food and medicine we gave him. Even though he had a, *um*, superior view of himself."

That's Gramps, all right. I squirmed a little as both Abuela and Myriam gave me sideways glances to see how I took that information. Judging from the look in Myriam's eyes, this was new information on an age-old story.

She was translating quickly, as if impatient for the story to emerge faster. Meanwhile, I detected anger seeping away in Abuela. Her voice began to soften.

"Despite his faults, I admired him. I was only seventeen. I didn't know better, but I came to love him."

What? Myriam's jaw loosened as Abuela hung her head. "When he left, he knew I was expecting his child. He swore he'd return. His parting words were 'I will find a way.'" Abuela's energy seemed to be fading.

Myriam and I were stunned.

"Papá?" Myriam finally asked, her voice a whisper.

"Of course," Abuela replied.

My head was spinning. Papá of the soft green eyes, face paler than the other men in the village, his strong build so much like Gramps'. *Papá was my mother's half brother?*

"So Papá is . . . my uncle?" I blurted, trying to compute it all. "And Myriam and I are . . . second cousins or something?"

Myriam didn't translate the question. She didn't need to. We stared at each other. *No wonder Abuela was so upset!*

"The village elders found out, and a few of them went to talk to him. I guess that scared him. . . ."

Rex tried to imagine his grandfather scared of anything. "And they chased him down the mountain?"

Abuela glared at me, shaking her head *no*, both pain and anger in her eyes. "That's what he claimed? He said nothing else? Nothing of me?" She was struggling not to cry.

I sat forward and pulled Abuela's hands into mine. I wanted to assure her Myriam was innocent. I wanted to put things right somehow — to apologize for all that Gramps had been and still was. I was willing to bet he'd never even told Abuela he was married to someone back home, someone expecting — my own mother.

I didn't have the Spanish or English to do it. And even if I had, it was too late. Abuela pulled her hands away, rose, and ordered Myriam to rise.

"You, go!" she said in terse English, her anger and energy returning.

Abuela speaks some English words? I stood there, feeling torn and helpless as I had that first day in Myriam's village. I was an outsider.

"But I want to say good-bye, and thank you," I mumbled. I'd paid them; I'd fetched food for them; I'd left most of my possessions with them. *I hadn't exhibited a superior attitude, had I?*

"You said your good-byes last night," Myriam said in a cold voice that cut me like a machete. She must be still thinking of the necklace . . . must be still angry. And the necklace was back in my hidden boat, along with Gramps' journal of lies. She moved alongside Abuela, away from me. "Go finish your river!" she shouted.

Abuela's story had clearly rekindled Myriam's anger at me. *Do we really have to part this way?*

Panic reached my throat as they walked out of sight. A girl with a swollen ankle, a worn-out eighty-something woman leaning on her cane. It was a long walk to the village, probably more than an hour's journey at the rate they were going.

"I could fetch the mule for you," I called out. They didn't answer, didn't look back.

I eyed the bike sprawled in the dirt with a flat tire. They'd send someone back for it. *But me?* No one was coming back for me. To them, I was worth less than a bike with a flat tire. And I was guideless – totally alone in a foreign land.

I headed downstream, my heart heavy, rain flowing down my face. I walked listlessly, no longer caring I was beside the Furioso, no longer caring I was moving towards what could be the Furioso's most dangerous rapids. It didn't matter now if I paddled them or not. Maybe I should abandon the kayak and not attempt the canyon, as Myriam had begged. That way I'd return alive to face Gramps – let him know what I thought of him, let him know that he owed Myriam's family. It was time to build my life around not becoming like him.

The faster I walked, the more certain my resolve. Mom believed I was better than Gramps. And I believed it now too. I would deliberately put an end to this first-descent game.

I reached down, picked up a fistful of wet dirt, and slung it towards the river. Reached down again, slung more, and more.

First descent, I raged bitterly to myself. *Oh, yes, Gramps, you had multiple first descents in Colombia, all right. Or did you decide Mom and I were "first" and Papá and Myriam "second" among your descendants?*

"You like the dark ones, eh? We're not meant to mix with Indians," I mimicked him as I ran faster and faster along the trail towards my kayak. "You pathetic two-faced hypocrite! You *liar*!"

I didn't realize I was screaming until I thought I heard someone shouting back, far behind me. I paused.

Is the earth shaking, or is that the pounding of boots? It was like an entire army running at me from the direction of Myriam's village. My heart seized up. I veered off the trail, my heart catapulting in my chest, searching for somewhere to hide.

A hollowed eucalyptus tree appeared between me and the river. I sprinted to it, hoisted myself up inside it, thankful for all that upper-body strength training. Breathing heavily and sweating bricks, I wriggled farther up to ensure that my dangling feet wouldn't show. I managed to find a crack through which I could see what was on my tail. It was only moments before a large battalion of soldiers began marching past.

My body grew cold and shivers ran up my spine. Their feet were clad in black leather lace-up military boots; their uniforms were green camouflage; and their faces were covered by black bandanas, cowboy style. But this was no western movie. I was in Colombia, a stone's throw from dozens of soldiers moving in a column through sheets of rain. Although lots of them were younger than me, the deadly serious way they held their machine guns dispelled any notion of child's play. I had no idea whose side they were on, but I vaguely recalled Tom saying that the Colombian Army never came up here because there weren't enough of them to fight the other two armies, and they didn't much care what happened to the *indígenas* anyway.

Alberto had joined the guerillas, which must mean guerillas were the ones fighting for the poor. The paramilitaries worked for the rich to get rid of the guerillas. *Isn't that what Gramps said? One thing's for sure: I need to stay clear of all of them.*

The problem was, the soldiers didn't seem to be passing by. They were spreading out, positioning themselves along the trail. *How long can I hang out, soaking wet, in a hollow tree?*

CHAPTER SIXTEEN

Myriam, shaken by Abuela's revelation and the unpleasant parting that it had forced on her and Rex, tried to focus on just one thing: getting Abuela home before she collapsed.

Myriam's ankle still throbbed, but she was more worried about Abuela, who needed to stop and rest so often that Myriam feared it would be dark before they reached the village. The rain beat down relentlessly.

When she smelled smoke on the wind, Myriam reminded herself they were close. *The men must be burning another field to prepare it for planting*, she thought. *Strange they would try to do so in the rain.* But when she heard shouts, she roused herself to a higher state of alertness.

"Abuelita," she whispered, tugging on her grandmother's elbow. "I think I hear soldiers. We need to hide."

Abuela allowed herself to be led to a thicket of brush. Myriam removed Abuela's plastic rain poncho, helped her lie under some low thick bushes, lay down beside her, then pulled the plastic over the two of them.

The shouting grew louder; the smell of smoke stronger. Tensing, Myriam raised her whistle. Then she heard the spit of machine-gun fire.

"No," she groaned, dropping the whistle and throwing her arms around Abuela. They lay like that for a long time, Myriam trying not to weep, Abuela falling asleep as if unable to hear the distant fighting.

Then came the sound of boots crunching stones on the trail only yards away. Myriam dared not move as a column of soldiers marched by. She froze when she heard boots leave the path and move towards their hiding place. Spanish voices exchanged words as soldiers searched the brush. She held her breath, pressed her body closer to her sleeping grandmother, and prayed.

They came ever closer. She opened one eye and could see the muzzle of a gun hanging from a soldier mere feet away. From the leather lace-up boot, she guessed he was a paramilitary. She held her breath. Only when the boots and voices retreated did she let it out.

Moving her ear over Abuela's mouth, she felt no breath. Panicked, she leaned closer, then started as a jagged snore arose.

Best to let Abuela be until I'm sure it's safe, she thought. She crawled away from her and slithered through the mud to a better view of the trail. She saw only muddy boot prints.

Moving as silently as she could, Myriam crawled farther, closer to the village. The first body she came across was that of her dog, Capitán. His head was crushed as if by a gun butt. One hand flew to her mouth in disbelief as she cradled her beloved pet in her arms. The paramilitaries had been here to avenge Alberto joining the guerillas, she understood with a sob.

Her breath came jaggedly as she raised her head and saw half a dozen bodies strewn in the wet field. Her first instinct was to run immediately from one to another to see who was injured and needed help. But she forced herself to hold back the longest ten minutes of her life, until she was sure no soldiers had stayed behind to lie in wait. Finally, she could hide no longer.

She moved through the field in slow motion. Her spider bite forgotten, she dragged herself from one body to another, her fingers checking for a pulse, sobs bursting from her throat. She made the sign of the cross over each. Uncles, cousins, and other males she had known from birth were lying there, motionless. They were all adults; the soldiers had either let the boys flee, or had "recruited" them to their cause.

"Papá? Papá? Papá?" she found herself crying.

She discovered him under a pile of three men. They must have surrounded him in an attempt to protect their leader.

"Papá!" she screamed, rolling the other bodies off to wrap her arms around his big chest. Her tears dripped on his lifeless eyes as blood from his head wound seeped onto her wet, muddy blouse.

"No!" she shrieked to the angry gray sky, releasing him and limping to the plaza. There, smoke was still curling from the burned buildings. No women or children were in sight. They and some of the men had been allowed to flee to the next *indígena* village, Myriam guessed.

She looked about the plaza. The soldiers had smashed up the looms, and she could still smell gasoline from where they'd poured it to start the fires. She bent down and picked up Rosita's fiber bag. She pictured a terrified Rosita running, the twins in her arms, guns aimed at her.

Myriam backed away, shaking, screaming for someone to answer her, to comfort her, to help her guide Abuela to safety.

Only a ripple of thunder and a hard pounding of rain replied. She gulped between sobs and walked up to her family's scorched hut. Stepping through the doorway, she spotted Freddy's little red hat and clutched it to her breast. As tears streamed down her face, she turned and fled down the trail, back to Abuela.

Abuela was stirring. She sat up and stared dazedly at Myriam.

"You have blood on your blouse," she said, looking down to Myriam's ankle as if that might be to blame. Then her eyes rose slowly, scanning Myriam's trembling body and shell-shocked face. She reached her arms up to her and pulled her close as Myriam sank to the ground, spilling every tear that had ever thought to form.

It was nearly dark when Myriam led Abuela to the cave over the river. They had no energy to make it to the next community that night. Myriam had neither food nor appetite, and she couldn't face sleeping in the remains of her village – nor did she have the physical or mental strength to bury the bodies of the men who had fallen.

She could barely move. It had taken all her remaining energy to walk Abuela to the cave by a circuitous route, to prevent her from witnessing the devastation.

"I will go. I must see," Abuela had insisted, but the frail woman was no match for Myriam, who was capable of just this one act: preventing her grandmother from seeing the carnage.

Now, Myriam had the presence to accomplish one more goal: getting the two of them up the steps and into the cave, coaxing herself and Abuela to drink some water, peeling off some of their wet clothing, and covering the two of them with the dry blanket Alberto had kept in the cave's corner. They clung to each other, both crying.

Just before she fell into a deep sleep, Abuela lifted Myriam's face close to hers. "Myriam," she said, "you must tell people. You must do as you planned: Go to university; find a way to tell the world."

Myriam's eyes flooded, and she stroked her grandmother's wrinkled face. Salty tears ran past the old woman's lips. "I love you, Abuelita," Myriam said, choking on a sob. She could not tell her grandmother it was too late. Everything was too late. The world had ended.

CHAPTER SEVENTEEN

During my hour in the tree, I determined several things. First, I was no more than a ten-minute walk from my hidden kayak. Second, the soldiers spread along the trail weren't spending any time by the river itself. And I knew from Myriam that only rarely did the trail offer a view of the river. Even if someone spotted me once I started kayaking, I'd be long gone by the time they ran to river's edge. And while they could take potshots at me if they wanted to, something Papá said stuck in my mind: "You're worth more alive than dead."

I was frightened, yes, but saw no future in staying in the tree. My plan to abandon the river and portage along the trail had just been scuttled. I was better off getting out of this hot spot by kayaking the river. Suddenly, portaging seemed more dangerous than paddling without a safety-rope assistant. In fact, the biggest danger would be stepping onshore to scout.

Can I paddle a series of difficult rapids while scouting only from my boat? It was unwise and heightened the danger, for sure.

And I'd have to get out of my boat at the waterfall. But with soldiers around, I was best off getting out of here as fast as the river could take me. For better or worse, the continuing downpour was making the river flow faster by the minute. Besides, I had no sleeping bag and almost no food left, so dared not spend any time looking for figs or berries. Never mind that Abuela had banished me from the village.

I tried not to think about that, or the fact that during the abrupt parting with Myriam, I hadn't had the necklace to give her. Not that it would have helped mend things between us, even if I'd handed it over. The damage was done. By thinking only of myself and a first descent, I'd brought this misery on myself. It was time to leave this country to its troubles. Survival, not a first descent, had become my top priority. I'd hand the necklace over to Jock to deliver to Myriam and Abuela on their next market day.

Slowly, noiselessly, I eased myself from my uncomfortable perch. Crouched, almost tiptoeing, I worked my way down to my boat and breathed a sigh of relief to find it and my paddle undisturbed. I pulled on my helmet and paddling jacket, running my hand over the bulge of the necklace. I double-checked that I'd stowed the rescue bag in my boat before I carried my kayak silently to the river. *My camera!* It was in Myriam's pocket. Maybe, if she ever forgave me, she'd e-mail me the photos I'd taken.

I stepped into my kayak, affixed my spraydeck, and searched the shore for soldiers pointing guns at me. *None.* Then, taking a deep breath to steady my nerves, I peeled away into the welcome embrace of the current.

The rapids. Concentrate on the rapids. No rescue-rope helper meant nailing every single move, and never, ever missing a roll. In a way, I was thankful for the demanding water, the peals of thunder, and the distraction of the rain. They obliterated any other thought or emotion.

Gramps and his expedition party did this section in much less maneuverable kayaks, I told myself. Skirting a large boulder, I found myself in a minefield of exploding waves, keeper holes, and rocks waiting to bash me. *Wham!* A wave tossed me against a boulder, but with a flick of my hips and a well-planted brace, I stayed upright, using the new boat angle to power to a safer route on the left. Heart stuck in my throat, I thrashed my way through churning white, searching for a route like a lab mouse in a maze. The rapids' constant roar deafened me.

One rapid followed another, with a barely defined pause in between. I'd have given anything to see Myriam waiting for me at those calm breaks, concern on her face, rescue bag in hand. Instead, I ploughed right through them to the next monstrous set.

Water slapped me in the face at regular intervals, blinding me as I stayed in marginal control. In the third rapid, determined to catch an eddy to inspect what was coming up, I spun too fast into a behind-rock surge that rammed my bow against stone. As my boat and body reverberated from the collision, I tried to brace in what felt like lava lifting from a volcano under me. My attempted brace failed. I was over, the water dragging my kayak and me upside down out of the troubled eddy.

I reached, positioned my paddle, and rolled up. Gasping, I saw a huge boulder in front of me and tried to turn too late. Over again. Rocks banged against my helmet and clawed the length of my life jacket in a shallow section. With my face plastered against the deck of my kayak, I stretched my arm out and rolled again. This time I had no time to shake water out of my eyes before a five-foot wave lifted me. Its trough stalled me, and the next wave picked me up, windmilling me end-over-end like giant watery hands delighted to discover a plaything.

When I had another chance to roll, I found myself in one of the first quiet pools I'd met since launching an hour before. Breathing heavily, I clung to a root that hung from the rock wall beside the pool, staring back upstream at a rapid I'd have considered portaging if I'd had the luxury of examining it first.

I'm still alive, I reminded myself. *I'm still in my boat. And once I get to the waterfall and find a way down into Dead Man's Canyon, I'll be safer. From capture, at least. Rapids, I can deal with. As for being the potential object of target practice, that's something I can't do anything about!*

I kept on paddling, rapid after wicked rapid, adrenalin spewing from my weary body. *How many rapids until the falls? How long till dark?* I had to get to the falls and find a way down to the canyon.

To my relief, the next rapid was Class III, a welcome reprieve after what I'd been through. But as I wound through it, taking no chances with my chosen line, I had the eerie feeling of being watched. Once, when the only safe route took my kayak close to the right shore, I thought I caught a movement there. Then I spotted a turquoise bird Myriam had told me was a "honey creeper" perched on a tree branch, watching. *Just a bird*, I told myself. *Anyway, the paramilitaries are on the left shore, right?* No one lived along the right shore, Myriam had informed me. "Never, ever land there," she'd added. "Too many land mines and guerillas trying to protect themselves from paramilitary attack."

Great, just what I need. Paramilitary soldiers on my left. Guerillas and land mines on my right. Killer rapids in between.

I was hungry, thirsty, and in desperate need of relieving myself, but I took only micro-breaks for gulps of water and ignored my bladder's growing pressure. My feet had long since fallen asleep. My upper body felt like I'd abruptly doubled the weights in a gym workout.

Finally, I came to a rapid with a suspicious-looking horizon line at its far end. I eyed a cloud of mist hovering over that line. Though I could barely hear the rumble of the falls, my instincts told me I was about to tackle the last rapid before they loomed. *Should I get out now and walk along the right shore? No. Don't want to get blown to smithereens.*

I grabbed a midriver eddy that allowed me to scout the last rapid over my shoulder as my boat faced upstream. This time, I wasn't just looking for a conservative path through a long, complicated obstacle course; I was also looking for a surefire getting-out spot before the plunge. The left bank offered no such possibility. Almost twenty-four hours of hard rain had raised the river such that eddies were disappearing. The right bank was high and overhung, but a decent-sized eddy presented itself beneath an over-hanging cliff that featured a canopy of roots. I plotted a route to that eddy, figuring I might even be able to lift and stash my kayak in the tangle of roots above it, a tangle that formed a sort of "cage" beneath the overhang's ceiling of dirt. That would put the boat out of sight from above, and make it pretty tough to spot from the left bank, too.

I took my time memorizing the moves between where I lingered and the target eddy. "Zero tolerance for error," I muttered. I ran the rapid mentally like it was the do-or-die section of an Olympic slalom racecourse. I drummed my fingers on my bow, then touched the pocket containing the necklace. I took deep breaths. *Gotta do it now, Rex.*

Down the center of the rapid I went and cut left. *So far, so good.* The noise of the falls grew. *Time to U-turn around that nasty whirlpool. Go! Go! Farther left, yes left! Harder! Pull, pull, pull.*

Sweat squeezed from my skin as my bow spun too low into the eddy. The strong current tried to suck my stern out of it. I dug my paddle in hard and put every ounce of strength towards pulling myself up into it. When I realized I was losing the battle, that I was about to be sucked backwards over the lip of the falls, I took one hand off my paddle and grasped in desperation for a root hanging from the dirt bank. It didn't break off in my hand. Breathing heavily, hardly daring to hope, I let my paddle clatter onto my deck as I clenched that root with both hands and began to pull on it. I willed it to hold the weight of my body and kayak as I struggled to ease myself upstream into the calm piece of water over which the root was anchored.

Slowly, the tug-of-war got me halfway into the eddy, where I grabbed another root and finally pulled myself clear of the downstream drag. Shaking, I freed one hand to pop my spraydeck off, then stood, knees wobbling, in the kayak. Rain-soaked dirt never smelled better as I leaned against the tall bank and found a foothold, keeping my kayak captive with the other foot. As soon as I'd gained reliable handholds on the bank, I lifted my kayak with my remaining foot and shoved it and my paddle into the overhead tangle of roots that formed a sort of "luggage rack" below the overhanging cliff. My efforts had me sweating so heavily that I felt a need to shed my life jacket and paddling jacket, too. I shoved them and my helmet into the kayak, knowing I'd return for them in a minute — as soon as I figured out how to get around the falls. I opened the waterproof bag in my kayak long enough to grab Gramps' plastic-wrapped journal. If I read it while gazing at the falls, I'd know which portions were truthful.

Looking up, I saw a vision of Gramps standing on the bank. "You almost missed the eddy, you idiot. Got lucky the root was there."

"I knew you'd make it," a vision of Myriam countered, smiling and giving me a thumbs-up. "Good job, cousin."

My heart caught on her words. *If only she were real right now.*

Like a rain-drenched rabbit emerging from a burrow, I raised my head slowly above the overhang and looked left and right to ensure no one was around. My hair dripped water into my eyes as I scrambled up to pee. Feeling much better for that, I crammed the journal into my wetsuit trousers and crawled along the bank within a foot of its edge to avoid land mines. Wet grass cushioned my palms and knees.

I could taste the waterfall's spray now. The falls pulsed enough to make the ground beneath me tremble like the floor at a rock concert. I was deafened and drawn by its powerful, throaty roar and veil of fine spray. Pretty soon, it was impossible to distinguish rain from spray. I crawled to the ledge that extended to the right of the falling water, my eyes scanning for a glimpse of the canyon's start below. I stopped, dropped to my stomach, and reached ahead to clutch the ledge a dozen feet to the right of the pounding pour-over. Trembling, I thrust my head past the ledge and stared down into the gathering gloom.

No rocks or logs were piled up at the bottom of the falls, but that didn't mean it was runnable. Safer, I thought, was to hurl my kayak from the very spot where I was now lying – well to the right of the falls – then jump in after it. We'd both land safely in the deep, dark pool directly below. It looked clean and rockfree.

To test that theory, I wrestled a nearby log that was roughly the weight of my kayak and shoved it over the cliff's edge, taking pains not to fall in after it. I waited as it hit the water, counting as it bounced back to the surface. *Deep and clean.* I even spotted a crevice in the wall over the pool that I might be able to spend the night in. Pushing another log into the river directly above the falls, I watched and counted as it reappeared in the froth below. The time and way the log reappeared indicated that the falls, fifty feet as Myriam had described, were runnable.

But what is beyond the pool? I could see only the rain-washed, horseshoe-shaped sheer rock wall that dropped fifty feet to form the pool beneath me. It ran from where my hands clutched it to the right in a semicircle, until it stopped directly across from me, on the other side of the pool. The

far end of the horseshoe stuck out into the current. A headlong rush of water from the falls curled around its toe,
beckoning me, daring me to ride it. I ruled out walking along
the cliff around the pool. It would be dark before I could get
back to the boat. The land-mine threat discouraged me, and
who knows whether soldiers might be lurking around here?

I realized I should retreat: fetch my kayak, get it and me
down there, not attempt to scout further. But the Furioso
was trying to tell me something. It was urging me to shuffle
to my left on my stomach, closer to the deafening falls, for
a view beyond the pool. There was urgency, even desperation in the falls' voice. I had to obey.

I inched left, towards the steep cascade. I inched and
inched, getting more spray-soaked by the minute, until I
was at dire risk of falling in; my left pinkie dangled over
the hurtling water. Still the wall on the farside of the pool
blocked my view, but only barely. I stretched my neck left
and spotted a yellowish shadow in the river. Lurking just
downstream of the toe, it looked like a flat boulder a foot
beneath the river's swift current. I arched my neck one final,
treacherous inch. What I witnessed made my breath whoosh
out of me and my stomach feel like it was free-falling over
the lip of the falls.

I screamed and pounded the wet ledge with my fists,
shaking my head and filling the foggy air with my fury and
frustration. Strong arms grabbed me and pulled me back,
back, back, away from the ledge . . . away from the devas-
tating sight I'd barely glimpsed.

Just beyond the pool, beyond the yellow underwater
rock, behind the tall wall, the entire Furioso River turned

into a giant, deadly whirlpool, seething and spinning in front of a cul-de-sac. I knew exactly what that meant: Somewhere below the surface of the whirlpool, the entire river writhed like a python and dove underground. It was sucked into a massive natural-rock tunnel, leaving nothing but spatters of itself on the cul-de-sac's skyscraper-high rock walls. Out of sight, the mighty Furioso bulged sinuously into a black hole, converting itself into every kayaker's worst nightmare: an underground river.

CHAPTER EIGHTEEN

I cy terror shot through my veins. The shock of what I'd just seen was instantly displaced by searing pain where someone's rubber boots connected hard with my ribs. At first I tried to fight them off, but soon found myself curling into a ball. Even before they yanked a course piece of rope around my hands to tie them tightly behind my back, I felt fear and despair descend.

When they rolled me onto my back, I found myself staring at Alberto's cold eyes. Beside him stood a square-shouldered man in a black beret.

"Where's your kayak?" Alberto demanded in Spanish.

"Lost," I managed to choke out as I jerked my head towards the falls.

He smiled listlessly and mumbled something to his commander, who patted him on the back. My heart still clenched, I watched Alberto fall back into a lineup of look-alike soldiers, way too many of them young kids. Even in my unnerved state, I took in how belts held their fatigues on their skinny bodies, guns hung proudly on their shoulders, rubber boots and berets bobbed as they marched me into the darkening forest. Pain jerked through me as a gun's muzzle jabbed into my back to hurry me along. My heart sank with the sun and I shivered as, dressed in nothing but neoprene shorts and boots, I walked in a half-stupor in the middle of Alberto's unit.

The first wave of panic slowly loosened its hold on me, and I turned to look at Alberto. He returned my stare with passive, sunken eyes. *Something is different about him*, I thought. Even in the shadows, I took in his slumped shoulders and sallow face. He marched with a lethargy I'd never seen in him before. *So being a guerilla isn't all he dreamed it would be . . . but maybe he'll be rewarded for my capture*, I thought bitterly.

An hour later, it was pitch-black except for the dim, bouncing beams of flashlight that a few members of the troop switched on. No one spoke a word to me, not even when I asked for a drink of water. I marched with my head tilted back to collect raindrops on my tongue. Now and again someone called out in a low voice, and a hidden voice in the surrounding woods responded.

I was all but stumbling with exhaustion when the procession slowed, then halted. Ahead I could see two campfires burning, despite the rain. The crackle of their logs reached my ears. The orange glow silhouetted a huddle of soldiers around them and the edges of tents, tarps, and huts.

A group from the campfire surged forward with flashlights and spoke to the commander in rapid-fire voices, like they were informing him of something. A bunch of soldiers turned towards Alberto. I heard Alberto give a throaty cry of distress. A flashlight flicked over him just in time for me to see him sink to his knees as if in shock. The commander turned my way, barked a command, jabbed Alberto, and pulled him to his feet.

Someone spun me around and shone a flashlight on a wooden hut not much larger than a two-seater outhouse. They pushed me in and shoved the door closed before I'd even fully moved from the door frame. I heard a padlock click into place. Whirling around, I felt for the door latch, wanting to cry out. *But what's the use?*

"Agua?" I asked through the door. "Water?"

I put my arms out to feel around, fighting against the numbness and dejection taking over my body. A sliver pricked my right index finger as I slid it along the rough plank walls. A metal basin slid noisily across the dirt floor as my foot ran into it. I crouched down slowly and felt for the object. Enamel-covered bowl. Smelled like urine. I set it back down and continued shuffling around the space. I tried not to picture poisonous spiders scurrying about, or poisonous snakes hiding in the rafters. I could hear nothing but the rain pounding on the corrugated tin roof above me.

I was waiting for my knee to hit a mattress or bedsprings, but no such luck. By the time I'd done three rotations of my hut, I'd determined it had no furniture. Nothing on the walls. Just the bowl and a musty-smelling blanket thrown in a corner. I sat down, leaned against the wall, wrapped the blanket around me, and stared into the blackness.

Throat parched and stomach rumbling, I shivered and shivered until finally, somehow, I fell into a fitful sleep. I dreamed that the men of Myriam's village washed over the waterfall and were sucked into the abyss, despite my frantic efforts to save them. I was left swirling in the whirlpool, endlessly circling. In my dream, Myriam's necklace was around my neck, tightening slowly, ever so slowly — choking me even as I clawed at it.

Dim daylight filtered in between the wall boards when a soldier unlocked the door long enough to shove a big jug of water, a tin cup, and a tin plate of lukewarm rice and beans at me. I crawled to them, clutched the five-gallon jug by its two big handles, and lifted it straight to my lips. I drank and drank, trying not to let even one precious drop escape. *How long do they expect the jug to last me?* I wondered. I set it down and spotted a plastic spoon sticking out in the center of the beans. I ate until not a single bean or kernel of rice remained.

The commander, flanked by two soldiers, let himself in somewhere around midday. The door shut on a curtain of gray rain and wet forest behind them. He barked questions at me in Spanish. I tried shaking my head, but it didn't produce any English words from him. "Speak Spanish!" he ordered.

Slowly, painfully, we began to communicate. I understood the words "mother" and "father," and when he waved a pencil and pad of paper at me, I knew he wanted Mom's and Gramps' contact information. My spirits sank.

"No money," I tried to tell him in Spanish. "They have no money."

His sneer indicated what he thought of that. He shoved the paper into my hands.

Trying not to picture Mom's or Gramps' faces when they learned I'd been kidnapped, I slowly penciled their names, address, phone number. *What choice do I have? Will I be freed when the guerillas figure out my family can't pay whatever outrageous sum they are asked for? Killed? Tortured? Will my government intervene? Will the Colombian Army come up here and swoop in for an attack and rescue?*

After the commander left, I huddled back in my corner. Memories of the day before played like a looped tape. Kissing Myriam. Myriam finding the necklace and turning angry eyes on me. Myriam running away. Abuela's accusing finger. Abuela revealing her story. Abuela banishing me. Abuela and Myriam leaving.

I had nothing to do but play these scenes over and over in my mind, hour after hour. *My fault, my fault, my fault!* my mind screamed at me. *Who do I think I am, coming to Colombia for a first descent, like nothing here exists but a river and me? Who do I think I am, pursuing a girl with troubles I can't even imagine?*

Slowly, my thoughts turned to the falls. That was where Gramps had fallen ill. That was where his legacy ended and I had imagined mine would begin. I shuddered as I pictured the Furioso all but imploding as it protested being fed into the dead end. I pictured the hideous, foaming swirl that resulted from too much water attempting to slide down an unseen drain. Such a feature was a monumental death trap. There had been no eddies on either side, nothing to stop a kayaker from being sucked into the hole, drowned and possibly decapitated in one massive plunge. To exit the pool below the falls was to hurtle to one's death. End of story.

I leapt up and paced around my tiny hut. Gramps had never seen the falls or whirlpool, I was sure. Otherwise he'd never, ever have let me come here – to my potential death. *But how can I be so sure?* From knowing my grandfather for seventeen years. From knowing deep down that he loved me. From pure instinct. From the way the dark Furioso was whispering the secret to me even now. He'd heard the falls, returned to camp, then fallen ill.

I stopped my pacing abruptly. *The journal!* Stuffing my hand down my pants, I felt it still lodged there. I drew it out and removed it from its sealed plastic bag. Slowly, almost fearfully, I opened it to its last pages, pages I'd read hundreds of times before by flashlight, as a boy and as a youth, enthralled.

Finally we approached a sharp bend, beyond which I thought I could hear a thundering waterfall. Tomorrow we will find out, but tonight I returned to camp exhausted and somewhat feverish. Once we get past the waterfall, I anticipate a half day of very challenging paddling to reach the point where the Furioso joins the Magdalena. Must sleep now, feeling a little off. – Malcolm Scruggs

"You had a parasite from drinking bad water, Gramps. You almost died." I tried to picture Abuela shyly visiting his site with a fiber bag of herbs, no doubt initially accompanied by male chaperones. I pictured her as a double of Myriam: seventeen, beautiful, proud. "You were ill for two months, Gramps, long enough to know you'd gotten Abuela pregnant. Long enough for village elders to know it, too." I double- and triple-checked the next entry's date. The next day. *Liar!*

They came at dawn, a rabble of angry savages. They had loud voices, sticks and rocks in their hands. My companions ran off in fright and never returned. — Malcolm Scruggs

"No, Gramps, your companions abandoned you much earlier, leaving you and a young, admiring seventeen-year-old way too much time together. You would have died if the village hadn't allowed her to tend to you. You didn't pay them for their food or medicine; you treated them like dirt. When you realized you'd knocked up someone who thought she loved you, you panicked and ran. The elders would've been angry, all right. *Angry enough to run you off the mountain?* Maybe, maybe not. *Who'd blame them?* Or maybe you just slunk away without so much as a good-bye and made up a dramatic story."

When a man is alone and outnumbered by a vicious lynch mob, it's time to retreat. Sadly, I was forced to abandon my tent and my beloved kayak. — Malcolm Scruggs

"Nothing else 'beloved' but your kayak? Funny how you managed to retain the journal and necklace, though, and whatever else you needed to fly home to your pregnant wife and family."

I escaped only by the skin of my teeth, running hard, hiding well, and using my best survival instincts in that hostile mountain environment. Who'd have thought the natives of these parts would be so uncivilized, so wild? By the time I made it into town, I decided it was time to return home. I never saw my expedition companions again, but in subsequent correspondence, I was able, of course, to determine they had also narrowly escaped. — Malcolm Scruggs

I moved the journal closer to my face to see whether he'd altered the entry's date. No sign of that. I ran my fingertip down the stitches of the binding. *A slight gap, or was I imagining that?* More space between these last two pages than elsewhere in the book. For just a second, my grubby fingernail caught. I opened the journal up as wide as it would go and kneeled on it, one knee on each margin. I leaned down so that my nose almost touched the binding. Yes, there it was, the tiny fragment of a torn page. He'd been meticulous in trying to leave no evidence, but he had torn out at least one page. A page Abuela had just filled in for me.

Still a question nagged at me: *Why had he been so reluctant for me to come, and yet, in the end, had allowed himself to be persuaded by my mother?* It was definitely not so I could complete his only failed first descent. It was definitely not to help me launch my career or fulfill my dream of taking on his legacy.

I thought about the necklace still hidden in my kayak and suddenly knew: A sliver of guilt over leaving Abuela had surfaced in Gramps when my grandma died. He'd all but admitted it to my mother when he'd said, "Your mother was a good woman. And I was a bastard of a husband and father sometimes, Anne. I'm sorry. Guilt is a terrible thing to live with."

He'd stopped short of asking me to return the necklace, but he'd wanted me to meet the Calambás family. *So what am I? An unwitting messenger sent sixty years too late on the chance Abuela still happened to be alive? Or is it for me to find out the truth that he can't bring himself to tell?*

Our conversation came back to me in mocking tones:

"Anyway, try, and if you fail, maybe it'll be out of your system."

"I'll do it, Gramps. I'll finish that river for you."

"Or you'll come back with your tail between your legs."

I slumped down on my blanket, turned my face to the wall, and felt the sting of tears. Maybe he wanted me to fail so his legacy wasn't threatened. But it wasn't really about failing or succeeding, in the end. It was all about sending me to discover his other family.

I slid the journal into its plastic bag and hid it back in my shorts. "I hate you, Gramps!" I shouted. I banged my head against the rough wood until blood dribbled from my forehead. I banged it some more until my guard unlocked the door and shouted at me.

"Quieto!" he ordered.

My head sank into my hands. My salty tears mixed with the blood, stinging the small wound. I didn't care. I was too numb to care. I slumped into a ball and stayed there until sleep came again, about the time the rain stopped.

Three days passed in a blur. I hated myself. I hated Gramps. I banished all thoughts of Mom and Myriam from my mind. I didn't deserve their pity. Mom especially didn't deserve the pain I was inflicting. I felt I shouldn't be set free, even if anyone had the money or force to free me. I worked myself into such a state of self-hatred that I started refusing the food they shoved into my hut twice daily. I knew that the hunger pains would eventually subside. I drank from the big jug with handles, but that was all. I wanted to shrink to nothing, to disappear from the earth. Even if someone opened the door, I didn't think I would move from the corner where I lay, day and night, staring at my four walls without talking to anyone. I pledged that if I didn't die, I would never kayak again. And that when I returned home, I'd get a job and send a portion of my savings to Myriam and Papá and Abuela. It wouldn't be much, but money went a long way here. It would be something.

After three days of not eating, I had little hunger. Once, a soldier tried to spoon-feed me, coaxing me in Spanish. I closed my eyes and turned away.

The next day, they sent Alberto. They opened the door, slid in the plate of beans and rice, and let Alberto walk in, locking the door behind him. Even in my numb state, I registered the irony. *Do they think we are friends? That he'll be the one to persuade me to cooperate? Alberto, the one who probably got me kidnapped in the first place?*

Alberto stood there, barely looking at me. Then he sank down and sat slumped against the corner opposite mine. He stared at the floorboards. He sat there silently for so long that, eventually, I began to study him. His army fatigues were ragged. His rubber boots were faded. His face was gray. He seemed to have as little energy as me, and his body was so slight that I wondered for a moment if he'd been fasting, too.

Someone shouted at him from just outside the door,

which seemed to jar him out of his stupor. He looked at me.

"Eat," he said in Spanish.

"Go to hell," I said.

He nodded, like he'd expected that.

"Papá and many men are dead in my village," he said, raising his eyes to mine.

I stared at him. *What is he trying to pull?*

"A massacre. The paramilitaries. Revenge for me joining the guerillas."

My shrunken stomach balled up. *Is it possible?* I searched his eyes, which had gone watery. I saw his body trembling and felt my veins freeze. He was speaking the truth.

My mind flashed back to working on the trout pool with the men of the village. I pictured Papá, the gentle giant. *Papá, murdered?*

Alberto slid towards me slowly, the plate in his hands, his eyes darting once towards the door as if measuring whether the slits between the boards held prying eyes.

"Eat. Eat because your mamá and papá would say eat."

"Go to hell."

"Eat because your cousin says eat."

"Go to . . ." I stared at him, blinking stupidly.

"Your cousin who wants to go to university." He lifted the plate of food and held it out to me. I shrank away. But his eyes held mine in an almost pleading fashion. Then I noticed that the hand holding the plate had a scrap of paper peeking out from it.

"Eat everything," he said as I accepted the plate, my hand folding around the note. "Everything," he repeated, with the slightest of nods at the note in my fist.

I was still looking intently at him as he left. The note sat balled in my sweaty palm, the plate of food atop it. As the door opened to let Alberto out, I lifted the spoon and dug in, shoveling the beans greedily into my mouth. The soldier guarding my hut nodded approvingly, first at me, then at Alberto. Alberto walked away, shoulders slumped. The door slammed. The padlock clicked back into place.

I couldn't finish the food in one go. My stomach had shrunk too much, and I was reeling from Alberto's news. *His village attacked by the paras? Lots of men murdered? If it really was in retaliation for his defection, the guilt weighing on him must be overwhelming.*

I placed the plate on the ground and curled back into a ball on my blanket. If anyone was peeking through the cracks, they could not see me staring at my hand. They could not see me unrolling the tiny piece of paper. They could not see me reading it, could not know I was ready to swallow it unread if anyone interrupted me.

"Rex: I am hiding near your camp. I am hoping to slip this to Alberto. Many from our village have died in a massacre. Abuela and I were spared, but now she has passed away. Alberto will find a way to free you if you will help Alberto and me escape down the river. I know I begged you not to kayak the canyon, but now I must trust that you can do it and can take us with you somehow. The paras and guerillas have blocked all other ways. They will catch me soon. Please, Rex. Trust Alberto. Myriam."

I read it twice. The food in my stomach tried to lurch to my throat. I lifted my hand to my face, shoved the note into my mouth, and swallowed it between gags. *Paddle the canyon? Take two others with me? Trust Alberto?* She had no idea what ludicrous things she was asking.

I crawled to my toilet bowl, lingering on all fours with my head over it. *Must not retch. Must keep the food down to grow stronger. Myriam is alive.*

I lay down and began to sob. I felt the hut whirl around me. I was in the whirlpool below the falls again – whirling, whirling, choking, choking. They would capture her because I couldn't help her. I deserved to die.

I fell into a troubled sleep. This time I dreamed of ziplining, my hut door opening, and me stepping out to find a zipline attached to it. I stepped up, hitched on my harness, and slid away from the guerilla camp on a long cable. I ziplined across the Furioso's falls, over the tree-tops, all the way to Jock's place. He greeted me with a big smile. "See how beautiful Colombia is? A great place for tourists to come."

I eased myself off the zipline and saw a deer grazing on Jock's lawn. A *pudú*, a Colombian miniature deer. The tiny deer lifted its head and gazed at me with almond-shaped eyes. Gramps raised his rifle to shoot it.

"Deer season's open. Let's get us one. I'll make a man of you yet."

"No!" I shouted, leaping over to lift the barrel of Gramps' gun as it went off. "No, Gramps!"

———

A key turned in the lock on my hut and the door opened. My guard was checking on me. I'd probably shouted out in my sleep.

"I'm okay," I reassured him, rousing myself to drink some water.

I looked at my five-gallon plastic water jug and its funny handles, which resembled *pudú* ears. I thought about the *pudú* under the zipline that day with Tom, the *pudú* that the stream had sucked into the underground cavern but that had emerged alive on the other side. I sat bolt upright and pictured the Furioso's falls, its pool, the nightmarish whirlpool. I ran my filthy fingers through my greasy, uncombed hair, thinking, thinking so hard that it hurt.

The next day, I refused to eat again. They sent Alberto, tailed by the commander.

"Eat," Alberto pleaded. The commander looked on.

I took my time considering as Alberto cajoled me in a soothing voice. Finally I put my spoon into the rice like an obedient child.

"It's good. It's good," I mumbled as Alberto's eyes and mine met.

Then my eyes slid to his feet. "You should wear shoes, not boots," I stated, pointing to his feet like it made sense for a prisoner to take on the role of fashion police.

The commander's eyebrows knit as he looked from me to Alberto's rubber boots.

"I need another water jug," I addressed Alberto, pointing to make sure he understood. "And a rope to hang myself with." I made signs for a length of rope and for hanging myself.

Alberto was quick enough to shake his head and pat my shoulder. "You're okay, you're okay," he murmured with appropriate sympathy as the commander watched. I was pleased he'd caught on to the game. He'd quickly realized that the other soldiers thought he was the only soldier to whom I'd respond. This was pretty ironic, given that there was a time Alberto would have told me to go right ahead and hang myself. The commander gazed at me as if trying to assess how suicidal I really was.

After they left, I lay back on my blanket listlessly for anyone peeking through the cracks to see. I waited through the midday heat. I waited through the night and all the next day, conscious of nothing except that it wasn't raining – and it mustn't rain before Alberto came for me. *What is he waiting for?*

More days and nights passed. I ate any food shoved into my hut. At dusk one evening, I peeked out between the boards to see that fog engulfed the camp and made the campfire's glow a watery image. Fog was good. *Is Alberto thinking the same thing?*

It was not quite dawn when I heard the padlock click. I sat up, every nerve electrified. Feeling my way to my water jug, I lifted it to my lips and nearly drained it, leaving only a few swallows. Holding it in one hand, I moved on my hands and knees towards the door. Silence. Nothing but silence. Then the door creaked ever so slightly as it came ajar. Shivering, I stuck my head out.

The inky blackness engulfed me, but I could feel the shroud of fog. An arm gripped my wrist, and I nearly cried out.

CHAPTER NINETEEN

"Follow me," Alberto whispered, his breath prickling my ear.

"Did you bring some rope?" I whispered back. I felt a length of rope being pressed into my hand. "And another water jug?"

He pressed another five-gallon jug against my chest. It was full. He hadn't understood. I removed the lid and poured most of the water into the grass. Then I clutched it in my other hand, careful not to let the two precious plastic containers knock noisily against each other. Looping the rope over my shoulder, I allowed Alberto to pull me by my wrist again.

I stepped as lightly as I could, pulled by the ghostly arm, guided by short flicks of his flashlight. I noticed he was wearing his threadbare basketball high-top shoes again, not boots. Good, he'd gotten that message, too. *Does he know where the land mines are planted? One mistake and we'll both be blown sky-high. How can he know in this darkness, in the closeness of this damp night cloud?* I shivered, but Myriam's words echoed in my head. "Trust Alberto."

He was deserting his unit and freeing a kidnap victim in the process. I could only imagine how seriously he could be punished for this. He was placing his life in my hands as much as I was placing mine in his. Soon, we'd be placing our lives at the mercy of Dead Man's Canyon. *If* a glance from the falls confirmed my latest, reckless theory.

Dawn broke all too fast. While it allowed us to see the path underfoot, even in the fog, it also increased the chances of guards or followers spotting us. My feet felt heavy, and the near-empty water jugs felt like iron weights as I jogged behind Alberto. My days of not eating or moving had weakened me. Alberto, on the other hand, was as fast as a puma in his holey shoes. I was glad of my neoprene boots against the rocks and sticks on the path. I was especially glad of them when we veered off the path at unexpected intervals – whether for land mines or guards, I was not about to ask.

The dampness gave the forest a distinctive smell, which mixed with Alberto's and my sweat. No birds chirped in the first rays of light, as if the fog gave them permission to sleep in. There was only the snap of twigs underfoot as we hurried along.

After an hour of running without pause, I doubled over with nausea and a side cramp. I raised my hand to warn Alberto I needed a moment to recover my breath.

"Where's Myriam?" I asked between panting.

He put his finger to his lips, his eyes darting around.

"Where's Myriam?" I repeated in a whisper, suddenly suspicious.

He stiffened as he stared into the surrounding forest. I rose and twisted my head to look and listen. *Is that the faint pad of soldiers' boots?*

Alberto grabbed my wrist, and we sprinted through the fog now like Olympic runners, my cramp forgotten. I followed his every footstep, as fearful of a fatal foot plant as of being shot in the back.

Sweat streamed down my face and chest; wind whistled by my ears; my heart pounded like a drum. Once or twice, my water jugs brushed against bushes, making a racket. My ears strained for our pursuers' footfalls, but what I heard instead was the welcome sound of running water.

As we reached the falls, I saw her. Crouched in jeans and blouse behind a boulder in the still-dense fog, terror on her face. Her shoulders relaxed for a split second as she saw us, and she handed me my camera as she caught sight of the water jugs in my hand. There was no time to greet her or explain.

I handed the jugs to Alberto, then sprinted to the right-hand edge of the falls, lay down, and stretched my neck leftward. My heart sank. Fog, nothing but fog. *What did I expect?* Then a tiny piece of mist moved to give me a peekaboo view of what I sought. A sigh of relief escaped my chest.

I leapt up and sprinted back to Alberto and Myriam. I ushered them to the point on the cliff just right of the falls. Anchoring Alberto's rope on a rock, I let it dangle to where it ended, halfway down the cliff face. That would have to do. We stood with our toes just back from the edge, gazing down to where a blanket of fog hid the pool.

"I'm getting my kayak. I'll be back in a few minutes," I instructed Myriam, hoping she'd have time to translate for Alberto. "Climb down to the end of the rope, then toss your jug in, push out from the cliff, and jump – body absolutely straight, toes pointed downward, arms at your side. When you come to the surface, grab the jug – it will help you float. Swim across the pool *away* from the current, hold on to the rock wall, and wait for me."

Myriam's eyes grew huge. "Jump down there?" She had no way of seeing where she'd be landing.

I placed one hand on her shoulder and used my other hand to point straight down. "Trust me, Myriam. Please trust me."

She was translating for Alberto as I left them. I ran upstream, keeping as close to the river's edge as I could. My heart climbed into my throat. *Will I recognize the overhang? Can I get my kayak to the cliff before the soldiers arrive? What if high water has washed the kayak away, or someone has stolen it?*

I climbed down the bank to where water lapped, certain I had the right place, but saw no kayak hidden in tree roots. I looked upstream and thought I saw it. I was making my way in that direction, trying not to slide into the river, when I was thrown half into the water by an explosion.

My ears rang; faraway shouts followed. I grabbed a piece of riverbank before the current could snatch me away. Shaking, I registered that a land mine had gone off, but not from my movements. A guerilla must have taken a misstep. Others must be close. I tried to tell myself it couldn't have been Alberto or Myriam. They'd have jumped by now.

Three seconds later, I'd traversed the rest of the way upstream to the overhang where I'd left my boat. My nerves were shattered by the land mine. I tugged out the gear in my kayak and stowed the camera and journal back in my waterproof bag, which also held a headlamp, my passport and wallet, a pair of shorts, duct tape, and my space blanket. I buckled that bag and my throw rope to my kayak seat. Then I donned my paddling jacket, life jacket, helmet, and spraydeck and clicked the two halves of my paddle together. Finally, I yanked on the boat until it came free from the tree roots.

I hesitated. Popping up to level ground and carrying the kayak to the cliff so I could jump off it might put me face-to-face with soldiers. That left only one option. I placed the kayak in the water, climbed in, and snapped my spraydeck around the cockpit. My stomach was tight, my heart banging like it wanted out of my chest. But I had to take the gamble. I plunged my paddle into the water and sped to the lip of the falls. Shouts and belated machine-gun fire filled the air as my kayak and I dropped like a log over the falls, fifty feet through fog-draped air.

Five minutes earlier, Alberto and Myriam were crouched beside the rope, the plastic jugs loose in their hands. As they peered over the edge of the cliff, they trembled.

"I can't do it," Myriam confessed.

Alberto nodded, looking about for another way. "There could be rocks where we land."

"They might get Rex before he gets back here."

"Do you really think he has a plan?" Alberto asked. "He told me his kayak had washed over the falls. And he's an idiot."

She smiled wanly. "Not about rivers."

He squeezed her hand. It may have been to reassure himself, but she was conscious only of how good it felt, how right it felt, how calming to have him beside her. He was almost all she had left now. She had chosen the extreme danger of finding him over trying to fit in with her other grandmother's village. They'd been good to her when she'd stumbled to them for help, the morning after Abuela had died peacefully beside her in the cave. And it had been a relief to reunite with Mamá, Rosita, the twins, and baby Alejandro. But she hadn't stayed long, and Mamá hadn't tried to make her.

Myriam was haunted. She was too frightened to wash clothes in the river. She never joined the women's conversations while going through the motions of pushing yarn through a loom or lifting pots from the fire. Her embroidery looked like a child's effort. And when left to look after the twins, she merely clung to them, crying into their hair, until someone relieved her. Nightmares robbed her sleep. Worst of all, long after Mamá had scrubbed her only remaining blouse, she continued to see and smell where Papá's blood had stained it.

Finally, she'd said her good-byes and used some of Rex's pay to persuade a guerilla on sick leave in the village to lead her around the land mines to the outskirts of Alberto's camp.

The noise of the falls made it difficult to listen for the soldiers. *Will it be too late when Alberto and I spot them?* Her heart drummed in her ears. She'd witnessed so much death recently that she should not be afraid of it, she told herself, peering down at the white puffs of mist that clung to whatever was below.

"You go first," she finally said.

Alberto looked like he was going to kiss her. Instead, he held on to his water jug and crawled over the cliff's edge, clinging to the rope. He half-slid, half-climbed down the rope, peering over fearfully as if trying to determine when he'd come to its end.

Myriam watched him disappear. She waited a few seconds, then climbed on as he had, shaking, the jug in one hand. The rope burned her hands as she slid down it, but she managed to slow herself before reaching its end. She dropped her jug and used her bare feet to kick out, took a deep breath, and dropped into nothingness. She fell with her body straight as an arrow, toes pointed so she wouldn't injure her back. Slicing into the water, she felt herself sinking forever, then slowing, then rising. When she broke the surface, gasping, she grabbed for the floating plastic container and used her arms, like she'd seen Rex do, to maneuver herself away from where she'd dropped in — and away from the waterfall.

Alberto's head appeared in the mist and he dog-paddled towards her, jug holding him afloat. They moved together across the pool until they could cling to the cliff.

There, they waited anxiously for the third splash. A land mine's explosion made them turn in terror, followed by the burst of gunfire. Myriam was not prepared for what happened next. She saw Rex in his kayak drop like a missile from the fog ceiling and plunge into the water at the base of the falls. The kayak disappeared almost entirely, then shot back up like a torpedo and rested for a split second upside down, shuddering in the foamy turbulence. As her hand went to her mouth, she saw a paddle and Rex's wrist break the water's surface, and the boat's occupant roll up. He shook water from his eyes and sprinted out of the current into the calm of their pool.

As he neared them, Rex executed a broad sweep stroke to come beside them, not unlike a rider whirling his horse around by the reins. "You're both fine?"

Myriam shook her head with awe. "We're okay. How about you?"

"Okay. Now comes the hard part."

Myriam translated his words for Alberto, whose fingers were curled around a bulge in the cliff wall like he had no interest in ever letting go.

"I'm going to ferry across that current below the falls."

"What does 'ferry' mean?"

"Cut across it on the diagonal so it doesn't wash me downstream immediately."

"Oh."

"Then I'll take a good look at what's around the corner and signal you with a thumb's-up from the other side of the falls if you're to follow, okay?"

Myriam stared dubiously at the jet stream below the misty falls. She ran her eyes along the walls of their pool. Wet, mostly vertical. She looked across the river, past the jet of current. Though the rock walls were mostly hidden by fog, she knew they were just as tall and impossible-looking to climb.

"After I give you a thumb's-up, I will disappear around the corner. Wait five minutes. There is a big flat yellowish boulder there. It was underwater the first time I saw it. But because it hasn't rained for days and the river has dropped, it's above water now. I will stop there, pull myself up on it, and get ready with the throw rope. You'll need to catch it as you float near it. Don't both come at once. Leave five minutes in between the two of you. It's essential that you catch the rope, understood?"

Myriam agreed and explained to Alberto, who looked petrified. Both could swim, but not very well, especially in currents among boulders.

"Back up and throw Alberto the rescue bag now, so he knows how it works," Myriam suggested. "I've done it before," she reassured Alberto. "It's not difficult."

Rex paddled backwards and tossed the rope to Alberto. Alberto watched it uncoil in the air, nodding as the sack with one end attached landed beside him. He grasped the bag, and Rex pulled on the rope until it was taut between them.

"I understand," Alberto said.

Rex looped the rope back into its sack and buckled the sack back into his kayak. He snapped his spraydeck into place and paddled slowly towards the falls.

Myriam didn't like how close he was to the falls, but had to trust he knew what he was doing. Facing the falls, already looking ghostly in the heavy mist, Rex suddenly went into a sprint, like he was trying to paddle right into the heavy cascade. Barely had the front tip of his boat crossed the line of current, however, when the water shot him across the jet stream diagonally, so fast that she drew in her breath.

Just as abruptly, the pool of water on the far side halted him like power brakes. *So that's what "ferry" means in kayak language*, she thought.

From there, he could survey what was downstream. But half-hidden in the fog, his face was impossible to read. She could only feel her stomach tighten as he raised his thumb, arced downstream, and disappeared at high speed, fully at the mercy of the current. She locked eyes with Alberto.

"I'll go first," he offered, staring at his empty jug.

Which is worse, going first or being left here alone for five minutes? she wondered.

Myriam leaned in and kissed him. He looked surprised, and pleased. They waited what seemed like five minutes. Then he dog-paddled across the pool towards the frightening froth of the falls.

She bit her tongue as the current grabbed him, pulled his head underwater for a second, then washed him out of sight, a head and a jug and a massive amount of water heading for Dead Man's Canyon.

She waited and she waited. *How long is five minutes? An eternity. What are the soldiers doing high above me?* she wondered. *Probably making the sign of the cross out of respect for the loss of three people's lives.* The commander, of course, would be cursing for his loss of a prisoner, whom he must have imagined represented money for lots more guns.

When she could wait no longer, Myriam let her fingers slide off the cold rock wall. She struck out for the current, water jug in hand. She gulped what she hoped wouldn't be her last breath as she hit the well-defined line between the still pool and the jet stream. Then she felt herself pulled under, ripped from the calm, manhandled by terrifying currents. She didn't know left from right, up from down. Even when she surfaced, splashes to her face blinded her to the flat yellow boulder she was passing at high speed. But, somehow, she managed to grab the rope that fell across her chest in the monstrous current. She grabbed it with both hands, even as the fingers of one hand stayed curled around the handle of her water jug.

The rope tightened. Her grip tightened even more. Then her body ploughed upstream, dividing waves as it went.

Water went up her nose and drenched her face. But not for a second did she lessen her death grip on the rope, her only lifeline to the two men reeling her in.

CHAPTER TWENTY

I felt my stomach muscles relax. All three of us were standing on the big, flat yellow rock, facing the rock-wall cul-de-sac. Both Alberto and Myriam stood white-faced at the scene in front of us: the river throwing itself at the towering wall as a massive volume of water sloppily attempted to feed itself into a natural rock tunnel. The water fit so tightly into the opening that only a tiny dark arch, the size of a person's head, remained above water level. It was like viewing a mouse hole at the bottom of a wall, the "floor" being rushing water.

"We're not going in there, are we?" Myriam asked, voice quavering.

"Good thing you didn't see this section during that heavy rainfall," I said. "Right before I got kidnapped, the water level was several feet over this rock we're standing on and higher than the top of that tunnel. There was no airspace identifying the tunnel at all. Just a massive, ugly whirlpool – like what forms when water goes down a bathtub drain."

"How long is that tunnel?" Myriam demanded. "And how do you know it's a tunnel rather than a dead-end cave?"

"Rivers always find a way to keep moving," I said. "They'll carve out what doesn't give way faster. That current is moving downstream; it has found a way out. What we don't know is whether we can follow it."

"Why did you bring us here if you don't know?" Myriam asked.

"Because I know how to find out."

She studied me for a minute. "Is this like when you went under the bridge on *El Furioso*?" she asked. "You plan to turn upside down and hold your breath just before you go under that arch, and then roll up on the other side of the tunnel?"

"I wish it were that simple," I replied. "I will need your help now. You're going to ease me in there on the end of the throw rope, letting it out as far as it will go. I'll have my headlamp on my helmet. I will find out what's in there. Hopefully I'll see light at the end of the tunnel before you haul me back."

Myriam's eyes narrowed as she looked from me to the rope to Alberto. She translated for Alberto, then engaged in a lively debate with him.

Finally, she turned to me. "It's better if you put me on the end of the rope. I'm the lightest weight."

I opened my mouth to argue, but nothing came out. I could swear the Furioso itself had jumped up to clamp it shut, to slap sense into me. She was right. I had been worried about Alberto and her having the combined muscle to haul me back upstream, against the current. But I hated to put her at risk. On the other hand, we were all at great risk in a high-stakes game now. The morning mist was thinning, lifting. That meant if any snipers had positioned themselves on the cliffs above, we'd soon be sitting ducks for being picked off. Alberto and I would have the strength to haul her back up to this midriver rock for her report.

I saw the surprise in Myriam's eyes when I agreed. But before she could reach for the rope, I pulled the necklace from my paddling jacket pocket and placed it around her neck. As my fingers touched her soft skin, they tingled slightly. But any lingering romantic attraction was gone, dispelled by Abuela.

Alberto, his wet army fatigues clinging to his skinny body, looked at the necklace, his jaw hanging slightly open. Myriam lifted her watery eyes, then placed her hands over mine in the same manner that Abuela had so many times. "Thank you, cousin," she said in a choked voice.

I fashioned a makeshift harness for her out of one end of the rope. I slipped the headband-mounted flashlight around her head. Alberto muttered to her, gave her a quick hug, then signaled that he was ready.

As Alberto and I held on to the rope, Myriam lowered herself from the rock, her eyes fiery with courage, the necklace glinting at her neckline. Then she floated through the dark mouse hole as we fed the line out gradually. After the tunnel had swallowed her, Alberto and I continued to feed out the rope until our calloused palms ached. My own hand was super-alert for the slightest change in tension. When the rope was fully played out, we sat there like nervous puppeteers. I counted to twenty, then ordered, "Now!"

Together, Alberto and I hauled and hauled, adrenalin fueling our efforts, like fishermen bringing in a net – an empty net, she was so lightweight.

Alberto cried out joyfully as she appeared, pinching her nose to keep water out.

When she flopped onto the rock, Myriam took a few deep breaths before bursting into a rapid-fire news report. "I can see light at the end. We can float right through. The ceiling goes high right after the entrance. There's even a rock shelf to the right, several feet beneath the cave's ceiling."

"Yes!" I cried, reaching my arm over the edge of our rock to touch the water reverently, as if to shake hands with our enemy-turned-friend, the underground Furioso.

"We should hide in the tunnel until the soldiers have decided we've drowned," Alberto suggested through Myriam as I disassembled her harness and recoiled the rope. "If they haven't decided that already."

I nodded agreement as I positioned my kayak for a launch off the rock and moved the headlamp from Myriam's head to my helmet. "I'll go first. I'll stop on the rock shelf and get ready to toss you the throw rope as you float by so I can tow you to the shelf if I need to. Hold your water jugs to your chest, with your arms wrapped around them. Keep your feet up, ready to spring off rocks. Stay where the most current is, if you can."

As I was speaking, I attached my spraydeck to my kayak, positioned my paddle, and slid off the rock into the current. I didn't expect this walrus-style entry to flip me over, but it did. I rolled back upright fast, glimpsing Alberto's look of respect. Then I aimed for the tiny piece of breathing space in the entrance archway. As the bow of my kayak entered beneath it, I purposely tipped over to allow my kayak to slide under without decapitating me.

After a count of three, I rolled up into the darkness of the cave, noting with relief that the rough, scalloped ceiling was more than a foot over my head, rising the farther I went. I swiveled my head left and right to let my headlamp light up the cavern. When my paddle hit a midriver rock, it echoed eerily through this spooky catacomb. The *thunk*, *thunk* of water dripped from the ceiling onto my boat and droplets flicked onto my face. Still, it smelled fresh in here. It felt as cool, fresh, and wondrous as an ancient cathedral.

I spotted the rock outcrop to my right and swung hard on a sweep stroke to detach from the fast current. I needed to get myself in a position to leap out onto it.

Pebbles crunched under my neoprene boots as I hauled my boat to safety and grabbed for the throw rope. My headlamp's thin beam picked up a wet body floating towards me, fast. With his jug atop his chest, Alberto resembled a dead body with a severely distended belly. I shouted and tossed the rope; he caught it and I hauled him up.

Again, pebbles crunched as they moved under our feet. The second misshapen body showed up, writhing as she tried to maneuver herself our way.

"Myriam," I called, and the tunnel echoed her name.

Soon three glistening human forms sat shivering on the dark shelf, listening to the gurgling river hurl by, our eyes on the light at the downstream end of the cavern.

"Do you think they're watching for us on the other side?" I asked Alberto. As Myriam translated, her soft voice ricocheted off rock walls. The three of us leaned together for warmth and to hear each other over the noise of the river and echo.

"It's possible, but not likely," he said slowly. "Rock and brush make the cliff edges hard to get to, and no one ever climbs down here. The elders tell of people in past generations who've fallen over the falls or cliffs. Not one ever came out alive. But the soldiers know you are different," he said, turning to me, then looking at my kayak. "It's possible, and a sharpshooter's bullets could reach us, for sure."

"They will kill you for deserting?" I don't know why I bothered posing it as a question.

Alberto lowered his gaze in my light's beam when Myriam translated. She wrapped an arm around his trembling shoulders.

"They will do far worse than kill me." He rolled up a sleeve to display scars that looked like cigarette burns all up his arm. He removed his wet shirt and turned his bare back to my headlamp. I winced at the angry welts and scars from beatings. Hearing Myriam's strangled cry, I watched her chest heave as she leaned into Alberto and ran her fingers down his scarred arm and back. She translated between sobs.

"They torture for the slightest offense in camp," he said in a flat voice. Myriam lowered her forehead to his knees.

He lifted a hand to stroke her hair. "You were right," he whispered, his throat heavy with emotion. "You tried to warn me."

I didn't need to ask why he'd helped capture me. In fact, I wondered if he'd managed to persuade them not to do it until I was free of Myriam. I also wondered what Alberto would do when we reached Jock's. Surely the Colombian Army would not treat an ex-guerilla kindly, or employ him.

"There are organizations that protect ex-guerillas," Alberto said as if reading my thoughts. "There are some in Popayán. They will help me while Myriam starts university there."

As Myriam raised her head, Alberto pressed a finger to her lips. "You are meant to go to university. You are meant to help our people. Even Abuela told you so," he reminded her softly.

I turned away to grant them privacy for a moment. Then I spoke: "We'll spend the night here." I pulled my space blanket out of the kayak. "At first light, we'll float out."

CHAPTER TWENTY-ONE

None of us slept well. We lay in a tight huddle, the space blanket barely reaching across us. Chill wet stones dug into our backs. The impenetrable blackness was accentuated by the constant slapping and sucking noises of the flow beside us. Hunger gnawed, thirst bit. Only our combined body heat provided any relief from the cold. There was comfort in being part of a threesome, I reminded myself – but not much.

I woke numerous times, fearful that a rainfall might make the water rise and flood our shelf, which would force us into the canyon in the dead of night. Fearful my kayak might float away. Fearful a mad guerilla might climb down the canyon walls, ninja-style, float in, and stab us. Fearful, even, of what lay ahead – the tremendous responsibility I had for two people as well as myself. On the other hand, once I'd seen the cave entrance, I'd never have attempted the canyon if not for the need to get my companions to safety. Nor would Henrique or Tiago ever have considered it.

When the first pricks of light lit the two ends of our cavern, I felt Myriam stir. "What would you have done if you'd found that this tunnel wouldn't let us through?" she asked.

I flicked on my light and turned it towards her. I'd been waiting for that question. "I'd have been forced to free-climb the canyon walls on the river's left side and help you up with my throw rope. Then we'd have had to take our chances with the paramilitaries, I guess."

Myriam shivered. She couldn't imagine taking their chances with those who'd slaughtered the men of her village.

I walked to the downstream end of the shelf and listened. The roar of whitewater was not sweetness to my ears. The prospect of big rapids no longer drew or thrilled me. My only goal was to get Alberto and Myriam out of the canyon alive.

I returned to our shelf. We each took sips of water from the little bit we'd left in the jugs. No one had food.

"Here's how it's going to work," I said. "You'll float in the water on your backs with your jugs on your stomach and your feet up. You'll keep a death grip on your jugs with one hand, while using the other to maneuver left or right. Aim for the deepest-looking channels, unless I signal otherwise."

"Could we tie our jugs to us?" Myriam suggested.

"Dangerous," I replied. "If anything catches, you could get strangled or drown. I'll be well ahead, picking the best route. You'll do what you can to follow that route. It's very, very important you try to go where I go. In Class V, the wrong route can kill you. The most important thing to remember . . ." I paused for effect ". . . is to keep your feet up and pointed downstream. If you lower them, they can catch between rocks and drown you."

The memory of nearly doing that when paddling with Jock and Tom was all too fresh.

"Plus, you need to use your feet to spring off rocks as the river hurls you towards them. Bend your knees and bounce off them the way a frog floating on its back would."

A vague smile pulled at Myriam's face.

"Alberto's shoes will protect him as he does this. Myriam, I'm giving you my neoprene boots so you don't cut your feet."

"Okay," she said, tugging my boots on after I passed them to her. I omitted saying that this added to the many reasons I must not – absolutely must not – eject from my boat. As their leader, and as someone with no one to rescue me if I messed up, I felt intense pressure to succeed in rolling up every time the violent rapids capsized me.

"If I see something super-dangerous, I'll attempt to land on a rock and position myself to toss you the throw rope. It will guide you the right way or pull you to safety. If you get ahead of me, try to back-stroke into a calm spot until I pass you."

"Okay," they said.

Secretly, I feared for them. Even if they'd been expert kayakers, following my lead was going to be tough. Doing so while immersed in tossing water, with no more than a slapping hand to steer with, and while clinging to a floating jug, was going to be somewhere between brutal and impossible. But critical for survival.

"Kayakers use river signals," I added, and shone the headlamp on myself to demonstrate the hand and paddle signals that would warn them to maneuver themselves left, right, or center down a rapid.

"And if I raise my paddle like this . . ." I lifted it high above my head horizontally ". . . it means get out of the water onto a rock as fast as you can, and wait for further instruction, okay?"

My headlamp illuminated their nervous glances towards our cave's exit.

"Alberto, I have a pair of shorts you should change into."

He looked at me questioningly.

"You don't want your guerilla uniform on anymore, do you? You don't want the guerillas or paras or Colombian Army to identify you as an ex-guerilla."

"You're right," he mumbled, and accepted my shorts. As he changed, I switched off my light. The blackness was creepy. I wanted out of this tunnel.

"Ready?" I asked, flicking the light back on.

"Ready," Alberto answered in English. I saw Myriam look at him with surprise and pride.

"No matter what is ahead," I pronounced, "it's only a few miles to the Magdalena. The Furioso will batter us, but stay with my line and it will flush us out into the Magdalena alive. Maybe even before noon."

My hand brushed against my paddling jacket pocket before I remembered the necklace was no longer there. Myriam saw me. She reached out for my hand and touched my fingers to her necklace. Then she did the same for Alberto.

I climbed into my kayak. They placed their only possessions – the water jugs – on their chests.

I paddled out of the tunnel exit, which was just high enough that I didn't need to roll to slip under it. The daylight blinded me. Even as I positioned myself for the first rapid, I glanced warily up canyon walls that reached high towards the blue cloudless sky. Though I'd never have seen a hidden sniper, one thing was for sure: I was about to become a super-fast-moving target. Dead Man's Canyon lay before me like a seething minefield of whitewater. It was tough to identify a safe line at all, let alone on the fly. But I was committed, now, and determined to fight the battle with the best muscle and instincts I had.

Whoosh, wham, bang. My boat felt pellet-sized in the massive waves, which picked it up, slammed it down, and threw it against house-sized boulders. I got thrown over; I rolled; I got tossed into a backwards cartwheel; I rolled again. My heart moved to my throat. My eyes darted everywhere, searching for passage between boulders. I scouted frantically from the tops of waves and looked in vain for eddies into which I could turn and breathe, check on my mates behind me, and gauge what was coming up.

I turned violently into a micro-eddy at the end of the first rapid, craned my neck, and saw my compatriots come bobbing, crashing, and hurtling towards me. Like ducklings caught in a hurricane, they searched frantically for their leader and flapped madly to follow in my path.

I peeled out again, got sideswiped by a wave, and skittered down a frothy, rock-studded path, barely upright. In the havoc of current at the rapid's bottom, I was thrown over, the collision of my helmet on rock reverberating around my skull. I rose back upright on one quick paddle arc. Hardly had I blinked water out of my eyes when I found my kayak charging towards a line of rocks that divided the river into two. One look and I knew that the right-hand channel was the way to go, but my best efforts to sprint over there turned my boat backwards in the left lane. *No!* Frantically, I signaled for my followers to head right, even as I was forced to negotiate – backwards – the tricky water in the rockier channel.

Loud smacks against rocks unnerved me, but failed to damage my boat or the touch-and-go course I selected. *This is the butt-bruising, foot-entrapment capital of the world if my two river-mates make it down here*, I thought.

At the bottom, I put in a hard spin and sprinted to the end of the other chute in time to help steer Myriam and Alberto to a calm patch.

"You went the right way," I congratulated them. "Are you okay?"

"Y-y-yes," Myriam said, shaking as Alberto eased his stranglehold on his jug. "Can we rest a minute?"

"For sure."

Hauling themselves up on a rock, Myriam and Alberto glanced upstream and downstream. The towering canyon walls cast reproving shadows on the invasion of its ancient, undisturbed space.

"So far so good," I tried to reassure them, treading water with my paddle to stay close by.

It was several moments before either spoke.

"This is nothing like the rapids near our community," Myriam said in a low voice, rubbing her back like it had been bruised by multiple rock hits already.

"No. Canyons tend to be crazier. Too much water squeezed into too narrow a space."

Myriam turned and studied me as she fingered her necklace. "You were looking forward to this?" she said with a note of disbelief.

I was holding up, but was far too concerned for our safety to be enjoying it. I squinted downriver. "If you get ahead of me and can't grab a rock, what are you supposed to do?" I coached.

"Keep to the deepest channel, and keep our feet up," she recited.

"And never, ever let go . . ."

". . . of our jugs," she finished, looking down at hers.

"Tell me when you're good to go again."

They sat there, pale-faced and silent, for a full five minutes. Then they eased back into the water together, faces turned bravely toward me.

I smiled, with what I hoped communicated confidence, and plunged my kayak back into the heart of Dead Man's Canyon. Once again, the Furioso flung me at boulders that seemed to rise at will and turn passing water into a simmering stew of instability.

I lost count how many slap-braces gave me narrow escapes from capsizing. I lost count how many times I had to roll. My neck grew stiff from the tension of scouting upcoming catastrophes and swiveling around to check on Myriam and Alberto. *Surely we are at least halfway down now?*

I sighted a decent-sized eddy and darted towards it, adrenalin fueling my overworked shoulder muscles, only to find myself sucked into a whirlpool that knocked me over and held me, even after I rolled four times within it. It ground my helmeted head against an underwater rock before I finally rose, gasping, and side-surfed out of its grip.

There! A moment's reprieve in a patch of calm. My breath was coming fast. My throat was dry. I stretched my neck high to look for my companions. I saw Alberto's jug come barreling towards me – his head, shoes, and hands extending out from it like turtle appendages.

"Grab hold of a rock and wait for me," I shouted, pointing and pantomiming so he'd understand. His face was white, but he'd made it past the whirlpool. *That's something.*

"Myriam isn't behind me!" he shouted. "She went . . ." He pointed to a different channel.

No! I thought. She hadn't been able to see me or judge which way to head, while I was upside down.

I searched the waves for the second jug, my chest tight with worry. Then I saw it – floating high and alone – no Myriam clinging to it. Charging out of my eddy, I ferried back and forth, back and forth, as Alberto managed to halt his downriver journey by clinging to a rock in an eddy near me. Neither of us was in a position to catch the jug, even if we hadn't been more focused on sighting Myriam. Finally, I heard a shout and saw her clinging to a small boulder upstream – well away from where I'd carved a path. She was struggling to maintain her hold.

"Myriam!" I screamed.

She raised her head.

"Stay there!" With no flotation or help, she could not carry on down the steep, agitated channel. I looked about frantically, found a rock I might be able to climb onto, and took considerable effort to get to it. After I hugged the rock, I crawled up onto it and pulled my boat to safety. I aimed the throw bag to a point just upstream of Myriam. It took two tries, but she finally grabbed it as it floated by. Then, after great hesitation, she slid off her rock and into the roiling water. When she dropped into the whirlpool that marked the joining of the two channels, I pulled and pulled, praying she wouldn't lose her grip.

Finally, I guided her to my rock and pulled her up by her armpits. She allowed me to lay her on her back. She was so bruised and waterlogged, she resembled a rag doll. I turned and felt immensely relieved to see Alberto and his jug still waiting in their eddy. Downstream of him, I noted, the rapids let up a little.

I squatted down on our tiny rock to study Myriam, whose braid was in disarray. Hair hung over her face. She didn't bother to move it. "Are you okay?"

She stared dully at me, not responding. She looked defeated. Without the jug, she was lucky not to have drowned. I noticed her shivering uncontrollably. I unzipped my life jacket, sat her up, helped her arms into it, and zipped it back up. She didn't move to help me; she seemed almost lifeless. I wrapped her in a warm embrace to reassure her. Alberto would have to understand. She didn't resist, nor did she respond. I kept my arms around her until I felt the shivers subside. Then I placed my hands on each side of her face to lift it to mine.

"Myriam, with my life jacket, you'll float okay. Are you ready to get back into the water?"

She shook her head firmly and dropped her eyes.

Alberto looked concerned, but had no way of getting to us. I held up a finger to tell him we needed a minute. "Myriam, you can ride on the back of my boat, okay? I'm going to get into my kayak and turn it so that its tail end is near you. Slip into the water and grab my waist as you pull yourself up onto the boat, one leg dangling into the water on each side. Keep your weight even or we'll capsize, understand?"

She nodded numbly.

"If we do, you need to slide off and stay near until I roll back up. You'll float, because you're wearing my life jacket. Then I'll tell you when it's okay to climb on again."

Her eyes showed her agreement.

I eased my kayak off the rock, then shoehorned myself into it. I back-paddled and waited for her to slide on. She did as I'd requested. With her hands clasped about my waist, I left the eddy below the whirlpool, aiming for the most conservative routes to minimize my chances of flipping.

Alberto dog-paddled out into the current to join us and said some encouraging words to Myriam.

We traveled like that for a mile, me capsizing only once, and Myriam sliding off cooperatively when I did.

Lightweight as she was, it was awkward having a passenger – it definitely compromised my paddling style and safety – but I sensed that she was slowly regaining her confidence.

Then came a big one.

"Myriam, you need to slide off now and float through this on your own. I will hover as nearby as I can. We'll get through it, I promise."

She slid off wordlessly and positioned herself on her back, feet up. Her eyes scanned the whitewater ahead.

"I think it's the last one!" I shouted, spying a place where the canyon walls seemed to open up.

I saw her body relax, even more as Alberto floated up to us and took her hand.

Then I was off, sprinting around rocks, punching through backwashes, route-finding on the fly once again. My empty stomach churned with the whitewater as the rapids battered me about. Once, while I was trying to sprint left, my downstream side slammed against a rock. Despite my best efforts to lean downstream, the river tossed me over upstream and plastered me and my kayak against the rock, the plastic of my boat shuddering as if about to wrap around it.

I held my breath, told myself to stay calm, and waited. If I came out of my boat, I would have no life jacket to float me and no boots to protect my feet from high-speed collisions with sharp rocks. Worse, Alberto and Myriam would have no guide to trailblaze through the violent whitewater. I waited until all my breath had run out. Just as I was about to eject, a surge of water decided to free the boat. I rolled up, executed a fast sweep stroke to keep from wrapping around another rock, then dashed down the left side of the angry rapid just behind a couple who were holding hands and working in sync to stay in the deepest channel, feet up.

The Furioso disgorged us into the Magdalena together.

I towed my companions to shore, where Alberto helped Myriam out of the water. Then I went searching for the boats left by the mule at the start of this journey for Jock and one of his guides to join my Brazilian friends and me.

We couldn't expect them to still be there. We were days late. So I emitted a cry of joy when Alberto dragged them out from under the bushes and hauled them to the water's edge.

He was a in a big hurry, I noticed, and looking over his shoulder frequently. He pulled the break-apart paddles from each boat, clicked them together like he'd been doing it all his life, and seated Myriam before helping launch her into the river. Then he tossed his jug into the water, got in his boat, and dug in his paddle like he was afraid paramilitaries would burst from the trees any moment. He capsized, tumbled out of the boat underwater, and surfaced spluttering. I helped him back in.

I gave them both the briefest lesson in history on how to kayak, suppressing a smile as they spun and rocked and flailed for several seconds before reaching the center of the river.

Within half an hour, after I'd given them more words of encouragement and advice, both my kayak students were looking competent.

The Magdalena was gentle here, a fast and easy flow for miles. During the journey, Myriam relayed bits of her story, of finding the men in the field and of Abuela dying peacefully in her sleep in the cave. She wept between sentences. I was unable to stem a flow of tears myself. But hardly had they dried than I felt anger rise – anger and a sense of helplessness.

CHAPTER TWENTY-TWO

We reached Jock's shop in the early afternoon with seriously parched throats, shrunken stomachs, and drop-dead tiredness. No one had paid any attention to our party of three kayakers floating down the river. Even as we paddled through Jock's upper village, passersby had barely turned their heads. That was fine with me.

Jock came sprinting out of his shop before we'd beached all three kayaks.

"Rex! You're here! I can't believe it! The radio reports said you'd been —"

"Shut up, Jock," I said sharply, looking around. No one was in earshot, but I dared not take any chances, especially for Alberto's sake. "Let's get inside your shop, quickly."

He looked the three of us over as if just noticing our severe exhaustion. He stared at Myriam and Alberto, his eyes running up and down the scars on Alberto's bare back.

Jock shooed a guide out of his shop. "Go take lunch, okay? I've got a meeting with some customers."

The minute the guide stepped out, Jock turned the sign from OPEN to CLOSED and locked the door. By the time he'd turned around, I was busy rattling through his cupboard, grabbing coffee cups and filling them with water from the sink.

Jock watched wordlessly as we drank, refilled, and drank, water dribbling down our chins. He opened his desk drawer and produced guava sticky candy, which we swiped from his palm and loaded into our mouths.

"Thank you," I said. "Can I use your phone to call my mom? I'll pay you back. Myriam and Alberto can tell you our story while I do that."

He nodded. I grabbed the phone and dialed Gramps' number. It rang and rang, then, "Please leave a message after the sound of the tone."

"Gramps, Mom, I'm okay," I said, my voice cracking a little. "I've escaped and I hope to be on a plane tomorrow. I'm calling from Jock's. I'll phone again when I can, okay?"

When I turned back to my friends, Myriam was speaking so rapidly that I couldn't follow a word of their conversation. I walked to the window and looked out at the peaceful Magdalena, the stack of kayaks and rafts, the green grass, the delicate orchids, the waving ferns and yellow daisies, the mountain rising majestically above all.

It's a beautiful country, I thought as I felt my pulse slow. *Have I even noticed that before?*

The animated conversation beside me finished with Myriam offering to pay Jock for Henrique's and Tiago's kayaks still up in the village, if they hadn't been stolen or burned.

"No way. Forget them," Jock replied generously. "Look, first I'm running out to get you some *empanadas*, meat and cheese pastries. If you want to shower while I'm gone, there are towels in that cupboard."

I placed my wallet on the glass counter. "I'd like to buy three of your *Expediciones del Río* T-shirts," I said. "Two mediums and a small." I glanced over at my companions. "And Alberto needs some shorts or jeans, if you can spare a pair."

Jock half-smiled. "Excellent souvenirs," he said, gesturing to the counter as he tossed a pair of shorts at us: "Help yourselves." He moved towards the door. "I'll leave the CLOSED sign up and lock the door behind me. When I get back, I'll hand this afternoon's business over to my guides and drive you to Neiva. We'll phone your embassy and get you on a plane," he addressed me. "Then I'll help put Myriam and Alberto on the bus to Popayán."

"*Gracias,*" Myriam said, eyes filled with tears.

"Do you need money for the bus fare?" Jock asked Myriam.

She shook her head proudly and pulled some wet paper money from her jeans pocket. Alberto stared at it. I recognized the second half of my pay. She must have retrieved it from the cave on her way to find Alberto. I was glad it was going to help get her settled at university — free to *indígenas*, Jock had told me — and that Alberto would be there for her.

We showered and dressed, drank more water, and fell half-asleep in the sun streaming through Jock's shop window. The phone rang. On impulse, I picked it up. "*Hola.*"

"Rex?" My mom's voice leapt through the phone. "Rex, is it you?"

"Mom," I said, my voice catching. "I'm okay. I promise you, I'm okay. I'm sorry about all this. I should've quit and come home when my teammates did. I should've listened to people."

I heard some muffled sobs. Then she said, "Rex, I'm sorry I wasn't in earlier. Gramps was in the hospital. He was so worried about you. He kept saying it was all his fault. He was on the phone for days, ranting at government officials here and in Colombia. He even shook his hunting rifle at reporters camped on our lawn. Plus, we were busy trying to raise money to . . ."

I heard the key turn in the door. Jock entered with a basket of *empanadas* and Lina, his reporter friend, behind him.

I turned away, putting a hand over my ear as the others began talking.

"Mom, Gramps will be okay, won't he?" I asked, a bit choked.

There was no answer, just more sobs. Then, "He passed away this morning, Rex. I'm so sorry to have to tell you. So sorry you weren't here. But you know, don't you, how much he loved you? He always loved you."

I sank to the floor and turned my face away from the others. My hand reached out for my waterproof bag and touched the bulge of the journal. "Mom, thanks . . . for telling me. I . . . I'll be home soon. I love you. I'll call you back as soon as I know what flight I'm on. I promise. Gotta go now."

I hung up with a broken heart. *Gramps has passed away?* A part of me always believed he'd be around forever. I turned to see Lina interviewing Myriam and Alberto, snapping photos of them and me. I looked at Jock.

"Okay, dude?" he asked. "This is a big scoop for Lina. A kidnap victim escaping and –"

"Jock, Lina, Myriam," I said, "I just don't think it's safe for a reporter to be here."

Myriam, hair freshly washed and wearing her new, bright red *Expediciones del Río* T-shirt, rose and placed her hands on the hips of her still-damp jeans. "I'm telling Lina about what happened to our village. *That* is what is important."

I hesitated only a second. "You're right."

"The real story is the kidnapping," Jock interrupted. "If Lina quotes you about the massacre, Myriam, you know that all the officials, including the Colombian Army, will deny it. And no reporters will go up there to check it out."

"A reporter has already been up there," Myriam said, her jaw set. She took two steps over to the counter and placed her hands on my waterproof pouch. She pulled out my camera and handed it to Lina. "I took photos."

She sank to the floor as if the declaration had exhausted her. Alberto pulled her to him, allowing her to press her face against his shoulder.

Lina, not even thinking to ask my permission, switched my camera on and flicked through the photos. Her face drained of color. Jock moved to look over her shoulder. I hung back, not really wanting to see.

Lina's expression moved from pained to aghast. She lowered the camera slowly and squatted down to eye level with Myriam. "We will tell your story," she said.

"But —" Jock tried to object.

Lina shook her head at him firmly. "It is a story that must be told," she said, her hand reaching out to touch Myriam's shoulder gently. "It may scare away some of Jock's precious tourists, but it must be told."

I watched Jock nod, his eyes cast to the floor. Myriam looked gratefully at Lina through her tears.

"Myriam is going to be a reporter," Alberto announced to Lina, pride in his voice.

Myriam looked at Alberto, then shifted her gaze to Lina. "I'm going to be a reporter," she repeated.

"Colombia needs *indígena* reporters," Lina said. "And you can speak English. That means I can help you get interviews with international news agencies when you reach Popayán. Shall I make some calls?"

"Yes," Myriam replied bravely.

I stood awkwardly, still shell-shocked about Gramps' death, but feeling a sense of pride in my cousin, too.

Lina interviewed Myriam and Alberto some more, then turned to me. Myriam translated her words. "So, Alberto and Myriam broke you out, and the three of you jumped over a waterfall to escape the guerillas. Then you guided them by kayak through Dead Man's Canyon to here? And that's a first descent?"

I was startled to realize I hadn't even thought about the first-descent aspect for days. It no longer interested me. I stood up. "We escaped from the guerillas, and we found our way to here. I have no comment as to how. All that's really important is that Myriam and Alberto are safe now and have a chance to tell the world what is happening on their *resguardo*." I knew Lina would leave out mention of Jock's connection because it could endanger him.

Myriam sat silent for a moment, then gave me the slightest of smiles and translated for Lina. "It was a first descent," she added, clearly enough for me to understand. "Rex should get that credit, whether he wants it or not."

"I agree," Jock spoke up.

I shrugged. "Whatever." I didn't care. Too many things were more important.

I sank my teeth into one of the pastries Jock brought us. It made my taste buds dance and awakened a suddenly voracious appetite. I ate it in two big bites and reached for more as Myriam and Alberto did the same.

The food must have had something in it, because as the three of us climbed into the back of Jock's red Toyota Hilux pickup truck, we all began nodding off. As I lay my head against my pack, I felt the bulge of Gramps' journal. I wouldn't be writing in its last pages after all; I no longer viewed my journey as an extension of his. Indeed, I had no further need for the journal, yet it would always be a part of me. When I got home, I'd have lots of explaining to do to Mom. But she'd come to terms with my discovery of Colombian relatives, and she'd be proud of me for helping where I could.

I raised my fist to thump the journal so it wouldn't poke into my head and drifted into a deep, comforting sleep. We all slept like babies as the Hilux bounced over ruts. The space blanket did little to keep off the dust, but we didn't care. We were free. We were headed down the mountain. We were on our way to new lives.

Acknowledgments

Just for the record, the Furioso is a fictional river; the Magdalena is real. All characters in this novel are fictional, even if, sadly, many of the issues depicted are all too real. Jock's village is very roughly based on San Agustin in Huila, Colombia.

I am deeply grateful for a B.C. Arts Council grant toward this project, and to Leona Trainer for encouraging me to "reach further" with my writing.

I also owe an enormous debt of gratitude to Colombian anthropologist Lina Gómez, who worked tirelessly with me through every stage of this project – from earliest conception through readings of the evolving manuscript, including assisting in collecting and translating material in Spanish. She emerged not only as a valued partner in my work, but as a Spanish tutor and friend. Even so, any errors are my own.

Warm thanks to Melanie Peck, my traveling companion and translator in South America, and our guide Miguel;

anthropology professor and filmmaker Laura R. Graham (see her documentary *Owners of the Water: Conflict and Collaboration Over Rivers*); Anna and Colombian refugee Ruby at Pastoral Imigratoria in Ibarra, Ecuador; my husband, Steve Withers, a fellow whitewater kayaker with a sharp eye for critiquing my manuscripts-in-progress; Cathy at XPAC Capilano Hatchery in North Vancouver, B.C., Canada; and Tao Berman of Washington state, who holds numerous first-descent records in whitewater kayaking and is the subject of *Going Vertical: The Life of an Extreme Kayaker*, by Tao Berman and Pam Withers. Barbara Berson, Bob Mayer, and Nan Gregory also offered valuable editorial input.

I appreciated information from ONIC (National Organization of the Indigenous of Colombia), CRIC (Regional Indigenous Council of Cauca), and ACIN (Association of Indigenous Councils of Northern Cauca): www.onic.org.co; www.cric-colombia.org; www.nasaacin.org.

Also, various Icarus Films documentaries and the inspiration of the report (available online) from the Mission to Colombia to Investigate the Situation of Indigenous Peoples, organized by Rights & Democracy, with the cooperation of the Assembly of First Nations (Canada) in 2001.

A portion of the earnings from *First Descent* will go towards organizations working for the rights of indigenous peoples worldwide. These include www.cs.org; www.intercontinentalcry.org; www.minorityrights.org; and www.survivalinternational.org.

Teen readers included Julian Legere, my niece Esther Tuttle of the Lakota nation, Suraya Clemens, and members of the Bibliophiles grade-eight book club at Christianne's Lyceum of Literature and Art in Vancouver, Canada, and Malcolm Scruggs of California, whom I met in Ecuador.

And, finally, thanks to Sue Tate and all the Tundra Books staff; Lynn Bennett at Transatlantic Literary Agency; and Chris Patrick, my speaking tours agent.